LIFELINE

ABBEY LEE NASH

TinyFox
PRESS

A Tiny Fox Press Book

Cover design by Alfred Quitevis.

Library of Congress Catalog Card Number: 2017949346

ISBN: 978-1-946501-06-6

Tiny Fox Press and the book fox logo are all registered trademarks of Tiny Fox Press LLC

Tiny Fox Press LLC
North Port, FL

For J

Before

SUDDEN DEATH.

First game of the season, and we're heading into overtime against our arch rivals, the Wolves. Four minutes left. First goal wins.

Four minutes to prove to Coach Wilson and smug President Schaffer that they made the right choice by finally naming me lacrosse captain this year.

My eyes are blurry with sweat. Something wet drips down my chin. My nose is running.

I yank up my helmet, swipe my nose across my sleeve.

Coach Wilson stands beside the bench, his thick arms crossed over his pot belly. He glances down at me. "You alright, kid?"

"Allergies," I mutter, lowering my helmet. "I'm fine."

"Still," he says, "better drink up." He tosses me a Gatorade.

I squirt blue liquid through my mouthpiece and look over my shoulder at the bleachers. The crowd's all riled up. I spot

Savannah with her friends, anxiously clutching a Frappuccino. She painted my number on her t-shirt: it's knotted up in the back, so it shows the tight skin of her stomach above her jeans.

My stepdad, Steven, is down front, working the crowd like he does at the country club, chatting up the other khaki-wearing tightwads that cheer on their high school alma mater. Mom's on the phone—a work call, probably. Benny's standing on the bleachers beside her. "Go, Lions!" he shouts, thrusting a sign into the air. The "S" is backward. He waves the thing around, nearly toppling over. Mom grabs his shirt before he face-plants off the bleachers. That kid is such a spaz.

The ref blows the whistle, and Coach thumps my shoulder. "You're up, Eli."

"Go, Eli!" Benny shrieks.

I give him a thumbs up, quick and low, then jog across the field to the center circle.

The Wolves' midfielder eyes me with cocky indifference.

Coach paces the sideline, chomping gum like it's rawhide. I know what he's thinking. The outcome of this game will set the tone for the entire season. It's a hell of a lot easier to stay on top than it is to claw your way up from the bottom.

"Down, set," the ref announces.

The Wolf spits in the grass by my feet. We get low, and our eyes meet. I am the dirt under his Nike cleats.

I am nothing unless I win.

The whistle calls the face-off, and the midfielder slams into me. I scramble for the ball, but this guy's bigger and stronger. His shoulder catches me under the chin. I fall back, recover, but it's too late. He flings the ball to an open attack player, and the Wolves charge our goal.

I follow, another midfielder close behind me. The Wolves take the shot, but our goalie makes the save. The bleachers erupt in cheers as he scans the field. "Alex!" I yell.

Alex whips me the ball, and I snatch it out of the air. Sweat stings my eyes, blurring my vision. Footsteps pound the field behind me. Up ahead, a Wolves' defender bounces on the balls of his feet, his body tense, ready to come after me. I fake the pass. In the split second that he pauses, I get my chance. I take two more steps, wind up, and shoot.

The goalie lunges, but the ball slips past his reach and streaks into the upper corner of the net.

I don't even hear the ref's whistle. My team mobs me, slapping my helmet, my back. The crowd floods the field.

Savannah's in my arms, her cheeks flushed pink and her blonde hair windblown. She pushes up my helmet, kisses me right there in front of everybody, not even caring that I'm dripping sweat.

Alex squirts a Gatorade fountain into the air, showering everybody with sticky blue drops, and Savannah pulls away from me, giggling. Gatorade spatters her cheek like blue freckles, and I gently swipe them away with my thumb.

"Party at my place tonight," Alex bellows, clapping me on the shoulder. "This asshole's the guest of honor!"

Savannah beams up at me, and for a moment, I'm the guy she thinks I am, the one Mom and Steven want me to be.

Mr. Joe Academy. Super-jock. LionsHeart material.

The high's incredible but short-lived.

Faking it is exhausting.

The house is empty when I get home. Mom has Benny, and Steven took President Schaffer out to lunch at the club to celebrate the win.

My win.

I dump my stuff in the smallest bedroom—the one place in this ridiculous McMansion that feels like mine.

I flip on Comedy Central and flop across my bed. My eyelids are heavy, but my body's still amped from the game.

There are footsteps on the stairs. Benny flings open my bedroom door and hurls himself onto my bed, his mouth ringed in neon blue. "Wanna watch SpongeBob?"

"What? No, I don't . . ." I shove off the bed. "Mom!"

Mom's standing at the bottom of the stairs, her hair pushed back with sunglasses, her hand on her hip. "Just for an hour? I've got to get back to the office, and you know I can't get anything done with . . ."

She tips her head toward Benny, mouths *you know who*.

Benny tugs on my jeans. "Did you know Mommy has a spinny chair in her office? And candy, too!"

I roll my eyes. "C'mon, Mom," I try. "I have plans . . ."

She lowers her sunglasses, hikes her work bag up on her shoulder. "One hour, okay? Two, tops."

Benny's wandering around my room, sticky fingers touching all my stuff.

"Fine," I groan.

"Thank you!" Mom chirps. Her heels click away from the stairs. "Dad will be home soon!"

"He's *not* my dad," I shoot back as Mom shuts the front door behind her.

When I turn around, Benny's at my dresser, grubby hands tugging at the top drawer. I dive, slam the drawer shut.

Benny's eyes get big, watery at the edges.

"Don't you need a nap or something?" I ask.

"Babies take naps," Benny sniffs. "I'm a big boy."

"Okay, then, big boy, you know how to turn the TV on, don't you?"

Benny nods.

"Go turn on SpongeBob, and I'll be down in a minute, okay?"

"'Kay."

Benny pads down the stairs. When I hear the TV, I open my dresser drawer, pull out the baggie I'd hidden in a pair of rolled up socks, and empty the contents into my hand.

A lone capsule stares up at me accusingly.

Only one left? I've been so careful to ration my supply—only on the weekends, most of the time anyway. Last week was a killer, though, with double practices on top of exams. But still . . .

I tuck the baggie back inside the sock, jam it into the back of my drawer.

I can save it.

I can wait.

But my legs don't want to move. And my fingers twitch with want. I just bagged the first game of the season—don't I deserve to celebrate?

"E-li!" Benny's back at the bottom of the stairs. "E-li!"

I peel away from my dresser, lean out my bedroom door. "Didn't I tell you to start SpongeBob?"

The remote dangles from Benny's fingers. "Yeah, but . . ."

"But what?" I snap, louder than I mean to.

"I want to watch it with you." His lower lip trembles.

I sigh, single-handedly defeated by a five-year-old.

"Fine." I cast one backward glance at my dresser before I head down the stairs.

I can save it.
I can wait.

After one bag of popcorn, two episodes of SpongeBob, and three games of old-school Mario Kart (I won twice, Benny once—a total fluke), Steven finally comes home.

"Daddy!" Benny flings himself at Steven who swings him up into his arms, ruffling his brown hair.

"Sorry I'm late," Steven says to me. He smells like sunscreen and Arnold Palmer; the tip of his nose is sunburned. "Schaffer never was any good at golf."

I shrug. "Whatever."

"Thanks for watching the Ben-ster here. How about I take you guys out to pizza, celebrate your win?"

Benny cheers. "Pizza!"

No doubt, Mom put Steven up to this. No matter how many times I tell her I'm not interested, Mom peddles "father/son bonding time" like street crack.

I shut off the TV. "I'm not hungry."

Benny's face falls, but I swear Steven looks relieved. "Maybe next time then?"

"Sure," I say on my way out of the den. We both know it's a lie. Neither one of us actually wants to spend any time together.

"Go get your jacket, Ben," Steven says.

Finally—a few minutes alone. I take the stairs two at a time. This time I lock my bedroom door. I could save it. I could wait.

But I don't want to.

I yank open my sock drawer with hungry hands.

Steven calls from the bottom of the stairs. "We're heading out, Eli. You sure you don't want to come?"

"Yes, I'm sure!" I holler. *Jesus Christ, leave already!* There's a pause; the front door opens, then closes. I exhale, roll the last capsule in my palm.

How can something so small make me feel so good?

I grab my phone, send a quick text to my best friend, Chase:

H X 3

I'll get a few more, and this time I'll make them last. Weekends only.

I crack the capsule, sprinkle the contents in a line on my dresser.

Totally in control.

It's after midnight when I wake up. I dig in my pocket for my phone and squint at the screen. There are three texts from Savannah and two from Chase:

10 p.m. Savannah: Party at Alex's babe. C u soon?

11 p.m. Savannah: Everybody's here. Where r u?

11 p.m. Chase: Got ur gear. Ur picking me up, right?

11:45 p.m. Chase: Don't back out of this one, dude. Ur my ride!

12:00 a.m. Savannah: Hellooo?!?!

I groan and force myself to sit up. I'm sore, and my stomach churns. Parties aren't really my scene. Too many people, too much noise. But being captain comes with certain expectations, and if my teammates knew I'd rather spend the night watching *SNL* reruns, I'd never live it down. Besides, I have to meet up with Chase. I send him a quick text:

On my way

In the bathroom, I squirt in eye drops, run wet hands through my brown hair until it looks halfway normal. I shake it down the way I like it, so that it covers the half-inch scar that severs my left eyebrow. Then I head quietly downstairs.

Steven's already asleep, but I hear Mom in the living room. Even though it's midnight on a Saturday, tax season means she's always working. I lean against the living room door frame. "I'm going out, Mom."

Her laptop rests on her knees, and stacks of paper are scattered on the couch around her. A pencil is knotted in the dark curls on top of her head, another clutched between her teeth. "A little late, isn't it?" she mumbles over the pencil.

"C'mon, Mom," I groan. "Don't start."

Mom gives me a long stare. I know she's trying to decide if it's worth the inevitable fight, worth waking Steven. I know she's thinking about another night a few months ago, the night of Winter Formal, the phone call that dragged her out of bed at 4am.

"I'm trying to give you the benefit of the doubt here, Eli, but sometimes you make it so hard. This new crowd you've been hanging out with . . . I don't trust them."

I fix my gaze on a worn spot of hardwood floor where the varnish is fading. With the tip of my sneaker, I nudge back the wool tassels of the rug to cover it. "It's just me and Chase tonight, Mom. Video games, pizza, nothing exciting. I'll be back by two, okay? Promise."

Mom loves Chase, the first friend I made after she married Steven, and we moved to the "good side" of town. Chase made life bearable, for both of us. But things changed last year when the lax team went state, and Savannah and I started dating. All of a sudden, people at school decided I was *somebody*— somebody they wanted at parties, somebody they wanted to know. It wasn't until this year that Chase found his own brand of popularity. It comes in the form of the dime bags that have kept him on LionsHeart's VIP list all year long.

Mom sighs. "Please be safe."

"Always."

The roads are quiet, and it's not long before I reach Chase's neighborhood. I pull up to the curb, tap my horn. Chase's door opens, and he jogs down the driveway to my car.

"Took you long enough," he mutters, sliding into the passenger seat.

"I fell asleep," I admit.

"Some king you are," Chase says. "The high school monarchy is totally wasted on you."

"Yeah, probably." I stifle a yawn. "Did you bring favors?"

Chase nods. "I never show up at a party empty-handed. It's rude." He pulls a small baggie out of his pocket and hands it to me.

The tan capsules are barely visible in the dark. With my fingers, I count them through the wax. "Three, right?"

Chase pretends to look offended. "That hurts. Really. Have I ever sold you short?"

I lean over Chase to hide the baggie under the floor mat. Then I dig my wallet from my pocket and fork over thirty bucks. Three pills to last me the week.

"Pleasure doing business with you, sir." Chase folds the money without counting it and stuffs it inside his coat. "That reminds me." He reaches into his other coat pocket and pulls out a small bottle. "A token of thanks for driving."

I give Chase a sideways stare as I pull away from the curb. "I always drive."

"And I'm saying thank you." He unscrews the cap and passes it over. "Wouldn't want you to go in unarmed."

I take the bottle gratefully. The first swig burns going down, and I take another before passing the bottle back. "Thanks."

Chase takes a few quick nips, then pulls a Marlboro Red from the soft pack in his shirt pocket and lights up. "What are friends for?"

1:00 AM

ALEX'S HOUSE GLOWS IN THE dark and throbs with bass. Cars litter the front yard like lawn ornaments. I glance down at my phone. Savannah hasn't texted since before midnight. She's definitely pissed.

Chase gives me a sidelong glance as we climb out of the car. "You alright?"

I slam my door shut and nod.

We head toward the house. The front door flies open, and Savannah's blowing down the steps toward me, her face a twisted mask of "I'm-so-happy-to-see-you" and "You-are-so-dead-to-me." Even pissed off, she's hot, her blonde hair all shampoo commercial. Plus, she's wearing those jeans that I want to pull off with my teeth.

"Eli . . ." she starts, but I rush her, pull her to me, and kiss her hard on the mouth before any other words can come out.

She softens a little in my arms, then pulls away from the kiss and reaches up a hand to push back my wet hair. I toss my head, shaking my hair down again.

Savannah's ocean eyes hide green rip currents. "What took you so long?"

Chase ambles up the stairs past us. "Just a little harmless pre-partying."

"Dude!" I spin around like I'm going to punch him, but he's already swerving into the house.

Savannah's eyes narrow. "You're not in trouble, are you? You know we can't take any more trouble." She means the kind of trouble we got in after Winter Formal. It was February before her parents would let us see each other again, and that was only because I showed up at her house on Valentine's Day. I wore my nicest clothes, took grocery store flowers for her mom, and swore on my life to her dad that I would never put his daughter in that situation again.

"Tell me," Savannah demands.

I hook my arms around her waist and make like I'm going to haul her off into the woods behind Alex's house. She giggles and punches my chest in that girly-way that's supposed to hurt but wouldn't dent a pillow. I tell her the truth—at least part of it. "I fell asleep."

Savannah fixes me with one of her are-you-lying stares that makes it hard to hold her gaze. "Really?"

"Really."

"I guess you do look pretty tired." Savannah relaxes in my arms. "You have sleep lines on your cheek."

I stifle a yawn, and she giggles. "I'm still mad at you," she says, but her eyes tell me otherwise.

I press my mouth to her ear, breathing in her smell, starburst sweet, and whisper that I'll make it up to her. She sighs, but pushes me off. "C'mon," she says, grabbing my hand and tugging me toward the steps. "Everybody's inside. I can't leave Katie by herself."

Katie is Savannah's latest project, a freckle-spattered strawberry blonde she's been trying to set up with Chase since Winter Formal.

I groan. "Freckles is a big girl. Can't she take care of herself?"

"It's *Katie*," Savannah snaps, shooting me a look.

I let her pull me inside.

There are at least fifty kids in the house. Bodies press together in corners and sprawl on couches. A beer pong tournament is in full swing. Chase is already up to bat, draining a red plastic cup. Freckles hangs off his arm. In the kitchen, the granite countertops are lined with empty glass bottles, and Alex is going ape-shit because somebody drank his dad's beers from Hong Kong.

"Gimme that!" he yells at some random girl I vaguely recognize from Pre-Calc. He snatches a half-empty bottle from her hand and shoves her out of the kitchen. "Cans, not bottles, people! Cans, not bottles!"

I start to inch backward out of the kitchen, but Savannah's fingers snake around my wrist and hold tight. "Oh, no, you don't," she teases. "I'm not letting you out of my sight tonight."

"There he is!" Alex shouts, noticing me for the first time. "The man of the hour!" He scrambles up onto the kitchen island, clapping his hands together until everybody's looking at him. "Ladies and Gentlemen, tonight we celebrate our first win of the season, against none other than the muthafucking Wolves!"

The crowd in the kitchen roars.

"And who do we have to thank for that?" Alex bellows.

13

The tips of my ears are on fire. Savannah leans in, tucks her arm around my waist.

"Raise your drink with me," Alex continues, "as we celebrate the man . . . the legend . . . Eli Ross!" He spins around to face me, almost falling off the island. Somebody hands him a red cup, and he holds it up, beer sloshing over the lip. "To Eli!"

"To Eli!" the crowd in the kitchen echoes.

Alex jumps down. He slides a beer down the counter toward me. "E-li!" He claps his hands against the counter, urging the crowd to follow suit. "E-li, E-li . . ."

Savannah gives me an apologetic smile, and I crack open the can.

The chant quickly changes. "Chug! Chug! Chug!"

I slam three beers, one after the other, until the chorus changes into cheers and applause, and the room tips slightly out of focus. Savannah tugs on my arm. "Alright, alright," she says, pushing back the fourth beer that Alex places in front of me. "That's enough."

The crowd groans, but they let me go, clapping me on the back as Savannah pulls me out of the kitchen. Somebody hands me a red cup. It's cheap piss-water keg beer, but I toss it back and ask for another.

Savannah leads me into the crowded living room. It's commercial-perfect, with white couches and glass-topped tables. It wouldn't last ten minutes with Benny around. And judging from the swaying brunette waving around a red wine cooler, it might not last the night.

Guys from the team shout my name, punch my shoulder as they pass. Across the room, Freckles is sucking on Chase's neck, and he lifts his vodka bottle to salute me. I'm the man of the hour, the fucking king of LionsHeart. So why do I feel like a fraud?

Alex's family portrait hangs above the fireplace. His mom and two older sisters. Alex and his dad wearing the same deep tan, the same starched blue button-down. All of them shooting Crest-white smiles at the camera. The picture-perfect family.

My family doesn't have any pictures like that, all four of us smiling together. Steven's living room is a Benny Museum. There's a picture of the day Benny was born, another of his first day of preschool. There's even a snapshot memorializing the one day he played soccer before he decided he didn't like it anymore. The only pictures of me are from before Steven, back when it was just Mom and me, and I was all the family she needed. The rest are boxed up in the attic somewhere, along with anything else that might remind her of my father. His old lacrosse stick. A weathered baseball glove. Everything's hidden away, like he never existed at all.

Somebody bumps into me and I stumble, sloshing beer on the hardwood. Suddenly I'm suffocating. There are too many people, too many bodies to move through, too many faces getting in mine. I'm fucking drowning in bodies.

"I need some air," I tell Savannah.

Cigarette smoke hovers over the deck like storm clouds.

I lean against the wooden railing, sucking cold air into my lungs.

Savannah presses a cool palm against my clammy cheek. "Are you okay?"

I shake my head. I'm not okay. Not even a little bit.

She leans against me, and I love the way her chin fits right in the spot below my collar bone. I kiss her on the forehead, *I'm sorry*. Because she can't make me feel better, but I know exactly what will.

"I'll be right back," I whisper.

15

She pulls me closer, because she knows what I'm going to do, and she doesn't want me to. "Stay with me," she says, her fingers trailing the waistband of my jeans. "We can go upstairs for a little bit, okay?"

I hesitate, but then the glass door to the patio slides open so hard it rattles the frame. Freckles is a dark shadow in the doorway, twin black lines streaking down her face like train tracks.

"Katie," Savannah gasps. She starts toward the door, then turns and holds out a hand like a crossing guard. "Stay there," she commands. "I'll be right back."

I nod, because you can't lie when you don't say anything. And because a few minutes alone is all I need. Savannah wraps her arms around Freckles, and they disappear together into the haunted fun house of lights and smoke and music. I slip down the deck steps and through the bushes to the front of the house.

2:30 AM

THE AIR OUTSIDE HUMS WITH music. All the lights in the house are on. If Alex's parents have gotten any smarter since the infamous rager we threw after Winter Formal, the neighbors are on the lookout for suspicious activity. Everything inside me says we're going to get busted any minute, and I have the worst possible timing in the world.

But right now, I don't care about the neighbors or the cops or even Savannah. I just . . . WANT.

A couple of minutes are all I need. And then I'll get Savannah out of the house, tell her to get home before the shit hits the fan. Just a couple of minutes.

I scrounge under my seat for the empty CD case, then reach into the glove compartment for the Burger King straw I've cut down to size. I hook a finger under the mat and feel around for the baggie. My phone buzzes in my pocket, but I ignore it. Sweat beads on my upper lip.

I crack open a pill, sprinkle it onto the plastic case. It doesn't look like very much, definitely not enough, so fuck it, I crack open another.

My hands shake as I cut the powder with my driver's license, scrape it into twin tracks.

A distant siren sounds.

Hurry, hurry.

There's yelling from the house, and somebody's turned off the music.

I prop the case on my knee, duck my head, and snort the powder through the straw.

One line. Then the other.

I squeeze my eyes shut until the burn in my nostrils fades to a steady chemical drip at the back of my throat, and the surge of heat spreads through my frozen body like liquid sunshine.

A siren screams; blue and red stars light up the night. Bodies flood out of Alex's house like it's on fire.

I shut my eyes and lean back against my seat.

The noise from the house fades. My body melts like crayons in the sun, colors merging in a puddle of rainbow wax. And I . . .

. . . can't . . .

. . . feel . . .

. . . anything.

3:00 AM

4:00 AM

5:00 AM

M Y EYES CRACK OPEN, JUST slits, but the light that comes in is a fluorescent torch. Everything hurts. My chest burns like I'm breathing pool water. Every inhale is agony. A noise comes out of my mouth, something like a groan, and then all of a sudden this face is hovering over me—purple eye shadow and a shock of shorn blue hair.

"Well, look who's starting to wake up!" she says, way too loud, like I'm 90,000 years old and deaf. "Are you gonna be nice this time?"

This time?

"Eli?" The voice that calls my name is so familiar it hurts, but the sound is lost in the lights and the pain and the little blue-haired fairy that's flitting back and forth around me, her mouth running 1000 mph.

"You were a real beast when the naloxone kicked in, I tell you what. I know how bad it can hurt, but you put up the biggest fight I've seen in a while. Gave your last nurse a black eye. That's when we had to put you in restraints. If you're gonna be good now, I'll take 'em off."

Restraints? I flex my fingers, try to move my arms, but they're buried under a mountain of sand. My legs don't move either, and suddenly I can't breathe at all. I twist and strain until my wrists and ankles are on fire, and the blue fairy is freaking out, but I don't care, I'm not listening.

The fairy grips my arm with tiny talons and bites down hard. Venom rushes through me, warm and fuzzy, dragging me under.

9:00 AM

THERE'S SOMETHING STICKING OUT OF my dick.

I feel it in the way you feel somebody trying to wake you up when it's 6:30, and your alarm was set for 5:45, and all you want to do is sleep for five more minutes.

Just five more minutes.

But this thing in my dick is persistent. It pinches, and I wonder how it got there, and who the hell was down there anyway?

Beep.

Beep.

Beep.

The air is an acrid mixture of chlorine and piss, like the locker room at the pool. I'm afraid to open my eyes.

Beep.

Beep.

"His EKG is the best I've seen after a code in a long time." There's a man in the room, and he's talking, but not to me. "Still, don't let that crash cart wander too far. Never know with narcotics."

Beep.

Footsteps. A door clicks closed. I crack open my eyes. The light burns, and my vision floods with water. I blink, and slowly the room comes into blurry focus.

The man who's talking stands at the foot of my bed. He's wearing a white coat and a stethoscope. A doctor. But why is there a doctor in my room, and why does my room smell like chlorine, and where the hell is that awful beeping coming from?

"Can somebody shut off my alarm?" I ask, but my voice doesn't sound like me. It comes out scratched and croaky like I'm floating belly up. Which is actually a pretty good description of how I'm feeling at the moment, like a truck backed over my ribcage.

The doctor's face is suddenly hovering too close to mine. "Eli, can you hear me?" he asks. "Do you know where you are?"

My heart starts to pound. I scan the part of the room I can see over the doctor's head. Curtains where a wall should be. And a TV screwed to a metal frame. "Am I . . . in the hospital?"

"Yes," the doctor says, like I just aced the oral part of the exam. "You're in our ICU. Do you know why you're here?"

I'm sweating now, and my heart is racing for real, because all at once the pieces are coming back to me. The game. The party at Alex's. Savannah leaving me on the deck. Getting into my car. The pills. The sirens . . .

And then it doesn't matter that I'm in the hospital because I may or may not have been unconscious. The only thing that matters this second, the single most important thought that explodes in my brain like fireworks is this:

I. Am. Busted.

"Please," I say, because it's very, very important that this dude listens to me. I grip his coat, straining to lift my head from my pillow, but there's a screaming pain in my chest, and the water in my eyes isn't because of the light anymore. "Please, no matter what you do, please don't tell my mom. Oh, god, don't tell my mom."

The doctor doesn't say anything. He gives me a pitying look and pats my chest real soft.

Another face hovers over mine. And I realize why the doctor looked at me like that. It's too late. My mom's here, but she's not yelling. She's crying. She's touching my face and my hair, and then she lays her head on my chest, forehead to sternum, and she's crying so hard. And that's when I know, oh, god, I know. My mom's been here the whole time.

My wrists are red and sore, and my hands land heavily on the back of Mom's head. Her hair's matted at the back like she just woke up, and then I realize she's wearing pajamas. I am the worst son in the world.

"Mom," I say in a horrible, sandpaper voice that I'm still not sure belongs to me.

She peers up at me, the skin around her eyes all blotchy and red, and her cheeks streaked with tears.

"Mom, I fucked up. I fucked up so bad."

Mom wraps my hands in hers and kisses them until my fingers are all wet. The doctor clears his throat. "I'm going to need to ask you a few questions, Eli," he says. "Would you like your mom to leave the room?"

Mom straightens, snuffles, wipes her cheeks with her open palms.

"She can stay," I say, dreading what's coming next.

"Are you aware of what's happened, son?" The doctor's an older guy, with heavy gray streaks through what's left of his

25

brown hair. His collar's open, and a frond of gray chest hair peeks out.

I nod. "I think so."

"So you're aware that you experienced an overdose?"

Mom makes a pitiful sound, something between a sob and a cough, and she grabs my hand and squeezes.

"Yes," I say, because I am now.

"What do you remember about last night?"

I close my eyes, because what I remember and what I'm going to say to this dude are two entirely different things, especially with my mom sitting right here next to me. "Not much," I tell him.

Doc clears his throat again, commanding my full attention. My knuckles are scratched, nearly white from how hard I'm squeezing Mom's hand. Or how hard she's squeezing mine.

"Were you, or have you ever considered, attempting suicide?"

A sound comes out of me, almost a laugh. "What, like killing myself? You think that's what happened last night?"

Doc's face is a mask of seasoned indifference. "Is it?"

What's with this guy? Not everybody gets high because they secretly want to off themselves. I mean, sure, the thought had crossed my mind a time or two, in the really dark days after Dad died. But that's normal, right? Plus, it was a long time ago. Before LionsHeart and Savannah. I use because I like how it makes me feel, but that doesn't mean I don't have boundaries. Needles never touch my skin—that's how you end up dead or in the hospital. Not from snorting every now and then. This wasn't supposed to happen.

I meet Doc's tired eyes. "Absolutely not," I say, and Mom's whole body exhales.

"How often would you say you use?" Doc asks.

The answer flies out of my mouth without an ounce of hesitation. "This was the first time. It was stupid, I know. I fucked up."

Doc's mouth presses into a thin line. "Is that really the answer you want to stick with?"

The only thing I *want* is to get the hell out of here. I want a handful of Advil and a gallon of Gatorade. I want my car, my phone. I want to call Chase. "I promise," I tell him. "This was the first time."

Doc and Mom exchange a look that's filled with silent conversation.

"I swear, Mom." I sandwich her hands between mine. "I learned my lesson, and I'll never do it again, I swear."

Mom lifts her free hand to my face. She pushes back my hair, and her fingers trace the scar on my eyebrow, the way she used to when I was little and wanted my dad. She'd sit beside my bed and stroke my hair and touch my scar with feather fingers. She'd tell me that we had each other no matter what, and that everything was going to be okay. I can't remember the last time she touched me like that.

"Eli, honey," she begins, but she's interrupted when a nurse slides open the glass door. "Dr. Henderson," he says, "there's a girl in the waiting room, and she's near hysterics. Says she's not leaving until she sees the patient. Is it okay if I send her back?"

Savannah.

I don't wait for the doctor to answer. "Yes," I say. "Now."

The nurse ignores me, waits for the doctor to tip his head in agreement. "We're almost done here," he says.

The nurse steps back into the hall, and the door slides closed.

"Just a few more questions," Dr. Henderson continues, but now all I can think about is Savannah. Was she the one who brought me here? Has she been here all night? Does her dad know?

"Eli," Dr. Henderson says my name impatiently. "Could you answer the question please?"

I squint at him, because I didn't hear the question.

He sighs. "Is there a family history of drug or alcohol abuse?"

I brush off his question with a shake of my head. My only family is Mom. And Benny, I guess, but he doesn't count. "No." What's taking Savannah so long?

Mom opens her mouth like she's going to say something, but then the door slides open, and all is I see is Savannah.

She's a mess, with raccoon smudges under her eyes and the same clothes she had on last night. Her face is red and puffy, and when I hold out my hand, fresh tears spill over onto her cheeks.

Mom stands up. "Could I speak with you outside for a moment, Dr. Henderson? There's something I'd like to discuss."

Doc nods. "Yes, that would be fine."

Mom leans down and kisses me on the head. She squeezes Savannah's arm as she passes, and they exchange the kind of look people give each other at funerals. Then she slips out of the room with the doctor and slides the door shut behind her.

I give Savannah's hand a tug, and she climbs onto the bed. We sit shoulder to shoulder, Savannah's knees tucked up to her chest and her head leaning on my arm. The only sounds in the room are the steady beeping of my heart monitor and Savannah's soft sniffles.

I nudge her gently with my elbow. "There's a tube in my dick," I say, hoping a lame joke will ease the tension between us.

"Gross." She doesn't even look up.

"I think everything's still intact. Wanna check?" I pretend I'm going to lift the sheet. Savannah swipes the back of her hand under her nose. "It's not funny, Eli. I thought . . . I thought you were . . ."

"I know." But I can't stand to hear her say it. I shift my weight and gingerly reach my arm around Savannah's shoulder. She burrows into my chest, startling when I gasp in pain.

"Easy," I say, wincing as she gently wraps her arms around my waist and curls her knees up tighter. She looks so small like this. Fragile.

"Hey," I say. "Hey." With my finger, I tip her chin up so I can look into her eyes. "I'm okay, Savannah. I'm fine. I'm right here."

She gives a little nod, but her arms grip my waist like I might disappear. She turns her face away from me, hiding it against my chest. "I've never been so scared in my whole life."

"Me neither," I whisper, even though I mean it different. It's the doctor and the questions and the 'what next' that scares me now. I rake my fingers through Savannah's hair and down her back. Kiss the top of her head.

"I'm sorry about your mom, by the way." Her words are muffled against my hospital gown, but I hear them perfectly.

My spine goes rigid. "What about my mom?"

Savannah sits up, shoves her hair out of her eyes. "I knew you wouldn't want me to call her, but . . ."

"*You* called her?" The words come out sharper than I mean for them to. But still . . .

Savannah's eyes narrow. The calm in her voice is a tightrope walker, wobbling above inevitable disaster. "Your heart stopped, Eli. You were *dying*."

A distant part of my brain tells me that Savannah's right, that she had no other choice, and that I would've done the same thing if she'd been the one who needed help. But another part, a louder part, says Savannah betrayed me.

I drop my arm from her shoulder, shrinking back into my pillows. "I'm not dead now." Now I'm stuck in a hospital room with a doctor asking me tricky questions, like how often I use, in front of my mom.

Savannah's face flashes fire, and she shoves away from me, scooting her body down the bed so she can look me in the face. "Everybody else ran from the cops, but I went looking for you. I found you in your car. Your eyes were rolled back in your head, and you were foaming at the mouth and . . ." She pauses, sucking in air like she's drowning. "You'd locked the door, Eli."

I don't want to listen to this. I don't want to know what happened. "Shut up, Savannah."

She shakes her head fiercely, pounding her open palm against the thin hospital mattress. Words spill out like white water over a broken dam. "The cops had to break the glass. And when they pulled you out of the car, you weren't breathing."

"I said, *SHUT UP!*"

"They did CPR, and they put you on a stretcher, and they took you away in an ambulance. So, yeah. I called your mom."

There's no air in the room. The space between Savannah and me is too wide, and I want to cross it, but I can't. I wrap my arms around my head, covering my face, and wish the whole world would disappear.

Savannah's voice finds me in my cave of skin and bones. "You need help, Eli. I care about you, but . . ."

Her voice wavers, and I know what's about to happen. I can already hear the words she's about to say. I lower my arms. "Are you breaking up with me?"

"I just . . . I don't know *what* to do."

30

The door opens, and Mom sticks her head into the room. Her eyes move from me to Savannah, reading the tension between us. "I'm sorry to interrupt, but . . ."

"No, it's okay." Savannah stands up, sweeps her hands across her cheeks, and straightens her clothes. "I'm actually super tired. I'd like to go home now."

"Of course you would." Mom steps into the room. Her arms are full of pamphlets and paperwork, and she drops it all on the counter and reaches for her jacket where it's slung over a chair. "I'll drive you."

"No, it's okay," Savannah says. "My dad's here."

My head shoots off the pillow, and pain stabs me in the chest. I flop back down. "Your dad?"

Savannah sighs. "Call me when you get home, okay?" The door closes behind her.

I cover my face with my hands.

The chair beside me creaks as Mom drops into it. "Can I do anything?"

"I want to go home, Mom."

"I know you do, honey." She hesitates, reaching over the metal bar of the bed to squeeze my forearm. Her thumb strokes my skin in time with the practiced words she forces out. "But I'm not sure that's the best idea right now."

I freeze.

Mom walks over to the counter and scoops up the pile of pamphlets. "I want you to take a look at these." She fans out the pamphlets across my legs like cards in a magic trick.

My mind goes numb as I scan the pamphlet covers. They look like college brochures, with pictures of smiling kids walking across manicured lawns and artful shots of stone buildings meant to showcase the architecture. Like anybody would pick a college because of the architecture.

Mom waves one of the brochures. "Dr. Henderson recommended this one," she says. "It's up in the mountains, a couple hours from here. I spoke to the social worker about it. She says she'll make the call for us, see if they have a bed."

I take the brochure. The cover boasts a view of a lake with fog-covered mountains in the background. LakeShore Recovery Center. Inside the brochure's glossy pages, there are pictures of smiling teenagers seated in a semi-circle, all eyes on an overly expressive adult in the center. There's a shot of the dining hall, but it's the picture of the bedroom that surprises me, shoots a bolt of nausea through my gut. Because this is a place people go to stay.

"Rehab?" I say the word because Mom can't. "Really?"

She avoids my eyes, shuffling through the brochures like she's putting her cards back in the box.

"Those places are for people with drug problems, Mom. I don't have a problem. I told you, this was the first time . . ."

Mom shoots me a sideways look. She knows I'm lying.

I hold up my hands to show her she's got me. "Okay, so maybe it's been a couple of times. But I don't have a problem. I can stop whenever I want."

Mom's eyes soften. "I know you think that, sweetie, but . . ."

I cut her off. "I *know* I can. Just give me a chance, Mom. Please."

Mom sighs and runs her hand down her face. "Steven spoke to the officer who pulled you from the car . . ."

My pulse throbs in my throat. I know what the cops would've found in my car. The plastic baggie, one lonely capsule inside.

"He's made a few calls."

Knowing Steven, the chief of police is his golfing buddy, and he's made some deal that looks like it's about doing what's best for me, but is actually about keeping his own reputation clean and shiny. A girlfriend from the poor side of town? That he can fix with a two-carat wedding ring and a walk-in closet the size of most living rooms. But a stepson who's a junkie? Now that just won't do.

"So if I go to rehab, the drug charges go away?"

"The officer agreed to sit on the case to give you a chance to get better. Do you have any idea how lucky you are? Your dad . . ."

"He's *not* my dad!" I glare at her, my voice cracking like some pimply junior high punk. "And I don't care what kind of deal he's made. I don't need Steven, and I sure as hell don't need rehab!"

Mom slumps in her chair, shoves her hands through her knotted hair until the skin on her forehead stretches, and her eyes seem to bulge in the strange half-light of the room. "I mean lucky to be alive," she says, her voice strained, a rubber band about to snap. "I knew you were drinking, suspected there was pot, too. I mean, it's normal for teenagers to smoke once in a while. Christ, even I did! But fuck, Eli! Heroin? Do you have any idea what could've happened?"

I stare hard at the pocked gray ceiling tiles, sterile and colorless, like the rest of the hospital. I know what could've happened. But real life is hard enough without worrying about what-ifs.

Mom slides her hands down her face; her fingers wipe the sides of her mouth. "It's just 28 days."

I cough out a bitter laugh. "28 days? That's a whole month of my life, Mom, and I don't even have a choice."

"You're eighteen, Eli. I can't make you go. But after the last time . . ."

Her voice trails off, but I know what she was going to say. The morning after Winter Formal, woken by the call from Savannah's dad, Mom was waiting in the kitchen when I showed up, reeking of smoke and sweat, Savannah's dried puke on my shoe. Mom's yelling woke up Steven, who made me drink a pot of black coffee and said the next time, I might as well not come home at all.

I roll to my side, turning my back on Mom. "Steven finally found a way to get rid of me, huh? The three of you can finally be the perfect little family he's always wanted."

"We're not a family without you, Eli." Mom's gentle voice reaches over my shoulder, tugs at me like a hand on my chin, but I don't turn around.

Mom stands up, leaving the pamphlets in a stack on the bed. "I'm going to go home, get dressed, and pack a few of your things. I'll be back in a couple of hours."

She waits a minute for my response, and when it doesn't come, she bends down and kisses the top of my head. "I love you, Eli," she says.

I hear the door close behind her, and I squeeze my eyes tight, until stars form behind my lids, and the tears stop stinging.

After

THREE DAYS, EIGHT CUPS OF JELL-O, and countless hours of daytime TV later, Mom and I step through the sliding glass doors of the hospital and out into the parking lot. It's raining; the weather's a perfect fucking cliché. Nobody steps out of the hospital into a beautiful summery day—not when they're going to rehab. When you're on your way to rehab, the sky is angry, and the clouds close in on you. There's no sun for miles.

Steven's Lexus is waiting by the curb; thin rivers streak the SUV's wide windows.

I ease myself down onto the backseat, the leather as smooth and creamy as one of Savannah's vanilla lattes. Steven's hair is wet from the shower; the inside of the car smells like coffee and dial soap. Benny's sitting in his booster, barefoot, a *Blue's Clues* coloring book across his lap.

"You brought Benny?"

Mom buckles her seatbelt and adjusts the shoulder strap. "He's missed you," she says, shooting me a pointed look. "And it'll be a while before he sees you again." She reaches for her coffee, turning her attention to Steven. "You know where you're going?"

I lean back against the seat and shut my eyes, but I can feel Benny staring at me. I crack one lid. "What?"

"You don't look sick." He eyes me suspiciously.

"I'm not sick. Who told you I was sick?"

Benny squirts blue razzleberry hand sanitizer into his palm and rubs furiously. "Miss Tyler is taking us to the aquarium tomorrow."

Miss Tyler, Benny's kindergarten teacher, has managed to instill a fear of germs in Benny that borders on obsessive compulsive. Last winter, Benny's hands were raw from over-washing. I'm just waiting for the day that Benny starts wrapping his school supplies in aluminum foil.

"You can't go if you're sick," Benny says. "Miss Tyler says no germs on the bus."

"I'm *not* sick, Ben. Mom, you told him I was sick?"

Mom's arguing with Steven about the best way to get to the turnpike from the hospital parking lot, but she pauses long enough to give me an apologetic look. "We weren't exactly sure what to tell him."

Benny touches my face with small hands still glistening with sanitizer.

I swat him away. "What are you doing?"

"Checking for fever. Miss Tyler always checks for fever."

"I told you, I'm not sick!"

Mom sighs. She tucks her seatbelt behind her and twists around to face us. "Ben, your brother's not *sick* like you're thinking of. He's just not feeling like himself."

That's the understatement of the century.

"He's going to take a little break from school until he feels better again."

Benny's eyes narrow. "Like Disney?" he asks, referencing the trip my family took spring break of my junior year. The little nerd-bomber was so upset that preschool would be closed for a week that his teacher gave him a special notebook, so he could tell his class all about his trip when he got back.

"It's more like summer camp," Mom tells him. "They have a lake and all kinds of fun group activities."

Benny's eyes get bright with excitement. He spent a week at day camp last summer and loved it almost as much as Disney World.

"Oh, yea," I say, my voice dripping with sarcasm. "Exactly like summer camp."

Steven's dark eyes meet mine in the rearview. "I know it doesn't feel like it now, but you're making the right choice, son."

"You know I don't have a choice." My words are fists, and I'm aiming for soft tissue. "And I am *not* your son."

Steven's face tightens, but he swallows his words like bitters in his whiskey sour. His fingers drum the steering wheel, tapping out all the things he'd say if Benny wasn't here.

Mom reaches a hand across the center console and massages the back of Steven's neck. As if he's the one who needs her.

"When will you be back?" Benny asks me.

My throat suddenly feels tight, and my eyes sting. I'm grateful when Mom offers her phone to Benny.

"Here, Ben," she says. "Why don't you watch some *Blue's Clues*, okay?"

He takes it eagerly, and I prop my packed duffel against the foggy window, carefully positioning it under my neck like a pillow.

"I packed your green hoodie," Mom says. "The one with the fleece lining. That's your favorite, right? And your slippers. I did all the laundry, so I probably packed more than you'll need."

I nod absently, wishing for my phone and headphones so that I could disappear into a world of sound. Although the worst of my withdrawal symptoms are over, my stomach still churns around my hospital breakfast, and my whole chest aches. Doc said that's from the chest compressions, that I was lucky the paramedic didn't crack a rib. People have thrown that word around a lot over the past three days. But I don't feel lucky. I feel like my life is falling apart.

"They provide all your meals and snacks," Mom continues, her fingers toying the lip of her Starbucks cup. "I'll put money on your account, so you can get candy or soda or whatever."

I close my eyes and push Mom's voice to the background, like the steady whirring of a white noise machine. And I go to the secret place inside me that's for Emergencies Only, the place where there's so much nothingness that anything is possible.

It's the place where I keep my dad.

"Eli. Eli, wake up, honey. We're here." Mom's voice nudges me out of the dream. It's the same dream I always have. The one with the park and the swings.

I wake up reluctantly, even though I know how the dream ends.

My duffel bag is damp where I've been drooling in my sleep; my head is pounding.

I sit up, squinting out the window at the building ahead. Blue clapboard siding surrounds white window frames and doors. White curtains billow in a few open windows. The entrance is made entirely of glass, marked by two white pillars, and crowned with a large sign. The words *LakeShore Recovery Center* hover over a watery horizon, punctuated by a couple of painted pine trees.

Benny's snoring, his chin on his chest, a crayon loose in one hand. Blue, his favorite. I lift his head back against his car seat. He breathes easier for about half a second until his head flops down again.

Steven swerves into the lot. He parks, but leaves the car running. "I guess I'll wait here?" He tips his head toward the back seat, where Benny's already sawing lumber again.

Mom hesitates. Her hand flutters at her neck, frazzled. "Are you sure? It might be a while."

"We'll be fine." Steven tells her. His voice is soothing, and he offers a reassuring smile. "If he wakes up, we'll go for a walk or something."

Mom nods. She checks the visor mirror, absently fluffing her hair and swiping her thumb over the tired lines beneath her eyes. "Okay," she says, slapping the visor closed and collecting her purse. "You ready, Eli?"

Not in the least.

Mom climbs out of the car, closing the door behind her, and the sound nudges Benny from his nap.

"You going to Disney camp now?" he murmurs groggily.

"Yeah, Ben," I tell him. "Go back to sleep, okay?"

Benny nuzzles his face against the side of the car seat and closes his eyes. "Okay," he whispers.

I slip the crayon from his hand and put it back in the box, so he'll know where to find it.

Steven glances at me over his shoulder. "We'll see you soon, Eli."

"Sure," I mutter. "Whatever." Then I crawl out of the car, leaving Steven and Benny behind.

My body feels like an old man's when I unfold onto the pavement. I'm stiff and achy—my duffel's full of bricks. I hoist it onto my hip and follow Mom up the sidewalk toward the entrance. A wall of trees edges the property, as high and impenetrable as a barbwire fence. Green lawn stretches out from all sides of the building, like a cross between Alcatraz and Oz. This place is a freaking suburban island, but it was the only one close enough for Savannah to come and visit. That is, if her dad ever lets her see me again.

Mom stops outside the entrance. "So this is it," she says, the forced cheerfulness back in her voice. "Nice, right?"

Through the doors, I can see the curve of a reception desk and the artificial shine of potted plants. Like a fucking hotel lobby.

I just want to go home.

"It's only 28 days, Eli," Mom says. "You can do anything for 28 days."

"It's not that," I tell her. "This whole thing is so stupid. I mean, these places are for addicts . . . junkies. I'm going to miss half the season! Plus, it's senior year. How am I going to graduate if I spend a month here?"

Mom sighs. We're standing too close to the automatic doors, and the glass keeps parting awkwardly, sliding half-way open and then shutting again. Mom steps away from the door, runs her hand through her shoulder-length curls. "I told you we'll figure that out. You can do make-up work, even take a summer class if necessary. That's not important right now. What *is* important, is that you get better."

"You keep saying that," I plead. "But there's nothing wrong with me."

I see the exact moment that Mom registers the tremble in my voice. Her icy armor cracks, and I seize the opening.

"Dad wouldn't make me stay."

Mom's face hardens. Her words are frostbitten. "Then thank goodness he's not here."

She takes my duffel, tosses it up on her shoulder, and heads toward the door. The glass parts, then closes decidedly behind her.

For a nanosecond, I consider the wall of trees behind the building and wonder how far I could make it before they found me. But I'm pretty sure running would be next to impossible right now. Plus, my throat is so dry, and my head's throbbing like my brain is trying to escape my skull.

It's just 28 days. I can do anything for 28 days.

I follow Mom inside.

LakeShore Recovery Center
Detox Unit
Day 1

THERE'S A SPIDER ON THE ceiling. It's huge—the kind you'd need a tank to squish. With hairy legs, it dangles from an invisible thread, shimmying across the shadowed ceiling like it's flying. Show-off.

I'm lying on my back in a spectacularly UN-comfortable bed. I was assigned to it by a four-foot-nothing nurse named Rita, who dropped off my duffel (unzipped and searched through, my green hoodie hanging out) and wouldn't leave until I swallowed the pills from the little paper cup she pushed at me—ibuprofen and something for nausea. Every few hours, Rita sticks her head in the room to make sure I haven't gotten up and wandered away. Or that the guy in the bed next to me is still breathing.

Both are legit concerns in a detox unit, I guess, except for the fact that the dude next to me is mumbling so much in his sleep any idiot could tell he's perfectly alive. And even *if* I had the energy to get out of bed, I'd have no idea where to go. I'm stuck here, in Unit 7, Room 12, staring at a huge fucking spider on the ceiling and wishing I had spidey-senses so that I could shimmy up the wall and disappear through a crack in the plaster.

I'm seriously losing my mind. It's been like 10 hours since Mom and I finished up at intake—the pile of paperwork, the list of humiliating questions. *What substances have you used in the last 90 days? How often do you use?* I replay my answers, counting the times like sheep. Once a month, once a week, every three days, every two . . . That's insomnia for you, I guess. Not that I could sleep anyway, what with Jabber Jaws next to me, and Nosy the Nurse, and the obvious insect infestation problem. I just want to go home.

I don't belong here. People in this unit scream in their sleep, hooked up to so many IV drips that they can't even get up to take a leak. There are so many doctors and nurses wandering around that I might as well have stayed in the hospital—at least there, the metal bed was adjustable. Plus, they had JELL-O. And TV.

I miss Savannah.

Rita told me I'll only be on this unit for a couple of days. We had a nice long chat, she and I, while she took my blood pressure and temperature and did a couple of other useless tests that won't tell them anything. I highly doubt a well-controlled sniffing habit is going to show up on a blood pressure reading. It's like they're looking for medical proof that I'm sick, so they can make me "better." Pretty soon they'll figure out there's nothing wrong with me and send me home.

I'd said as much when Rita capped the little vial of my cherry red blood. Then I asked to use the phone. She flashed me a cutesy half-smile and told me detox residents are on blackout. No phone calls or visitors for the first five days.

Not that Savannah's dad would let me talk to her anyway. Even if she wanted to. I close my eyes and silently beg for sleep.

"Hey. Hey, buddy . . . you awake?"

I roll over and glare at my roommate. "You mean you *also* talk when you're awake?"

He grimaces, his ruddy skin coated in freckles. "Yeah, the sleep-talking, right? Sorry about that." He props himself up on his elbow, runs his hand across spiky red hair. "The nightmares are the worst. If I scream, just throw something at me. I won't be mad, I swear."

I flop onto my back, lifting my pillow so it covers my face, and grumble into the warm cotton. "Don't tempt me."

Jabber Jaws gives a hiccupy kind of laugh. I've barely crossed into drowsy territory when his voice tiptoes under my pillow.

"I must've been out cold when you got here, huh? Didn't even hear you show up. What's your name, anyway?"

I slap my pillow away from my face. "Dude! Can't you see I'm trying to sleep?"

"My bad," he squeaks.

I flop over onto my side, twist up my sheets in my fists, and squeeze my eyes shut. Sleep, please, sleep.

"My name's Ronnie, by the way."

You have *got* to be kidding me.

I flip over spastically, gritting my teeth against the stabbing pain in my ribcage that a little ibuprofen just can't touch. I'm fully intent on ripping Ron a new one, but when he stretches his hand across the chasm between our beds, I see how bad he's shaking.

I grip his hand and squeeze. "I'm Eli."

Ron gives me a jittery smile. "My friends call me Red."

No kidding. I roll onto my back and pull my thin blanket up to my chin. "So, Red," I say, stifling an enormous yawn, "Give me the lowdown. What do I need to know about this place?"

"It's alright, I guess," Red says. "Drugs have taken over the neighborhood, though." He laughs at his own dumb joke, a raspy chuckle, and I smile in spite of myself.

"Seriously, though," Red continues. "I've heard stuff about other places, bad stuff. Bed bugs, quack therapists, that kind of shit. Not here, though. Other than detox, I've only seen intake, but as far as I can tell, this place is pretty swanky. You and me musta got lucky."

I close my eyes and think about a conversation I'd overhead in the hospital, when Mom and Steven had assumed I was asleep. "There's the ambulance ride, all the tests. Not to mention two days in the ICU," Mom fretted, her voice a strangled whisper. "How much will it all cost?"

Steven had soothed her, whispering that money should be the last thing on her mind, and I'd remembered all the nights I'd stood as a little boy in the kitchen doorway, listening to Mom scream into the phone about rent money, child support, or unpaid bills. Dad would do his best, always showing up a few days later with a couple bags of groceries or his tool box to fix something around the house—a leaky toilet, a loose stair tread. Then Mom would be happy, and she'd let him take me for ice cream or a catch in the park.

I've never heard Mom and Steven talk about money because there was never any shortage of it. If it weren't for

Steven's money, Mom would never have been able to afford a place like LakeShore. Then again, if it weren't for Steven, I wouldn't be here at all. "Sure," I say to Red, sarcasm prickling my words with ragged edges. "Real lucky."

I stare into the dark as Red tells me all about the various medications available in the nurses' station *(Even something to help you shit if you can't. Imagine if they sold that on the street?)* and which nurse is his favorite (a super-hot brunette that brings him broth for dinner). His chatter is weirdly soothing, like a light on in the hallway bathroom or the TV on downstairs. Because it makes you feel less alone. I let my eyes close as Red talks, and little by little, sleep finally finds me.

Day 2

RED'S GONE WHEN I WAKE up. His bed is made up nice and tidy. I rub my face and squint at the round clock that hangs on the opposite wall. 11:00 A.M. I wonder where I can get some breakfast around here.

A cute brunette in clingy pink scrubs appears in the doorway. She's got a stethoscope around her neck, and she's wheeling a blood pressure monitor. "Glad to see you're up," she says, in the chipper tone of someone who wakes up much earlier than 11:00 A.M. She wheels the monitor to the side of my bed. "I need to check your vitals."

My ribs ache as I push myself upright and offer her my arm, wondering if this is the hottie Red told me about. "Where's Rita?"

The nurse's eyes stay fixed on the monitor as the strap around my arm squeezes tighter and tighter. "Night shift," she says. "She'll be back around 7."

Satisfied with the reading, she releases my arm, and I flex my fingers, pushing the blood back into them. She listens to my heartbeat, then takes my temperature. "Everything looks good," she says, tucking the thermometer back into the front pocket of her scrub shirt. "How are you feeling?"

"Sore," I tell her. "And hungry. Any idea where I can get some food?"

She gives me a couple more ibuprofen, then glances up at the clock. "Breakfast has been over for a while. I'll see if I can get you some juice."

She leaves the room, returning a moment later with a juice box of cranberry cocktail and a plastic wrapped two pack of graham crackers. "Best I could do," she says, offering me the tiny snack.

I tear into the crackers and suck the juice box dry.

"Better?" the nurse asks.

"A little."

She takes my crumpled juice box and gives me a half smile. "The kitchen opens in an hour for lunch. If you're feeling up to it, you can get up and get dressed. You'll probably be moving on pretty soon anyway."

"Moving on?" I crumble the plastic cracker wrapper in my fist, trying to ignore the whispering hope that all those tests have proven I was right. There's nothing wrong with me.

"Phase Two," the nurse says. She moves to the window and whips the curtains apart. A lazy ray of sunshine stretches across my bed. "No sense lounging around in here when you're well enough to start the program. Besides, we need the bed."

"People must be pounding down the door to get in this place, huh?" I paper-ball the graham cracker trash to the waste basket near the window. It bounces off the rim and hits the floor, scattering tiny crumbs.

The nurse purses her lips. "Something like that." She stoops to pick up the trash. I stretch my arms gently, easing my stiff neck from side to side. She gives me a discerning look. "Do you think you can manage in the shower?"

I freeze, my arms in mid-air. "What, like, *alone*?"

She rolls her eyes, but her voice is all business. "I can help if you need me to."

Not that being bathed by a super-cute nurse wouldn't be *awesome*, but given the circumstances, it'd be a new low. Even for me. "I'm fine," I tell her.

"There's an intercom in the bathroom. It calls the nurses' station. If you feel light-headed or anything, just press the button, okay?"

I nod. The fleeting fantasy of water-spattered pink scrubs fades into a mental picture of myself all "I've-fallen-and-I-can't-get-up!"

The nurse heads for the door, and I swing my legs over the side of the bed, pushing myself to standing before she can change her mind. The cart squeaks as she wheels it out of the room.

A quick mental survey of my body turns up wobbling knees and an aching chest and back. Dr. Henderson had told me I'd be sore for at least a few weeks and given me a long list of things I'm not supposed to do in the meantime. But other than that, I actually feel okay.

I'm still wearing my hospital bracelet. I don't remember anyone putting it on me in the first place. Because I was unconscious, I realize. The paramedics rolled me in on a stretcher, and some nurse slapped the bracelet on my limp arm.

With morbid fascination, I try to picture it, like a scene in one of those medical dramas Mom loves to watch. The ambulance squeals into the parking lot, lights flashing. The

EMS crew shoves my stretcher through the glass doors, shouting for the nearest ER doc.

The image sucks the wind out of me, and I sink back down onto the bed. To be somewhere one moment, and then wake up somewhere entirely different, with people who weren't there before asking you questions you don't know the answers to—it's like disappearing.

Or like dying.

I yank at the bracelet; it stretches, but doesn't break.

My duffel bag waits at the foot of my bed. I give up on the bracelet and rifle through the rumpled pile of clothes in my bag for the towel Mom said she put at the bottom. My fingers graze a hard edge. I feel around for whatever it is and pull it from the bag.

It's a framed picture of Mom and me, the one she keeps on her bedside table. I'm probably about ten or eleven—a total tool with ears that are too big for my head and huge gaps in my teeth. The scar that severs my eyebrow is a puckered strip of pale pink skin. We're on a lacrosse field—Dad had started teaching me to play as soon as I was big enough to hold a stick. "Any idiot can play football," he used to say. "It takes an athlete to play lacrosse. Are you an athlete, Eli?"

"I'm an athlete!" I'd holler, even though back then I could barely hoist the stick over my head.

Mom had signed me up for a club team as soon as I was old enough. We had just moved in with Steven—my green jersey reads Grandhaven Giants. Mom's squatting beside me, her face shiny and proud, her eyes tired.

I put the picture back in the bag.

I grab a pair of clean boxers and socks and toss them on the bed, and that's when it dawns on me that Mom went through my drawers.

Panic surges through me. My sock drawer was clean, I know that for sure. I mentally scan the other drawers until I'm fairly confident there was nothing else to find. Not that it would matter. I'm in detox, for Christ's sake. It's not like a hidden stash would come as a surprise.

I pull my towel from my duffel, and I head for the shower. And then I think about the lone pill left in my car, and I wonder if it'll still be there when I get home.

Fresh from the shower, I head to the cafeteria in search of food. My wet hair soaks the collar of my long-sleeve t-shirt as I weave through the grey fold-out tables in the dining hall. A few people cast curious glances in my direction, and suddenly, it's my first day at LionsHeart all over again. Only here, there's no hiding who you are.

I tug my shirt sleeve down over my hospital bracelet and briefly consider heading back to my room for a graham cracker/juice box lunch with Red. But then I spy golden-brown grilled cheese sandwiches and creamy tomato bisque on people's trays. My stomach whines, too empty and too nervous to muster a proper growl. I wonder if they have any chicken noodle soup.

On the far side of the cafeteria, two industrial-sized coffee makers bookmark a ginormous platter of cheese Danishes, muffins, and doughnuts. Residents hover around the table, picking at the platter of desserts and refilling Styrofoam coffee cups like it's desert water.

I snag a bowl of bisque and two grilled cheese sandwiches, topping off my tray with a shiny apple from the overflowing fruit bowl. Then I look around for a place to sit. My inner navigation system, forged by three and a half years of high school, clicks into high alert, and I grapple for a glimpse of the caste order in this place. But none of the pieces fit the way they should.

At one table, I spot a super-hot blonde, who looks like she walked right out of a Hollister's ad, chatting it up with a dude with more facial piercings than I have fingers. By the coffee table, a bird-sized guy in thick black glasses beams up at Oprah's doppelganger. This place is crawling with nobodies.

I head to the nearest table with an empty seat. A featherweight emo chick is talking with wildly expressive hands to a two-ton Hawaiian linebacker across from her. He glances up at me with mild interest as I drop my tray and pull out a chair. "Okay if I sit here?" I ask.

Linebacker shrugs. I plunk down next to him and dunk a cheesy sandwich triangle into my bowl of bisque. It's delicious, and my belly opens up to the food like it's starving. I forget about the people around me and shovel it in. It's not until I've started on my second sandwich that I realize they're both staring at me.

"You new?" Linebacker asks. A half-smile curls up one side of his mouth.

I nod, embarrassed. "How can you tell?"

"When you're an old-timer like me, newbies are easy to spot," he says. "Still a little green around the gills. Either they peck their food like starving birds or . . ." He glances at my ravaged plate. "They eat like you."

"I haven't eaten much the last couple of days," I admit. "Unless you count hospital JELL-O and something the nurses called oatmeal. I'm still not convinced."

The girl stifles a giggle. I give her the once-over. Cute, if it weren't for the black liner around her eyes and white blonde hair that Savannah would say was straight out of a bottle. A section of nearly black roots stripes her scalp, and she stares down at her uneaten food without acknowledging me.

"That's Libby," the guy says. He reaches out a meaty fist. "I'm Mo."

I put down my sandwich to shake his hand. "Eli."

"Pleasure to meet you." Mo twists in his seat, craning his neck for a view of the dessert table, which isn't as crowded anymore. "Now that the junkies have cleared out, I think I'll get myself some dessert."

He laughs at the look of confusion on my face. "*Sugar* junkies," he says, pushing back his chair and standing up. "Bad joke, I guess. You want something?"

Two sandwiches in, and I've still never been this kind of hungry. My stomach is a black hole; I could go face-first into a platter of sugar-glazed donuts and still not reach the bottom. "Donuts," I say. "Two? No, three."

Mo grins. "You got it." He side-steps between tables until he reaches the center aisle. Every few feet, he stops to talk to somebody, shaking hands and doling out bear hugs. His deep belly laugh carries across the cafeteria, bouncing from table to table like a freshly dunked beer pong ball.

"Nice guy," I say, more to myself than to the girl sitting next to me.

A small, rasp-stained voice pipes up. "The nicest."

Libby peers up at me from under a thick fringe of blonde bangs. Her ice blue eyes pierce mine.

"I think it'll be a while before I get my dessert, though," I joke. Across the dining hall, Mo's been offered a seat at another table, and he's deep in conversation with some dude with gaping holes in his ear lobes where spacers used to be.

Libby's lips part, and a row of slightly crooked teeth peek out from a hesitant smile. "Yeah, I wouldn't count on it if I were you."

I tip my head toward her tray. "I noticed he didn't offer to get you anything."

Her eyes drop. "I'm not that hungry." Her fingers draw into a fist. Her nails, more chip than purple paint, dig into sugar white skin. And that's when I see the scars.

Ribbons of puckered pink flesh crisscross the skin on her arms. There's no pattern to the scars—no obvious purpose in their making. It's like instead of tattoos, she decorated herself with pain.

She stiffens beside me, her arm darting under the table like a startled garden snake. I realize I've been staring, and that *she knows* I was staring. I'm suddenly super embarrassed, like I just got caught peeping an exposed thong. I have to say something—*anything* to fill this awkward silence. What comes out of my mouth is so socially retarded that I immediately want to punch myself in the face:

"I should see the other guy, right?"

Libby's eyes flash white-blue, like the crack of snow before an avalanche. She hisses at me through clenched white lips. "Fuck you."

"Hey," I try, reaching out almost automatically.

Libby slaps my hand away and jumps to her feet, shooting me one last electrified look before snatching her tray off the table and stalking away.

Near the exit, an orderly grabs her arm. She twists in his grip and lets out a scream like a slaughtered animal.

The dining hall freezes. It's completely silent, and everybody's staring. The orderly releases his grip. Libby slams her tray onto the floor. It lands with a deafening clatter that ricochets off the ceiling as Libby storms through the exit.

Silence hovers over the room. The orderly swipes tomato bisque off white scrubs with his bare hands. Spoons click against bowls. People return to their conversations. The orderly disappears into the kitchen. There's no alarm, no lockdown. Nobody runs after Libby. Everything goes back to normal. And that's the weirdest part of all.

I'm still shaken when Mo returns a minute later with a cup of black coffee and three donuts wrapped in a paper napkin. He slides the sugary package across the table with two fingers, then turns his seat backward and plops down. "What happened?"

I shrug, because it all happened so fast, I'm not even sure I know. But I'm pretty sure it's my fault. "We were talking." The image of Libby's scars flashes behind my eyes. "I guess I said the wrong thing. All of a sudden, she just . . . flipped."

Mo nods thoughtfully and sips his coffee.

I wait for him to press me for information, but when he doesn't, I ask the question that's screaming in the back of my mind. "Is she, like, crazy or something?"

Mo snorts, nearly choking on his coffee. "You mean, like, any more than the rest of us?"

I meet his even gaze. "Not me."

Mo laughs, but it stings. He shakes his head like I'm the world's biggest idiot. "Newbies," he mumbles.

I bristle, suddenly not so hungry. "What's that supposed to mean?"

Mo tips his chin toward my wrist. "How'd you get that bracelet, huh? Broken leg?"

I yank my t-shirt down to cover it and make a mental note to find a pair of scissors, stat.

Mo's white teeth flash in a no-bullshit smile. "You newbies are all the same. Blame, denial, blame, denial. Like somebody forced the fucking needle in your arm."

My muscles tense, and I shove back from the table.

"Relax, dude," Mo says. "I'm not looking for the details. We've all been there before. It's the cop's fault 'cause he pulled you over. It's the shit's fault 'cause it wasn't pure. We do the same crap over and over again, and then we wonder why we end up here."

I grit my teeth against the flood of memories that crash through my skull tsunami-style.

Savannah after Winter Formal, slung over my arm. The vile stench of stomach acid I was still scrubbing out of my car a week later.

Savannah on the deck at Alex's, begging me to stay with her. *We've got enough trouble already.*

Savannah's tear-stained face through my car window, fists pounding the glass.

I snatch my tray off the table and stand up. "I don't need this right now, okay?"

"What, you got something more important going on?" Mo asks. And then he laughs. I want to punch him, but he lets out this belly laugh like the whole thing's a fucking riot. "See what I mean, dude? Every single one of us. We're all fucking insane."

The lights are out when I get back to my room. The curtains are pulled shut, and a heavy shade blocks out the afternoon sun. Red is a snoring lump under the covers of his bed.

I stealth-walk past him, hands out in front of me to keep from slamming into anything. When my fingers brush my coarse cotton blanket, I lie down and bury my face in my pillows. I wish Savannah was here. Even better, I wish I was with her, wherever she is. Hopefully, her dad hasn't convinced her that I'm a horrible influence. Hopefully, she doesn't hate me.

I've just started to doze when the mumbling starts.

"Lisa . . . Lisa . . ." Red's thrashing around in his bed, kicking off his covers like they're knitted with thorns. His flailing arms nearly decapitate our bedside lamp, and then the mumbling turns to a guttural groan that starts low in his belly and rises to a primal keen.

I've had enough crazy for one day. I yank a pillow out from under my head and chuck it at Red, though the motion jars my ribs. He jolts—the scream cut off in his throat. He scrambles up, knocking the pillow away like he's afraid it might bite him.

"Red!"

He looks right at me, but his eyes are dead, and I know he's not awake. He's still with Lisa, and apparently, that chick really did a number on him. His body's twitching like he just took the scenic route through hell. I toss my other pillow at him. "Red, wake up! It's a dream."

He blinks a couple times, confused, and then his body relaxes. He slides back down in his bed and yanks up his blanket.

"Wait," I say, stretching over the space between our beds to punch his shoulder. "I need my pillows back."

There's a shuffling sound from Red's bed, and then a pillow soars through the air in a wide arc that ends on my face. "Thanks a lot," I mumble into the fluffy cotton. "There was a second one, you know."

I dodge this one in time, catch it before it hits me, and tuck them both back under my head. "You're welcome," I mutter.

"Thanks," comes the muffled response.

I roll onto my side. "Who is she?" I ask. "This Lisa chick."

Red turns onto his back, his profile sharp, his eyes dark hollows in the shadows of his face. "She's my girlfriend. Was my girlfriend, I mean."

"Must've been one hell of a breakup, huh?"

"We didn't break up," Red says. "We should've, maybe. I don't know. Anyway . . . she's dead. Flipped her car over a guardrail coming back from my house in the middle of the night."

"Dude." The word is an exhale, but I don't know what else to say.

Red rubs his hand across his face. "You want to know the crazy part? We didn't even party. I mean, we usually did. A lot. Backstage to catch the vibe before a gig, afterwards to celebrate. I mean, look at me." Red chokes on a bitter laugh. "I've got more scar tissue than blood in my veins. But not that night. That night we ordered a pizza and watched a movie."

Red's story unravels in dark whispers, shadows that cling to the corners of our room like spider webs. "We fell asleep on the couch. When we woke up the next morning, Lisa was late for work. She freaked out 'cause her manager was a real asshole, and then she took off."

Red gives me a weak smile. "It was probably the lamest date we'd ever had. I hadn't played a show in a while; all I had in the house was Safeway mac n' cheese. We pooled our change for one of those five-dollar pizzas and watched a movie on Netflix. But if I could go back, I'd do it all over again. I'd order pizza and a movie every night. I'd curl up on my couch with Lisa, and I'd stay there forever."

The heavy sound of our breathing thickens the air in the room. Wheels squeak outside our door, and footsteps crisscross the hallway. There are vitals to be checked and meals to be brought to kids who can't get out of bed. Life goes on even when it feels like it shouldn't, when everything should come to a screaming halt. Red and I lie here in the darkness, and we hold back the ticking seconds on the clock.

Lisa is dead.

Red is broken.

Five nights ago, I almost died.

Red's bed squeaks as he rolls onto his side. He shuffles his pillows into a ball and tucks his elbow under his arm. "What about you?" he asks.

"Me?" My girlfriend's alive. *If* I still have a girlfriend.

"Yeah," Red presses. "Prep school kid, for sure. Bet you spend Saturdays sailing, or play . . . what's the game like football, but more badass?"

"Rugby?"

"Yeah, that one. What are you in for, anyway? Oxy? Percs? Bet it's some real pricey shit, huh?"

I turn onto my back and stare hard at the ceiling. This is the last conversation I want to be having right now. But some part of me needs to say it out loud. "H," I tell him.

Red whistles through his teeth. "No kidding?"

"Honest to God."

"Shit. Needles?"

My spine goes rigid, and I glare at him in the dark. I'm not some itching, twitching junkie. I'm nothing like those "newbies" Mo mentioned. Nothing like Red. "No way, dude."

"Not yet, you mean." Red lets out a cackle that dissolves into a cough. "Still trying to keep it classy, huh? Up the nose or some shit like that. And you think 'cause you're not fiending yet, that means you're not like me?"

"I'm not like you," I tell him. "I mean, no offense or anything."

"None taken." Red's quiet, but I feel his eyes on me, and I can almost hear his mental wheels turning. "I don't envy you, dude," he says after a minute. "The itching was easy. It's *feeling* that sucks the hardest."

Red rolls onto his back and pulls the blanket up under his chin. His white ankles and toes stick out at the bottom, pale ghosts in the darkness. "Thanks again, by the way. For waking me up."

"No problem." I fold my arms behind my head, squeeze my eyes shut, and stare into the blackness of my lids until stars form. "I don't have anything better to do," I say. "If you want to try to go back to sleep, I can listen out for you. You know, wake you up if you need me to."

Silence.

I lean over the space between our beds until I can see the soft rise and fall of Red's chest beneath his blanket. Already sound asleep.

Day 3

A FOLLOW-UP VISIT WITH the staff doctor shows exactly what I knew it would—blood work and labs that say I'm healthy as a horse. My sore ribs are the only reminder that I'd ever been in the hospital at all. Mom was right about one thing: when I got here, I wasn't feeling like myself. But it turns out all I needed was a couple of days to sleep it off, rehydrate, and get my game face back on.

My sneakers squeak as I head back to my room. I do a quick two-step to avoid the janitor's mop handle as he swishes water across the hall floor. Any thoughts I'd been entertaining that Mom and Mo were right are pushed out of my mind like smudges on the tile as the mop sweeps by.

What happened at the party was a fluke, an accident. And now I have 25 days to figure out how to make it up to Savannah.

I'm still on blackout, which means zero communication with the outside world. Cell phones are contraband, almost as bad as sneaking in a blunt. From the nurses' station, I borrow a pencil and a piece of printer paper and head to the empty, sunlit lounge. A lonely shelf offers a couple of board games, a few decks of cards, and several tattered copies of books on addiction and recovery. No TV.

I settle into the couch and try to pen a letter to Savannah, but I can't decide how to start. Casual and upbeat? (*Hi! How are you? How's school going?*) Tortured and heartsick? (*If you're reading this, it means your dad didn't throw it away the second he saw the return address.*)

Jokingly sarcastic? (*It's been five days, twelve hours, twenty-seven minutes, and twelve seconds since I last saw you in the hospital. Not that I'm counting or anything.*)

I write and scratch out three different openings, and then I have to go back to the nurses' station for more paper. This time I write the only words there are to say:

> Savannah,
> I'm sorry.

I stare at the words, as flimsy as the paper they're written on, an echo of the apology I gave her after Winter Formal. Why should she believe me this time? Why should her dad? Mo's comment from lunch yesterday sneaks through the back door of my mind like some know-it-all narrator from an after-school special: *We do the same crap over and over again, and then we wonder how we ended up here.*

I crumple the letter in my fist. I can't fix this with a letter. I don't know if I can fix this at all.

On my way to dinner, I stick my head into our room. Red's propped up in bed, flipping through a white folder filled with paper. "You up for some grub?" I ask.

Red grimaces. "No solids, yet," he says. "But they do have some badass broth. One of the nurses said she'd bring me some."

"You mean the brunette? I see the game you're playing. You're hoping for a sponge bath, aren't you?"

Red gives me a wolfish grin. "Guilty as charged."

I leave him to his reading and head to the cafeteria. After what happened yesterday, I know better than to try to make new friends. This time I choose the only table with more empty seats than weirdoes. I'm almost finished when I catch sight of someone waving at me from across the room. It's a middle-aged man with a slight pot belly and a silver goatee. I point vaguely at my chest. *Me?* I mouth.

The man nods. He weaves through the tables until he's standing right across from me.

"Eli, I'm so glad I saw you. I was about to head out for the night."

I drop my fork and lean back in my chair. "Do I know you?"

He shifts an oversized mug to his left hand and reaches out with his right. "The name's Richard Fisher."

Richard Fisher wears a long-sleeved flannel shirt, open over a t-shirt from some band whose members probably died several decades ago. A tiny silver hoop hangs from one ear. I stare blankly at his outstretched hand. "So, Dick for short, right?"

Richard lets out a hacking smoker's laugh. "Call me Rich." He gestures to the empty seat across the table from me. "Mind if I join you?"

"Suit yourself."

63

Richard plops himself down and props both elbows on the table. He leans over his coffee mug, peering at the food on my tray. "What do we got tonight? Chicken parm?"

I push my tray away. "Look, I'm not trying to be rude, but who *are* you?"

Richard blinks. "Didn't I tell you? I'm your primary counselor."

"There's got to be some mistake," I say. "I don't need a counselor." Thanks to my parents' divorce and my dad's death, I've already seen my fair share of therapists. They peddle happy pills and stupid questions, and even if I was going to waste my time talking to another one, it sure wouldn't be this hippy has-been. "I'm just here to do my time," I tell him. "Isn't there like an opt-out form or something? I'll sign whatever I need to."

Richard's coffee-stained teeth show under his moustache. "Hate to break it to you, kid, but it's kind of a packaged deal. You're stuck with me for the next month." He takes a long draw from his mug, wipes his mouth on the back of his flannelled arm.

"Awesome."

"I would've been here yesterday," he continues, "but you came in on such short notice, and well, you know how it is. First day off in three weeks." His eyes flicker to my abandoned tray. "If you're done eating, why don't we take a walk?"

"Nah. I'm good here, thanks. Plus, I've got, you know, things to do."

"Funny. You're a funny guy, you know that?" But Richard doesn't look like he thinks I'm funny. The look on his face vaguely reminds me of ones I've seen on the lax field, usually on the faces of the opposing team.

He stands, lifts his mug in one hand and my tray in the other. "You're scheduled to be in my office at 8am tomorrow anyway," he says. "Might as well as find out where it is."

He heads across the cafeteria to the trashcans by the exit, where he pauses to scrape my tray, then hands it over to the waiting orderly with a tub full of dirty dishes in his arms. "You coming?"

Several people near me turn around to see who he's talking to. I sink lower into my seat and shake my hair down over my eyes like a shaggy shield. And then I see Libby, a couple tables up from me. Her ravaged arms are covered in a thin green t-shirt, and her frosty gaze meets mine with complete disinterest. But for some reason, I don't want to look away.

"Move it or lose it, Eli," Richard shouts. "I'm clocking out in five minutes whether you're in my office or not."

Somebody behind me chuckles. Heat rushes up the back of my neck. I shove off from the table and hurry to follow Richard out of the room.

Richard Fisher's office smells like day-old coffee and a dirty ashtray. Dog-eared books cling to an over-stuffed shelf on the rear wall. Two framed diplomas hang cockeyed behind Richard's desk. A worn sofa faces it, bumping up against a scratched wooden end table where a nearly dried-up water feature gurgles pathetically.

"Nice digs," I mutter. A black cruiser helmet with flame decals perches on a magazine rack in the corner. "You ride?"

Richard's shuffling through one of two towering stacks of manila folders and stapled paper packets on his desk. "Rain or shine. You know anything about bikes?"

"My dad had one." So did the first guy Mom dated after Dad moved out. A Harley. I hated the boyfriend, but loved his bike. Which makes it even weirder that I scratched a key through its shiny black paint one cold October morning on my way to catch the bus.

Mom didn't date after that—until Steven. The way Steven tells it, one of his golfing buddies referred him to the "best accountant in town," and it was love at first tax return. But Dad used to say that Steven wanted Mom to do more than his taxes, "if you know what I mean." The thought still makes me want to gouge out my eyeballs with a soup spoon.

"Bikes aren't my thing," I say. "Too dangerous."

Richard cocks a bushy brow. "Yeah, you strike me as a guy who likes to play it safe. You know, except for that whole heroin thing. A-ha! Here it is." Richard pulls out a thick white folder like the one I'd seen Red reading and hands it to me. A typed label on the front reads *STEP ONE: Honesty, Open-Mindedness, Willingness.*

"Flip through that tonight," Richard says, carefully patting the mound of paper on his desk back into a relatively stable pile. "It's your Step One packet. Go ahead and do some of the questionnaires. We'll go through everything together tomorrow, but it wouldn't hurt to get started."

I hold the folder loosely between my thumb and middle finger, flipping it up and down. "Nobody told me there was going to be homework," I mutter.

"What'd you think you were going to do for 28 days?" Richard asks. "Sit on your butt and eat chicken parm?" He gathers up a few things, hoists his briefcase onto his shoulder, and tucks his helmet under his arm. "Walk me out?"

Richard Fisher locks the door, and I follow him down the dimly lit hallway. "Mr. Fisher?"

He glances up at me, his thick fingers fumbling to hook the loaded key ring back onto the carabiner at his hip.

"I don't know why I'm here." The words I've been carrying around for the last 36 hours fall out of my mouth, followed almost immediately by gripping anxiety.

Richard Fisher scratches his chin. "I expect you know *how* you got here, right?" He gives me a pointed look, and I know he's talking about my overdose.

I fix my eyes on a dark spot on the carpet. "That was an accident. It wasn't supposed to happen. I'm not an addict, not like Red, or that girl, Libby. Those kids are seriously messed up."

Richard chuckles, not unkindly. He reaches under the folder in my hand and elevators it up to waist level. "Read through this tonight," he says. "There's a reason we start with Step One."

"Yeah, but . . ." I try again, but Richard's already heading down the hall. A red EXIT sign flickers at the far end.

"Just read it, kid." He lifts an arm overhead to wave without turning around. "We'll talk in the morning. My office, 8am." Then he pushes through the double doors at the end of the hall and disappears.

I stare down at the folder in my hand. "Thanks for nothing." My words echo in the empty hallway.

Day 4

*T*HE SUN IS BLINDING. THE tips of my light-up sneakers disappear into white fire as the swing carries me up, up, up. I shut my eyes, pushing backward against the wind, as I swoop back down into my dad's waiting arms.

"Higher!" I yell. "Higher!"

Dad grips the metal chains, and I jerk forward, suspended in midair. My back presses against his chest; his breath is warm on my cheek. "You sure?" he asks. "You won't let go, right?"

I shake my head furiously. "Under-duck! Under-duck!"

Dad's laugh rumbles through me. He pulls back on the swing until his arms are straight, and my legs are dangling nearly over his head. "Hold on tight!"

And then he's running, pushing me forward like wind in the folds of a paper kite.

"Under-duck!" I turn up my face to the warmth of the sun, so certain that I'm flying, that I forget my promise to my dad. My fingers uncurl from the chains that hold me in flight, and I let go.

A spasm shutters through my body, and I jerk awake, my heart throbbing against my ribs like I just ran laps. I push myself upright, rub my eyes. The dream slips away.

I peer up at the clock on the wall—8:05. Red's bed is unmade, and the bathroom door's shut, the shower running. I flop back against my pillows.

The water turns off in the bathroom, and the door opens. "Dude. Aren't you supposed to be somewhere?"

Red's standing in the bathroom doorway, a white towel wrapped around his skinny waist and water dripping into a puddle around his feet. Tattoos mark geographic regions on the pasty terrain of his chest and ribs—his arms are riddled with track mark scars.

"8am, right? The hippy biker?"

Shit. I groan and roll over to my side. The Step One folder stares at me from the bedside table where I left it last night, unread. I run my hand across my face and squint up at Red. "Do you think I have time for a shower?"

He glances up at the clock. "Depends, I guess. You going for sorry-I-overslept late or complete-and-total-asshole late?"

I reach for my dirty jeans, crumpled on the floor at the foot of my bed. "More like this-is-an-absolute-waste-of-my-time late."

Red laughs, shrugging his arms into a clean blue t-shirt. "Sure. I bet that's gonna go over *real* well."

Richard Fisher is pissed off. His fingers drum his desk beside an empty paper coffee cup, and he scowls up at the clock when I drop onto the faded brown sofa. "8:30," he announces.

I shove a chunk of cream cheese slathered bagel into my mouth. "I had to get breakfast."

Richard Fisher's voice is tightly controlled. "Look, Eli. I'm not exactly a morning person. As a matter of fact, I'm on my third cup of joe, and it's still taking every ounce of self-control not to toss you out of my office."

"I could leave if it's easier." I thumb the last bite of bagel into my mouth and push up off the couch.

"Sure, that sounds like a *brilliant* idea. Walking away from a get-out-of-jail-free card sounds like the kind of grade-A thinking that got you here in the first place."

My spine stiffens. The chunk of bagel goes down like concrete. "What's that supposed to mean?"

"The way I hear it, you walk out of here, your first stop is the courtroom. The judge decides where you go after that. Does that sound like a good idea to you?"

Richard's sarcasm nips at my self-control; heat pricks the back of my neck. "What's your problem, man?"

"No problem. I'm just calling your bullshit." A pair of reading glasses hangs from a chain around Richard's neck. He sits them on the end of his nose and flips open a manila folder, all casual, like he's reading Newsweek in a waiting room.

The couch cushions crunch as I sink back down. I eye the lopsided diplomas on the wall behind Richard Fisher's desk. "What kind of a therapist are you, anyway? Are you sure you're qualified for this?"

Richard glances at me over the rim of his glasses. "In more ways than one."

"Then help me out. Everybody keeps saying I need to get better, but there's nothing wrong with me. All this work you want me to do, it's a waste of time."

Richard leans back in his chair and takes off his glasses. "You got friends sniffing heroin?"

The question takes me off guard. "What's that got to do with it?"

"Just curious. I mean, you OD'd at a party, right? I'm thinking there was booze there, probably pot, maybe even a few pills getting passed around. But according to your intake report . . ." Richard Fisher holds his glasses over the open folder on his desk and peers through them like a magnifying glass. ". . . you were alone when the EMT pulled you out of the car."

"And?"

"*And* I'd bet a fifty that most of your *friends* at that party, maybe even a few of the ones popping pills, woke up for church Sunday morning, worked a lawn mowing gig, crammed for Monday's test, whatever. But not you. You overdosed and woke up in the hospital."

"That was an accident . . ."

"Sure, it was. An inevitable accident. You're not reinventing the wheel, Eli. I've been working this job for twenty years. You snort, you smoke, whatever. First, it's only at parties, but then you're doing it every weekend, alone, while your friends are out having lives. You use in the afternoon, in the mornings before school. When snorting doesn't get you there anymore, you turn to needles. Sure, your family's got money, but eventually they get sick of this shit—everybody does. They kick you out, or you run away. Next thing you know, you're blowing some crack head on a street corner for your next score."

My stomach twists in revulsion; my fingers curl into fists. "That's fucked up."

"Sure, it is," Richard Fisher says. "But it's the path you're on. Just because you're hovering at the starting line doesn't mean you're going to finish any different. You're on the cusp of a serious addiction, but you've been given an opportunity to choose a different way. If you're happy with the direction your life is taking, then by all means, go on home. But if you want things to be different, you're gonna have to show up and do the work. My office, every morning, *on time.*"

The old brown couch has folded up around me like it hasn't had springs for decades. I've heard this before. Savannah sitting next to me on the hospital bed, her cheeks streaked with dripping mascara: *You need help, Eli.*

Richard's staring at me, waiting for my decision. There's a smear of cream cheese on my thumb, and I wipe it on my already dirty jeans. If showing up here and talking about my "feelings" with this headshrinker is the only way to make it up to Savannah and get back to my life as it was, then I might as well get it over with. "Fine," I say. "When do we start?"

Richard's mouth curls into a crooked smile, and he shakes his head a little. "Like I told you last night, the only place to start is the beginning. I'm guessing you didn't look at your packet."

I stare at him.

He sighs, glances at the clock. "And we're almost out of time for today. Tell you what, fill out the Step One questionnaire by our meeting tomorrow, and we'll get started with the rest of the packet then. In the meantime, they tell me you're relocating today."

"Relocating?"

"To Unit 8. Phase Two. We need to get your schedule squared away."

Over the next fifteen minutes, as Richard and I go through a pile of pamphlets and paperwork, I gradually figure out that the next 24 ½ days of my life are going to be occupied in hour long increments, including daily meetings with Richard Fisher, large group lectures, small group counseling, art therapy, and "personal reflection time," whatever that means.

By the time I've left Richard's office, I've got a printed schedule, a map of the facility, and five minutes to get to my small group. But all I want to do is go back to bed.

"Remember," Richard says, as he walks me to the door, "Step One questionnaire by our meeting tomorrow. 10am, right after group. No bullshit. Got it?"

"Yeah, yeah," I mutter, squeezing sideways through the half-open door and almost bowling over Libby, who's standing in the hallway like a deer caught in the flash of headlights. She clutches a purple spiralbound notebook to her chest; the skin around her fingernails is puffy and red.

"Sorry," she squeaks. Her eyes trail past me to Richard Fisher. "I didn't realize you were in session."

"We don't meet until three, Libby," Richard says. "Everything okay?"

Libby shakes her head. Bleach-fried hair spills out of her ponytail and frames her face in subtle waves. "Something came up in group that I need to talk about." Libby's voice is scratched and sweet. It sounds like an ink black night with stars that go for miles. "Can I have fifteen minutes?"

"Of course," Richard says. He steps back, and Libby slips into his office.

I turn away from the door. Richard's voice catches me up from behind. "10 am, SHARP."

"I heard you the first time," I shoot back, but the office door has already closed.

My small group meets in the rec room. There's a Ping-Pong table and a couple of dingy couches that face a huge flat screen TV. In the center of the room, a few guys are already gathered. They lounge on metal folding chairs and slurp coffee from steaming white Styrofoam cups.

I spy the coffee on a table against the far wall. I'm adding a third sugar to my cup when a heavy hand claps me on the shoulder. "Eli, right? Nice to see you again."

I look sideways at Mo, who's beaming at me like we're old friends. I remember how he laughed at me, and I shove his hand off my shoulder. "Wish I could say the same."

Mo seems to take it in stride. "This your first group?"

I take a short draw of my coffee, testing its heat. "Yep." I turn away and reach for another sugar packet.

"Glad to have you." Mo waits while I stir my coffee with a red plastic wand and toss the empty sugar packets in the trash. "C'mon over," he says. "Meet the guys."

Mo says it like we're on a ball field or at a poker game—like the rag-tag group of junkies nursing black sugar water are his friends. "This is Eli," Mo tells the group gathered in the center of the room. "Just started Phase Two today."

I sink into an empty seat while the guys around me nod in acknowledgement or mutter introductions I can barely hear. I avoid eye contact.

"So what did you guys think of the speaker this morning?" Mo asks the group. A couple guys start talking. I sink lower in my chair and hope nobody asks for my opinion.

"The speaker was a counselor, ten years sober or some shit like that," the scrawny dude next to me says, filling me in. He's sporting a Kool-Aid blue faux hawk that looks fluorescent against his brown skin, and he reaches a skeletal hand to shake mine. "I'm Will. Just moved up yesterday."

"What do you think so far?" I ask.

Will gives me a crooked grin. "Too much talking. Everybody wants to tell you how they *feel*, and they want to know how you *feel*. I *feel* like I'd give my left nut for a stamp bag. You?"

I laugh. "I hear ya." Will's leg is bouncing up and down like he's working on his 18th cup of coffee. This kid's a junkie through and through.

"Got a roommate yet?" Will asks.

I shake my head. "I'm moving today—not sure where yet."

"Preppy over there's my roommate." Will points across the circle to a clean-cut dude with a popped collar. "He graduates in two weeks, and then I'll get a newbie." Will coughs out a crunchy sounding laugh. "Poor guy."

"Morning, folks." A tubby guy in a yellow button-up shirt and khakis strides across the room, legal pad in hand. His mousy brown hair is combed to one side, like how Mom used to make me wear mine for school pictures. "For those of you who are new," his eyes flicker toward me, "my name's Howard. I'm a counselor here at LakeShore, and I run this group." Howard drops onto a metal chair, his bulk protruding over the sides. "We usually follow a similar format to a 12-step recovery group. Each morning, I'll introduce a topic, and then we take turns with individual shares. Sharing is expected, not optional."

Will elbows me.

Oh no, I don't think so. I'll do the freaking worksheets, and I'll show up wherever to prove to Savannah and her dad that I'm "better." But showing up and participating are two completely different things.

As if reading my mind, Howard continues, his voice stiff and monotone, likes he's reciting a script. "If this is your first group, you may be feeling nervous about sharing, or even unwilling to do so."

That's the understatement of the century.

"I encourage you to keep in mind that each person here, including myself, was at one time in the exact place you are now. That's why we come together in this way, to learn from each other's experiences, strength, and hope. Don't worry about what you're going to say, just speak from the heart and try to keep an open mind. Okay?"

Several guys in the circle nod. I try to picture this straight-laced group leader toking a blunt or, for that matter, even drinking a beer that didn't come in a frosted glass.

"A couple things stood out to me during Cynthia's testimony this morning," Howard begins. He crosses one leg over the other, thick brown hair peeking out over the hem of a navy-blue tube sock. "Primarily what she said about finally facing her fears without relying on drugs as a crutch, and how that was a turning point in her recovery. Can any of you relate to that idea? Can you recognize any of Cynthia's avoidance behaviors in your own life?"

At this point, I go deaf. I don't know who Cynthia is, I didn't hear her "testimony," and I don't give a crap what she's afraid of. Mo raises his hand to answer Howard's question, and I let my mind wander. I think about Savannah, who's probably sitting in second period Anatomy right about now, and I wonder if she's thinking about me. I wonder what kind of hoops I have to jump through to get to use the phone.

And then I think about Libby.

What was in that notebook she was holding onto so tight? And what was so important that she couldn't wait a couple hours to talk to Richard about it? And, most of all, why the hell do I care?

"Eli?" An annoyingly nasal voice interrupts my thoughts. The whole group is staring at me, waiting for the answer to a question I didn't even hear.

I sit up straighter in my chair, feeling like I just got busted sexting Savannah in Pre-Calc. "Huh?"

Will snickers into his coffee.

Howard gives me a thin smile. "Seeing as this is your first time joining us, it'd be nice if we could get to know you a bit. Would you be willing to share your story with the group?"

"My story?" My mouth has gone dry, and my tongue feels like beef jerky.

"Yes," Howard urges. "Tell us about the journey that brought you to LakeShore."

My journey? Is this guy for real? Who talks like this? I glance around at the room full of strangers waiting for me to speak.

I hunch my shoulders and shake my head. "No, thanks," I say. "I'll pass."

"Sharing is an important part of the recovery process," Howard presses.

I shift forward in my chair and meet Howard's gaze, my voice a hard line that I dare him to cross. "I *said* I'll pass."

Howard blinks. "Maybe next time," he says.

After group, I carry my half-empty cup of now cold coffee back to my room. I should dump it, but it feels good to have something in my hand, like the red Solo cup at a party that magically makes you feel less like a loser and more like you belong.

Red's leaving our room when I get there. He looks more awake than I've ever seen him; his legs are sturdier, and he's shaking a little less. "I've gotta check in with the doc," he tells me. "Hopefully for the last time. I think he's gonna clear me for Phase Two any day now."

"There's no rush," I tell him. "It's no party up there, trust me."

Red laughs, bumps my shoulder with a loose fist. "Isn't that kinda the point?"

He shuffles down the hall, and I head into our empty room. The quiet is stifling, and the last place I want to be is alone. But there's nowhere else to go.

I drop onto my bed, prop a few pillows between my back and the headboard, and stare at the Step One folder in my hand. Might as well flip through it.

The Twelve Steps, written in the same cheese ball language as the books in the detox lounge, are printed right inside the front cover: *Step One: We admitted that we were powerless over drugs and that our lives had become unmanageable.*

I consider ditching the packet and hitting up that Ping-Pong table instead, but I promised Richard Fisher I'd do the stupid questionnaire. So I read on.

It's a load of psychobabble bullshit; the papers inside the folder read the way Howard talks. I can almost hear his post nasal drip as I skim a paragraph about the importance of answering the questions honestly. "This packet is an opportunity to explore the effects of drugs on the various areas in your life," Howard/the folder says. "Be honest in your answers. The only person you hurt by lying is yourself."

"Yeah, yeah, yeah," I say out loud as I rifle in the drawer of my bedside table for a pencil. The packet is several pages long, broken up into sections with headings like *Taking Risks*, *Self-worth*, *Relationships*, and *School*. The first section lists every drug under the sun (some I've never even heard of) and wants to know whether you've tried it, when you tried it, how old you were, and (my favorite question) how often you use it.

Under the column titled *I've used*, I check the boxes next to pot, alcohol, cigarettes, acid, and opiates. It's weird thinking back to the first time I tried all that stuff—it's like trying to remember your first kiss or the first girl you ever had a crush on. Twelve years old for cigarettes and alcohol, if the time Chase snuck a half-empty box of pink wine from his parents' fridge counts, and thirteen, I think, for pot. Fifteen for acid (that one terrible night when I freaked out at my own reflection, green-skinned with horns, and then watched South Park reruns for the next fourteen hours because I was afraid to fall asleep). But it's the opiates section that makes my chest get all tight.

My mind flashes back to the morning after Winter Formal, after the phone call from Savannah's dad, when Mom realized, maybe for the first time, that I was doing more than drinking. "Where are you even getting this stuff?" she'd shrieked, gripping my neck beside the bathroom sink and splashing cold water into my bleary, red eyes.

"Around," I'd told her. Had it been that long since Mom had been in high school? You only have to go to one party before you figure out exactly which lunchroom table to visit anytime you want to score. Once Chase ran into a supply-and-demand issue with his mom's medicine cabinet, he started tapping the neighborhood resources and went into business on his own. Lucky for me, Chase offers a Friends and Family discount.

The first time I'd tried pills had been in Chase's basement. I remember the chalky taste of the pills on my tongue, the burn of vodka as I washed them down with a swig from Chase's Red Bull can.

The fuzzy warmth that crept up my body like a plush blanket until every inch of my skin tingled with bliss.

I write '14' next to the word *opiates*. That time's not hard to remember at all.

It's almost noon when an orderly sticks his head through the doorway and tells me it's time to pack up so I can move to my new room. I glance down at the page, where I've checked the box marked "occasional usage" next to opiates. I flip the pencil over and erase it, my hand hovering over the box that says "regular usage."

"I'm kind of working on something," I tell the orderly. "Can you come back later?"

"Sorry," he answers, wheeling a service cart into my room. He hands me a black plastic bag for wet towels and dirty clothes. "Doc says you're good to go, and we need the bed. Got a rush case coming in this afternoon."

A rush case. An image of my hospital room flashes through my head, my mom hovering over me, and later, Savannah's tears. I wonder if I was a "rush case." I check the box marked "regular usage" and tell myself I'll explain to Richard later.

I glance over at Red's side of the room. He hasn't made it back from the doctor's, and I won't get the chance to tell him I'm changing rooms.

"Do you have a piece of paper I can use?" I ask the orderly. He's in the bathroom, gathering my "personal effects," and emerges with a bottle of shampoo and a toothbrush.

"What for?" he asks suspiciously.

I roll my eyes. "Unless there's a drug craze I haven't had the pleasure of trying, I doubt paper's contraband. I just want to write a note."

The orderly drops my stuff on the bed. "Pack up," he says. "I'll see what I can find."

By the time he's returned, my zippered duffel's waiting on the floor beside the trash bag with my dirty clothes. He hands me a piece of printer paper. "Will this work?"

I snatch the paper, scribble a hurried note that I leave on Red's bed before following the orderly out of the room.

No more nightmares, ok?
See you soon—
E

My new room looks a whole lot like the first. Both beds are neatly made, and clothes hang in a color-coordinated row inside the narrow closet beside the dresser. No sign of my new roommate, but he's obviously a neat freak.

The orderly drops my stuff on the second bed and tells me I better hurry up and unpack if I want to make it to lunch. I empty the black trash bag of dirty clothes and wet towels onto the floor of my own closet. The picture mom sent along stares up at me atop the pile of clean clothes in my duffel. I set the picture on my dresser, then dump the rest of my stuff into a single drawer.

I nose around the room to see if I can figure out who my roommate is. The small mirror hanging over the dresser is covered in pictures. They look to be pictures of a big family. A big Hawaiian family.

Oh. Hell. No.

Day 5

"**MO IS MY ROOMMATE?**" I launch myself through Richard Fisher's doorway like my heels are on fire. When Mo found out we were roommates, he HUGGED me. It was all I could do not to punch him right then and there. At group this morning, he kept calling me "Roomie," and I'm 99.9% sure this is all Richard Fisher's doing.

"Good morning to you, too," Richard says coolly. He gestures for me to take a seat, but I refuse.

"Don't even try to tell me this isn't part of your plan!" I growl, hovering over Richard's desk.

His mouth twitches slightly. "My plan?"

"Yeah, your plan! What is this—Sneaky Shrink 101? Put the kid who can't deal with his feelings with a roommate who can't NOT deal with them? You think that's going to make me talk? If anything, it's pissing me off!"

Richard peers at me over the upper rim of his reading glasses. "Can we ditch the paranoid conspiracy theories, please? No one's trying to *make* you talk. This isn't an interrogation."

"It sure as hell feels like one!" I drop onto the worn-out old couch, immediately arching back up because the frame pokes me in the ribs. "All anybody's done since I got here is ask me what I think and how I feel. I'm over it already. You said I have to do the work so I can get better, but all this talking makes me want to do is use."

The words stain the floor in front of me like blood spray from a punch in the nose. I've never said out loud that I want to use, not to anyone, not even Chase. I wait for Richard's *A-ha! I told you so!* But he gives me a soft smile instead. "That's called avoidance, Eli. Any idea why you avoid talking about your feelings?"

Here we go with the program-ese. I brush off the question, follow it with a question of my own. "You got kids?"

Richard Fisher blinks. "A son."

"Do you analyze him all the time or is that a special skill you reserve for your rehab captives?"

Richard Fisher folds his thick arms across his t-shirt, one of those Coexist jobbies, like the bumper stickers on the backs of Volkswagens. I take in his charcoal hair, the leather jacket slung on the tilting coat rack behind his desk, and wonder if he's got grandkids, and what his son thinks of this obvious midlife crisis thing Richard's got going on.

"What about your wife?" I press. "Does she let you screw around inside her head whenever you feel like it?"

A tight ball forms at the base of Richard Fisher's jaw, and for a second, I almost regret running my mouth. But then he clears his throat and leans back in his chair. "How about it's my turn to ask the questions, okay?"

"Hey, man, I'm just trying to make conversation."

"Are you?" Richard Fisher asks. "Or are you avoiding my question?"

"You're the shrink," I snap. "Why don't you tell me?"

Richard Fisher takes off his glasses, wipes them on the corner of his shirt. "Let's get something straight—first of all, I am not a shrink. I'm a board-certified substance abuse counselor, which is different. Second of all, I can't tell you why you're afraid to face your feelings. Only you can figure that out. What I can tell you, and I'm speaking from personal experience here, is that feelings are like zits. They usually show up when you least want them to, but you can't ignore them, and you can't cover them up. The deeper they are, the more they hurt, but one way or the other, they have to come out."

I wonder if Richard can even remember being a teenager, or if this acne analogy came right out of the latest edition of *Counseling Teens for Dummies.* "Wow," I seethe, sarcasm sizzling like raindrops on a hot sidewalk, "those most be some deep, dark issues you got there. What happened, Mr. Fisher? Your wife leave you?"

Fisher flinches, and I know I've struck a nerve. I press harder. "Did you fuck an intern or something? Or did your wife get sick of you shrinking her head all the time?"

"My wife left shortly after our son passed away. He was three."

"Jesus," I inhale, suddenly feeling like a first-class asshole.

Richard Fisher's tone is flat and emotionless, like he's telling someone else's story, reading it from one of those beige folders in the messy stack that hangs over the edge of his desk. "Viral meningitis. He was in a coma for two weeks."

"I'm sorry," I mutter, my anger doused like water over sizzling coals.

Richard waves my apology away. "You haven't cornered the market on pain, Eli. Everybody suffers. It's how you deal with your pain that matters. Honesty, open-mindedness, and willingness, remember?"

I stare down at my empty hands; the cuffs of my hoodie are dingy, and I rub at a spot that's darker than the others.

"Tell you what . . ." Richard swivels around in his chair and slides open a creaky metal desk drawer. He pulls out a purple spiral bound notebook, like the one I'd seen in Libby's arms. "You don't have to talk about your feelings until you're ready," he says. "But I do want you to start acknowledging them." He hands me the notebook. "Write them down. When you're in group, when you're doing your step work, even when you're at meals if you have to. Write it all down. And if something comes up that you want to talk about, that's what I'm here for."

I stare down at the notebook in my hand, flip through the stark white paper. Like Howard, the empty pages ask me to share my story, only this time without an audience. No one to listen. No one to judge.

I think about the notebook Benny's teacher gave him over spring break, the crayoned pages filled with pictures of Disney. Maybe I'll make up a story for Benny, *My Week at Disney Camp*. Bitterness burns the back of my throat like acid. *The Story of My Break(down)*.

I toss the notebook onto the couch beside me. "I'll think about it."

Richard Fisher sighs. "That's all I can ask. Now let's take a look at your step work."

I hand him my nearly completed Step One packet. He flips through the pages, asking me questions about my answers and taking notes.

I'd worked on it yesterday, in the crevices of time between lectures and group. Like I said, this stuff weasels into your head quick when it's all everybody around you is talking about. Each check box I marked held a kind of subtle relief, like ripping off a bandage. After schooling Will in Ping-Pong last night, I'd left the rec room to finish. It hadn't been until the section titled *Family*, that I quit.

"Why did you stop here?" Richard asks. He's pointing to a section that wanted me to write about the way using has affected my relationship with my family.

I shrug. "You can't affect a relationship you don't have. My mom's always busy with my brother, and my stepdad doesn't give a shit."

"Your stepdad doesn't give a shit, but he puts you in rehab to keep you out of jail? Your mom spends three days by your hospital bed, and you think she's not affected by your choices?"

I fold my arms across my chest. "It's complicated."

"We shrinks like to think of the 'complicated stuff' as gold."

"I thought you said you weren't a shrink," I shoot back.

Richard ignores the jab. "What about your father?"

Here we go. It's taken Richard Fisher all of thirty minutes to start asking questions about my dead dad. Figures. "He died when I was ten. Motorcycle accident."

"That's terrible," Fisher says. "It must've been very hard to lose a parent when you were so young."

I pick at the edges of a fresh scab on my wrist as memories of the funeral pour in. The closed casket so glossy I could almost see my reflection. The chill of the cold wood against my cheek and the overpowering smell of lilies. Mom's hand in mine, pulling me away.

"I survived," I say. Bright red blood oozes from the scab; I lick my thumb and swipe away the blood. "I don't really like talking about it."

"I see." Richard Fisher leans back in his chair, tucks his hands behind his head. "Tell you what—I'm going to give you a homework assignment for tonight. Finish up the packet, but when you're done," he gestures to the purple notebook on the couch beside me, "I want you to write about the worst thing that has ever happened to you. Write about it in detail and try to fully explore every feeling that comes up."

I scowl at him. "Do you actually get paid to torture people like this?"

Richard's mouth presses into a thin smile. "I know it hurts, but if you want to figure out why you're making the choices you are, the darkest places in your mind usually hold the most answers."

I let out a groan. "I don't write."

"Well, now's a good time to start." Richard glances up at the clock on the wall behind me. "Better get going. You've got art in five minutes."

The art room is a wide, window-lit space with walls made almost entirely of glass. The trees that border LakeShore provide a view that could almost make you forget you're stuck here. Almost.

A circle of easels outlines the hardwood floor, supporting canvases in various stages of production. People move in slow motion around here—they trickle through the door, gradually find their places behind canvases, choose brushes, and leisurely mix paint.

One painting grabs my attention. It's a person, I guess, but freakishly asymmetrical, its face and body parts composed of sharp, angular shapes and glaring colors. One eye is open, the other closed—the mouth a fractured line, almost like a zipper. But the most disturbing part is the arms. Composed of haphazard shapes, the arms are bent in several places at unnatural angles, giving the distinct impression of shattered bones.

"What do you think?"

I swing around. Libby's got a fresh palette in one hand, the other hand on her hip. She wears a black tank top under a paint-smattered apron. Her white blonde hair is piled into a messy bun held in place by a paintbrush. Her milky arms are bare, and two thick rows of jingly bracelets cover the places where I know there are scars.

She chews on the skin around her thumbnail. "If you're going to ogle my painting, the least you can do is give me your opinion."

I'm a mute idiot, with words like mush in my mouth. Her painting is freaky as shit, but the last thing I want to do is insult her again. "It's uh . . . nice," I say. "I like your use of, um . . . color and . . . line?" The words come out as a question, since I'm not entirely sure I'm even speaking English.

Libby giggles, and I realize that she's baited me, and like an idiot I fell for it. The laughter makes her cheeks flush pale pink, and she reaches a bangled wrist to sweep her hair from her eyes. Something about the gesture is so natural, so unprotected, that I feel myself relax.

"I don't know anything about art," I admit.

She flashes me a smile. "It's okay. It's supposed to be dark." Libby gazes at her painting like it's an actual person staring back at her. "She's broken."

"Who is she?" I blurt.

Libby's face tightens. "Do you ever *not* put your foot in your mouth?"

Not around you. I give her a sheepish grin. "It's a condition. Try not to judge."

Libby laughs out loud, and the sound is infectious. "You should do that more," I say. "Laugh, I mean."

Libby's gaze drops to her palette. She reaches for a plastic knife that she uses to mix the crimson and orange until it's the color of a burning sunset. Her eyes dart toward the instructor, who's hovering over someone else's canvas. "You should go."

It stings, this subtle rejection, but I nod and head off the instructor who greets me with a wide smile. "You must be Eli," she says, in a voice like warm milk with honey. Her nose ring sparkles in the light from the windows, and she's tatted up from elbows to wrists.

I nod, and she places a thin hand on my arm. "I've got a spot set up for you over here." I let her guide me to an unoccupied easel with a dauntingly bare canvas. "Right now, we're working on self-portraits."

I give a low whistle. "I think I'm in the wrong place," I whisper, leaning in so nobody else hears. "I can't even draw a stick-figure."

The instructor tips her head, flashing me the kind of smile that makes you think you can do anything. "That's the beautiful thing about art," she says. "There's no one right way to do it. Your self-portrait doesn't need to look anything like you. It's simply an invitation to explore the way you view yourself."

She shows me to the shelves at the back of the room where I can pick my paint and brushes and then hands me a plastic palette to fill. "Choose any colors you like, and then let your heart guide you."

It takes every muscle in my face not to roll my eyes at her.

"I can't wait to see what you come up with."

"Yeah, that makes two of us," I say, but I don't think she hears me. She's already moved on to someone else, leaving the subtle scent of patchouli behind her.

I stare at the empty palette and the sea of paint choices, wondering how the hell I'm going to pick colors that are supposed to describe me. I choose red, black and yellow—LionsHeart colors. The paint squishes from the tube like shiny toothpaste. I want to paint a guy who's cool under pressure and fierce on the lax field. I want to paint the guy I'm supposed to be, the one Savannah deserves.

But that's not the real me. I know I don't deserve the things I have. If it wasn't for Steven's money, I'd never have set foot in LionsHeart. I'd never have been made captain of the lacrosse team. I'd never have met Savannah. Inside, I'm still the same stoner freshmen with a dead dad. The last three years might as well have been a dream.

With a plastic palette knife, I push the red and yellow into the black, add more for good measure, and swirl the colors until they look like tar, like doubt and secrets. As I walk back to my easel, I spot Libby at the front of the room, only partially visible behind her canvas. Light spills through the windows beside her and pools around her feet. Her face is fixed in concentration, and her painting arm moves across the canvas like she's dancing. I think of the broken girl splayed across her painting, and I know that's how she sees herself.

I wonder how she sees me.

Day 6

'M STRETCHED OUT ON THE crappy couch in Richard Fisher's office while he flips through the rest of my Step One packet. Every now and then, he jots something down on the yellow legal pad on his desk. When he finishes reading, he peers at me over his glasses. "What about the writing assignment I asked you to do?" He glances at the purple notebook resting on my chest. "Anything you want me to read?"

I push myself upright and toss the notebook onto his desk. "Whatever. It's crap anyway."

Richard opens to the first entry. I count ceiling tiles while he reads.

I'd written about the day my dad moved out. That afternoon, he'd taken me to the park to play on the swings. I kept begging him for an under-duck, but when he finally gave me one, I was too excited to hold on the way I was supposed to.

I fell from the swing and landed face down in the dirt, hard enough to knock the wind out of me. I remember Dad rolling me onto my back, the sun so bright I couldn't see his face. There was something on my forehead, warm and wet. Dad scooped me into his arms like I was made of paper.

Mom met us at the hospital. It was only six stitches, but they'd bound me to the bed to keep me still. I could feel the anger rolling off Mom like heat waves. "I'm sorry," I'd cried, over and over again, straining against the binding. "I'm sorry!"

"It's not your fault, Eli," Dad had whispered, his breath hot against my wet cheek. "It's not your fault, okay?"

My fingers find the stretched skin of my scar, half-hidden under my hair. That night, Mom had stuffed Dad's clothes into oversized garbage bags, the big black ones used for raking leaves. I'd laid in bed, pressing pillows against my ears to drown out the words that ricocheted into my room like stray bullets.

Careless.

Irresponsible.

Dangerous.

It's not like this was their first fight; most mornings I'd woken up to Dad on the couch. But this fight was different. This fight was my fault.

"I'm sorry," I'd whispered into the darkness, where only my toys could hear me. "I'm sorry, I'm sorry, I'm sorry."

Richard Fisher takes off his reading glasses. "This is good stuff," he says.

"The devastation of a four-year-old? What are you, a sadist?"

Richard chuckles. "I'm saying I'm proud of you, Eli. You've finished your packet, and you're writing honestly about some of your painful experiences. You're starting the real work of recovery."

"Whatever." There's a rust-colored water stain in the far corner of Richard Fisher's ceiling, and if I stare at it long enough, it looks like it's moving. I remember doors slamming, footsteps pounding the stairs, the screech of Dad's bike peeling out of the driveway.

"Tell me more about your father," Richard says. "After he left, what was your relationship like?"

I shrug. "Normal, I guess. I saw him a couple times a week." A memory tugs at the corners of my mouth. "This one time, he showed up at school in the middle of the day. It was right before math, which was awesome because my math teacher was a total bitch. I climbed onto the back of Dad's bike, and kids were watching through the windows, pointing and gaping, like I was some kind of badass. We rode into the city and bought soft pretzels and cherry water ice. We spent the whole afternoon counting boats on the wharf."

"If I lived at home," Dad had said, dunking a pretzel into a squishy cup of yellow mustard, "we could do stuff like this all the time." I'd spent the whole ride back with my cheek pressed against his leather riding jacket, daring to imagine what that would be like—my parents together again, happy and in love.

The memory turns bitter after that, the taste of the water ice souring on my tongue. "Mom was pissed when we got home," I tell Richard. My happy family fantasy had dissolved the second I'd seen the look on her face. "She'd called the school when I didn't get off the bus."

"She must've been pretty worried," Richard says, tapping his glasses against his palm.

"Dad just forgot to tell her he was going to pick me up," I say, "but Mom had to go and make this huge deal out of it. I swear she was jealous that Dad and I actually had fun when we were together. That's what she was always complaining about anyway—that Dad got to show up whenever he wanted with gifts or surprise trips, and she was the one stuck at home, paying bills and folding laundry."

Richard nods thoughtfully and writes something on the yellow legal pad.

I pluck at the soft skin at the base of my thumb. "After that, Dad could only visit me at home with Mom around to 'supervise' or whatever. We mostly stuck to the backyard. That's when he started teaching me lacrosse."

Richard puts down his pen. "Do you ever talk to your mom about your dad?"

A broken spring in the couch pokes me in the back, and I shift uneasily. "I figured out pretty quick that she had no interest in talking about my dad."

"Why do you think that was?"

"She just didn't, okay?" My palm throbs, and I realize I've been pinching my skin so hard I've left a red half-moon welt that glares up at me. "She gave up on him a long time ago. She chose a new family, and I was just along for the ride."

"How do you feel about that?"

"Again with this crap?"

Richard Fisher fiddles with the earpiece on his glasses. "You're going to have to elaborate."

"Don't you ever wonder if sometimes things just are what they are?" I ask. "Shit happens, you move on. End of story. You should know that better than anyone, with what happened to your son and all."

Richard's chair creaks as he leans back, pushing out his buddha belly. "I still have feelings about what happened to me. Don't you?"

"Sure, I have feelings," I groan. "I'm just saying not everybody has some deep dark sob story waiting to pour out of them. My parents broke up, and sure, it sucked for a long time. But I'm over it now. Lots of people get divorced. It is what it is."

"Is that how you feel about using drugs?" Richard asks.

"Pretty much. Sometimes I want to use, sometimes I don't. It makes me feel good, it helps me relax, but it doesn't have anything to do with what happened to me as a kid."

Richard nods. He thumps his fingers on his desk one time, then another. The minutes tick by on the clock above his head. A little while longer, and then I can be done with Richard Fisher for the day. "I just wonder if . . ." he begins.

"What?" I snap. I've seen enough therapists to know when one of them has an agenda.

He runs his hand over his head, fluffing his nutty professor 'do.' "I'm willing to bet that four-year-old boy had some pretty strong feelings about his dad leaving that night. I wonder if you've been using drugs to cope for so long that you don't remember how to feel anything at all."

I open my mouth to say something, but nothing comes out. The room feels chilly, and I zip up my green hoodie, hike up the hood around my ears.

Richard stares at me for a minute. Then his expression relaxes. "But what do I know? Something to think about, right?"

"Whatever."

Richard hands me my first step folder and my purple notebook. "I'll be looking forward to hearing how your first step share goes tomorrow."

That gets me sitting up a little straighter. "Come again?"

"I know you're not big on group," says Richard, "but sharing helps build community. Every one of those guys in your group has walked the same roads you have. Believe it or not, your group will see you through some dark days ahead."

I wave the folder at Richard. "You never said I was going to have to read this shit to anybody," I say. "I don't share. Ask anybody. Ask my mom. Ask all four therapists she's taken me to. Sharing is not my thing."

Richard's mouth twitches. "Looks like you're going to have to develop a new *thing*."

"No way." The room is closing in on me, and I feel like I can't breathe. "This is a deal breaker, man. I want to call my mom. I want to call her NOW."

I lurch to my feet, ignoring the stabbing pain in my chest, and slam the folder face down on Richard's desk, knocking over a blue picture frame. A yellowing Polaroid stares up me, a young man with curly black hair, a baby in a backpack, a red bandana tied around his head.

Richard reaches to right the toppled frame. His voice is low and steady. "Why do you want to call your mom, Eli?"

"It doesn't matter! Just let me call her, okay?" I pace the floor, wearing tread lines into the already faded brown carpet. My head is a pressure cooker, and my brain is about to explode. I don't care what happens to me. I don't care about Savannah; I don't care about her dad. I just want out.

I want out. I want out. I want out.

Richard Fisher's voice finds me under all the noise inside my head. "Believe me, Eli, I know how you feel," he says. "You're miserable and terrified and downright pissed off. And you're convinced that not talking about it, not doing this work, will make all of that go away. But I promise it won't. The only way to the other side of this is straight through it."

I sink onto the couch, drop my head into my hands, and groan into my sweaty palms.

"I wish I could tell you this is as bad as it gets. But I can't."

I slide my hands down my face, peer at him over the tips of my fingers. "And that's supposed to make me feel better?"

"The work of recovery is some scary shit," Richard Fisher says. "You're going to feel vulnerable and terrified, and you're going to want out. But I promise you, if you do the work, if you feel those feelings, even the ones that threaten to rip you apart, I promise things *will* get better."

I tip my chin at the frame on Richard's desk. "That's your son?"

He nods.

"How can you look at that picture all the time? Doesn't it tear you apart inside?"

"Sure, it does, sometimes. But the sadness is only one part of the story, and I don't want to forget the rest. I want to remember."

I bite down on the inside of my cheek until the burning in my throat goes away. I will not cry.

"I'll make you a deal," Richard Fisher says. "You share some of your first step writing tomorrow, even just a little bit of it, and then I'll let you call your mom." He winks at me. "You can tell her all about it."

"Can't wait," I groan, already nauseated at the thought of reading aloud in group.

Richard Fisher lets out a hearty laugh. "That's the spirit."

There's already a handful of people in the gym when I get there—a couple of chicks on treadmills and one dude on the elliptical. Mo's in the free-weight section, spotting a guy with barbed wire neck tattoos who's straining to keep 350-pounds from dropping onto his swollen chest.

Will's bouncing on the balls of his feet, waiting to bench next. He's cut the arms out of his t-shirt, showing several amateur tattoos, smudged blue-black ink, like he tatted himself in the back of history class. "'Sup, Eli?" He tips his chin toward the bench press. "Want to work in?"

I'm pretty sure that weightlifting with bruised ribs is a no-no—definitely on the list of contraindicated activities, right next to running, sports, and basically doing anything other than walking. I'd planned on spending the next hour in a nice 3.0 pace on the treadmill, but before I can explain that to Will, the locker room door opens, and there's Libby.

Her hair's in a high ponytail, and she's wearing a pair of men's red basketball shorts that hang below her knees, a baggy t-shirt, and Converse sneakers with no socks. She makes a wide circle around the bench press machine and carefully lifts two light weights off the rack.

"Yeah," I tell Will, knowing I'll regret it later. "I'll work in."

"Good choice, my man," Mo says.

Prison Tat grunts out one last rep; the veins in his neck are thick cords that bulge under his skin. Will rolls his eyes.

Mo claps a heavy hand on my shoulder. "You're up, Roomie."

I steal a glance at Libby. She's doing like 400 reps of these teeny weenie Barbie weights. Our eyes meet, and she quickly looks away.

Mo's loading up the bar, and I almost tell him to take it easy on me, but the last thing I want is to look like a wuss in front of these guys. They're the closest thing to friends I've got in this place. I plunk down on the bench.

"I'm so happy to see you in the gym, bro." Mo's hands hover under the bar, and his thick body is pressed so close to my head that I have no choice but to stare at his armpits as I press the bar upward, gritting my teeth against the pain that instantly grips my chest like a metal vice.

"Recovery is such a mind/body thing," Mo drones. "You know there's research that suggests regular workouts can actually help you resist the temptation of drugs? It's like a chemical reaction or something."

"How . . . many . . . more?" I wheeze into Mo's hairy pits, pushing my screaming arms straight.

"You got another five in you, easy," Prison Tat says, the tear drop tattoo at the corner of his eye winking at me.

"Doing it for the dopamine, dude," Mo says, lowering the bar once more over my chest.

With monumental effort, I lift it again, and then one more time, in case Libby's watching.

"Just don't die," Will says encouragingly.

The laugh that rises in my throat nearly chokes me; my elbows buckle, and Mo catches the bar before I'm permanently pinned to the bench.

"That was only 150, bro!" Will sneers. "Aren't you supposed to be some badass athlete or something?"

Mo offers his burly mitt; I clasp it, and he hauls me to my feet, pounding my back with his other hand. I have to bite my lip to keep from crying out.

"Keep it up, brother," Mo says. "We get stronger every day."

"Thanks." I shoot him a wry grin, then punch Will in the shoulder. "Let's see you do any better."

"That's gonna have to wait a minute," Mo says. He's loading weights on the ends of the bar like they're marshmallows on a stick. He nods to Prison Tat. "Spot me?"

While Will hangs by the bench press, I make my way to the free weight rack. Libby's doing tricep kickbacks with a weight so light her arm's swinging like a pendulum. "You might want to go a little heavier," I say.

Libby drops her arm and glares at me. "Who asked you?"

"Nobody," I fumble. "I just thought . . . you're kind of swinging it? It's not going to . . ." What is it about this girl that turns me into some kind of speech-impaired idiot? "Never mind." I reach for a weight from the rack.

Libby watches me in the mirror for a second. "If you know so much, show me."

I falter, nearly dropping the weight on my foot. "Really?"

"Yeah, if you're not too busy showing off for your 'bros' over there."

I wince. "Sure, I'll show you." I put back my own weight and choose one for Libby. Bending over the bench, I show her the proper form. "Now you try."

Libby weighs the metal in her hand.

"You've got this," I tell her. "Trust me."

It takes some effort, but Libby pounds out ten reps. "See?" I tell her, as she stands up and swipes the fly-aways off her forehead. "You're stronger than you think you are."

Across the room, a heavy weight crashes to the ground with a primal groan, pulling my eyes away from Libby. Mo sits at the end of the bench, his cheeks red and his breathing heavy.

"Hey, Player," Will calls. "If you're done with the personal training session, I'm ready to school you in the art of the bench press."

Libby rolls her eyes. "Meat-heads await."

"Will's not like that, he's just being . . ."

"Anybody want to bet on it?" Will asks. "I've got ten bucks that says I can do 200 pounds."

Libby snorts. "Sure, he's not." She drops into kickback position, this time with her other leg on the bench.

Deflated, I head back to the bench press, where Mo's spotting Will as he powers through eight reps.

"Easy," I say when he's done.

Will gives me a lopsided grin. "Oh, yeah? Ten bucks says you can't do it."

I instantly regret teasing him. Coach says I'm an underdog with a Napoleon complex, always getting myself into situations I have to fight my way out of. It works out well on the field—you don't make captain by being a wimp. But sometimes I wish I could keep my freaking mouth shut.

In the mirrored wall, I catch a glimpse of Libby. She's got a free weight over her head, but I can tell she's listening. Three things go through my mind at once:

1. I don't want Libby to think I'm some dumb meat-head.
2. I don't want Libby to think I'm a wimp.
3. Why the hell do I care what this crazy chick thinks anyway?

"I'll see your ten and raise you five on Eli," somebody says. I look up to see Red winding his way through the cardio machines.

"Red!" I jog over to him, clasp his outstretched hand, and clap him hard on the back. "It's good to see you!"

After everybody's introduced themselves, Will gets back down to business. "So are we doing this or not?" His eyes glint with excitement. "We've got some serious money on the table."

"C'mon, guys," I try, fumbling around for an excuse. "It's almost dinner and . . ."

"How about a push-up contest instead?" Libby's voice cuts through the chatter in the gym. She's a feather-weight in this circle of jocks and body builders.

Mo chuckles, props his elbow lightly on Libby's shoulder. "You got money in this game, little sister?"

I can't read the look on her face. "Five bucks on Will," she says.

And then I'm pissed. I'm in, and I'm going to win.

We sort it out quickly—it's a 30 second countdown. The most push-ups by the time Mo calls it, wins. I throw in five bucks, Prison Tat bets a candy bar—Mo's the only one who doesn't bet. Odds are on Will with only Red in my corner. I don't mind. Will did bench more than me. What these guys don't know is that mad is how I play. It's not about strength; it's about who has something to prove. Screw my pain—mad is how I win.

Red claps his hands together like the crackling microphone of a sports commentator. "Alright, boys, assume the position."

Will and I are head to head, his arms stretched opposite mine. He winks at me, and then Mo says, "Go!"

Will and I are pumping them out at the same speed. I focus on how they all bet against me, even Libby. My triceps burn, and my lungs are screaming, but I pull ahead. Will is breathing hard. There's only ten seconds left, and I know I'm going to win.

Something heavy lands between my shoulder blades. Pain shoots up my back and into my skull—a bolt of lightning that blinds me. I cry out, and my arms buckle. I hit the rubber flooring, choking on chalk dust.

Mo lifts the weight off my back. I roll onto my side, whimpering like a beaten dog. Everybody's staring at Libby.

Her eyes are flat and hard, her mouth pinched. "Next time I want help, I'll ask for it," she spits. Then she turns and storms out of the gym.

Red calls after her. "Hey, you know you owe me fifteen bucks, right?"

Libby flips him the bird over her shoulder before the double doors slam heavy behind her.

Mo chuckles, reaches down, and carefully helps me to my feet. "You know what happens when you play with fire, don't you, bro?" He lifts my arm across his shoulder, supporting my weight. "You get burned."

It's almost lights out, and I'm stretched out on my bed, an ice pack spread across my sore ribs, thumbing through the pages of my Step One packet and trying not to think about the fact that I'm supposed to share it with my group tomorrow. Richard Fisher said I only have to read part of it, and then I'll get to use the phone. But how am I supposed to pick which part? The whole freaking thing is practically a burn book I wrote about myself. Page after page of admission—what I've used, how often, how using has affected my life. Each section has a culminating question at the end: *Have drugs affected your school work? Have drugs affected your relationship with your family? Do you use drugs to cope with difficult emotions?*

Yes . . . Yes . . . Maybe . . . I don't know. These are just words, scratched pencil marks on paper. But this is my life we're talking about. My real life. And the idea of reading it out loud to a room full of strangers makes me feel like I'm going to puke.

Hi, my name's Eli, and a week ago, I almost died.

Saying it out loud would make it real. It would mean that Savannah and Mom and Richard Fisher are right. It would mean there's something wrong with me.

I drop the folder on my stomach and peer sideways at Mo, who's lying on the bed opposite me, reading a recovery book like the ones in detox. Knowing Mo, it's probably his personal copy. He wears glasses at night—thick black frames that make him look more computer dweeb than linebacker, and it cracks me up.

"Mo?"

He lowers his book and glances over at me, his glasses cockeyed on the bridge of his nose.

"What's the deal with Libby?" I ask. I've been thinking about her ever since the gym and it's driving me crazy. She walked right past me at dinner and didn't say a word. I'm 99.9% sure she hates me, and I don't understand why. "I mean, one second we're having a nice moment, and then bam, she goes full schizoid. I can't figure that chick out."

Mo grins. "Don't you have a girlfriend?"

His question is a punch in the lungs. Of course I do. I have Savannah. I love Savannah. Libby shouldn't matter. Libby *doesn't* matter. But still . . .

Mo doesn't wait for my answer. "Libby's like a little sister to me. But she's had a hard road, man. The only people who've ever been nice to her, ended up playing her hard. I don't think she trusts anybody all the way, maybe not even me." He stares at me for a second. "You know she's not your problem, though, right?"

I fumble for my words. "Yeah, sure. I mean, of course . . ."

Mo grins. "You have to work on yourself, bro. Relationship drama only makes this shit harder." He turns back toward his book. "Trust me—stay far away from it."

I think of Richard Fisher's office, the blue frame on his desk, the baby in the red bandana. "Speaking of drama," I ask Mo, "do you know anything about Richard Fisher?"

"Fish?"

The nickname surprises me. "What's up with him? He's got this whole bad boy biker thing going on, and then today he told me about his dead kid." I think of the zit analogy, pimples oozing feelings like yellow pus. "I'm pretty sure he doesn't know what he's talking about."

Mo chuckles. "You know he spent time in jail, right?"

"For real?"

"Straight up. For a while there was a rumor going around that he used to be the leader of this motorcycle drug ring." Mo laughs. "I heard him speak one time last year; he gave a speech the day he got thirty years sober."

"Thirty years?"

"Hell, yea, bro. Fish is the real deal." He dog-ears a page in his book and puts it on our shared nightstand. Then he rolls onto his side to face me. "Apparently, he used to be some big-shot psychiatrist in New York or somewhere, I forget. When his kid died, he went *lolo*, crazy, you know? Started writing his own scripts, heavy shit, too—you remember that shit that killed Michael Jackson? Anyway, after a while, his lady had enough, so she bagged him, moved out. He wasn't seeing enough clients to pay the bills, so he started a side business."

Mo gives me a knowing look.

"Dealing?"

"Yup. Made a bundle writing scripts for high-end clientele—Manhattan housewives popping xannibars with their morning mimosas, porn stars pre-gaming on oxy—you get the idea. He was doing alright for himself until some rich bitch OD'd, and her husband went looking for her hookup. Fish got busted—judge hammered him hard. Lost his license, went to jail. Fish likes to say he found AA behind barbed wire. But he told me one time that the first time he saw *The Big Book*, that's the one that's like the bible for AA, was when he chased away some homeless guy that was rooting through the trash in front of his brownstone. The book fell out of the guy's grocery cart. Fish picked it up and tossed it in the bin. Next time he saw that book was when he checked it out of the prison library. Crazy, right?"

"Yeah," I say. "Crazy."

"Whatever Fish's done in the past, he's a damn good counselor," Mo says. "You're lucky to have him."

"Maybe," I mutter doubtfully. I tap my forehead with the folder, like maybe I can take it in osmosis-style. "He's making me read this at group tomorrow."

"No one's *making* you read it, bro. Howard, Fish—they just want you to try."

I roll my eyes. "Whatever."

Mo smiles knowingly. "Nervous?"

"Oh, you know," I say, "not really. Only mildly concerned that I might crap myself."

Mo's belly shakes with laughter. "I nearly puked the first time I had to do it."

The first time? "You mean we have to do this more than once?"

Mo's eyes twinkle. "This isn't my first time here."

"How many?" I ask.

Mo rolls onto his back, stares up at the popcorn stucco ceiling tiles. "Here? This is my third time. But I tried two other places first."

Mo has always seemed like the poster child for recovery, full of 12-step-isms and chipper advice. But then I think about how comfortable he is here, how he seems to know everybody, and it all makes perfect sense. He's been through it all before.

For a second, I feel like I've found a loop hole, a reason for my mom to pull me out and take me back to my life. "So you're saying this shit doesn't work?"

Mo's thick shoulders reach for his pierced ears. "I always leave feeling like this time it stuck. Like I'm never coming back.

But that's when the real work starts, you know? I go to a party, and there's beer, and I can probably handle one, right?" Mo closes his eyes, breathes in real deep, like he's imagining himself at a party, red Solo cup in hand, breathing in the smoky chaos of beer pong and popularity. I'm reminded of another party a few months ago. The one after Winter Formal.

Mo opens his eyes. "I think it does work," he says. "I think you get a little better each time around. Some of us just have farther to go than others."

I drop the folder over my face and groan into pencil-marked pages that smell like school. "I don't think I can do this."

"Sure you can," Mo says. "It's like in the weight room. We push through the impossible. We get stronger every single day."

He takes off his glasses and sets them neatly on the bedside table. "Turn out the light when you're done, okay?"

"Sure."

Mo rolls over, and soon the only sound in the room is the steady rhythm of his snoring. But I'm restless. It's like talking about this stuff has shaken something loose; I can't stop the flow of memories. The night of Winter Formal plays out on repeat like a bad cable TV movie. I glance sideways at my purple notebook where it waits on the bedside table.

Maybe if I write it down, I can stop thinking about it for a little while. Maybe then I can get some sleep.

I grab the notebook, flip it open to a fresh page. And I begin to write.

Day 7

"THE FIRST TIME I USED heroin was three months, two weeks, and five days ago." I did the math last night, the memory crystallizing as I scrawled it in ink across a blank page. My hands shake, fluttering the pages, and sweat beads on my upper lip. I stare at the floor, the concrete wall behind Howard's head, the grease-smudged corners of my notebook—anywhere to avoid making eye contact with the other guys in the group as I dump my life history out on the floor in front of them.

I'm not the first one to share my story with the group. After a week at LakeShore, I've heard a handful of guys read from their own packets, starting from the beginning, the inner cities or suburban paradises they were born in, the pot they smoked, the coke they snorted, the meth they cooked in kitchens like rabid scientists with crumbling teeth. I hadn't planned on reading much, but once the first few sentences scratched the surface, everything else came pouring out. I told them about my parents splitting up and about my dad's death. About moving to

Grandhaven, about Steven and Benny. I told them about the pills in Chase's basement, how the oxy I came to depend on eventually became a habit I could barely afford.

The guys in my group slurp coffee from their Styrofoam cups and bob their heads every now and then, like 'been there, done that.' Nothing I say surprises anyone.

"It was the night of Winter Formal. My girlfriend, Savannah, and I had been dating for almost nine months. She looked bangin' that night. I wore a new suit, and Savannah kept telling me how hot I looked, kept running her hands in my pockets. That suit was gonna get me laid for sure."

A couple guys laugh, but Howard shushes them with a condescending glare.

"We cruised by the dance around 9 p.m. My friend Alex's parents had rented us a limo. There were eight of us altogether. We stayed at the dance for about 45 minutes, then left the gym to the losers who wanted to sip pink punch and slow dance with the mandatory six inches between them." I hold my arms out straight, miming the awkwardness of slow dancing at school, and earn a chuckle from Howard.

"As usual, Alex's parents were out that night. It was only supposed to be the eight of us, but Chase has a big mouth. He told everybody where the after-party was. People showed up with trunks full of beer and a quarter keg. I swear, half the school was there. The music was pumping, and people were dancing, grinding on each other like they can't do at school. Savannah pulled me into the living room, but I didn't want to dance. I wanted to take her upstairs."

What happened next is like stained glass in my memory, each detail frozen in time. Savannah's shoulders are bare, her hair down loose. I pull her close, and the heat between us is a magnet. She moves her hips, and I sway, too. I push back her hair, run my fingers down her back. She gives me this warm, sleepy smile, and I know she wants me, too. My lips brush her ear.

Let's go upstairs.

"We were headed upstairs when my buddy Chase stopped me, told me there was something I had to see. I knew he was going to score that night; he'd been telling me about this amazing stuff his neighbor hooked him up with, better than pills, cheaper, too. I don't even think I asked him what it was called. I don't think I cared. I left Savannah on the stairs, and I followed Chase down to the basement."

Savannah's on the stairs, that blue dress hugging her body in all the right places, but I walk away from her. She shouts after me, furious, and I pretend not to hear. The stain glass splinters, shattering into a thousand glittering pieces.

"Chase was right—the dope was incredible, but it knocked me on my ass. I found out later that Savannah came downstairs and found me and Chase nodding off on the basement couch. She was pretty pissed." I chuckle at the memory, and a few guys echo the sound. Not that it's actually funny or anything, but more like, *of course she was pissed, I'd be pissed, too.*

"I woke up a few hours later, I don't really know when. Alex's mom shook me awake. Her makeup was all smeared, and she was wobbling around on these crazy heels, screaming at me to get the hell out of her house." I laugh, remembering how deranged Alex's mom looked, her hair all messed up in the back and her breath reeking of booze, more like a drunk New Jersey housewife than the school's Parent Council president. Not at all like the prim and proper mom in the picture over the fireplace.

"I'm barely coming down," I continue, "half-asleep, and all around me, people are freaking out—scattering like squirrels in the road. Total cluster-fuck." A couple of guys laugh, and I know they can relate.

But the story's not so funny after that. The basement stairs blur in my memory, and I remember Savannah, passed out in the fetal position on a leather recliner.

"Apparently, Savannah was so pissed after she found me, she went upstairs and pounded the rest of the vodka. I picked her up, carried her to my car, and somehow drove her home. Now that I think about it, I can't believe Alex's mom let me drive anywhere—I mean, what a bitch, right? More worried about her oriental rugs than she was about her kid's friends."

From across the circle, I catch Red's eye. I see the muscles in his jaw flex, and I wonder if he's thinking about Lisa. Thinking how lucky I am that I could be so stupid and yet my girlfriend's still alive.

Another image rises above the dusting of shattered glass. Steven, roused by Mom's hysterics, calmly makes me a pot of coffee and a piece of plain toast. And somehow, with the kind of certainty that twists my gut, I know that if the party had been at my place and Steven had busted it up, nobody would've driven that night. Nobody.

While the coffee was still brewing, Steven brought me a glass of water and sat down beside me at the kitchen table. "Next time, don't come home," he said.

I'd heard what I wanted to, what I thought he meant. *Don't come home at all.* But what if he meant it differently? What if Steven meant that I should've stayed where I was? To sleep it off. To get home safe the next day.

Somebody coughs. Next to me, Will stares hard into his coffee, stirs it over and over again with one of those little red straws.

"Anyway," I continue, "we made it to Savannah's house. The lights are on, and her dad's waiting on the front porch swing. He stands up when I get out of the car, and I swear to god, I think he's going to hit me. But then Savannah pukes, right there in the middle of the driveway, and it splatters on my new suit and on her dad's bathrobe. And he takes her from me, slings her up into his arms like she's four years old, and he yells over his shoulder that I'm never gonna see her again."

My throat burns, but I force myself to finish because maybe this pain is kind of like resetting a bone or popping back in a dislocated shoulder. It hurts, it hurts so bad, but when it's over, you're not broken anymore.

"The worst part," I say, "is that I knew her dad would call my mom. I knew she'd be waiting for me—I knew she'd be worried, pissed off. I probably even knew I shouldn't be driving. But only one thing mattered to me, more than my mom or Savannah. I called Chase, and I asked him if he had any more."

Humiliation threatens to pull me under. Saying it out loud is different than writing it down. It's harder and colder. It's fucked up.

I'm fucked up.

The back of my neck burns, and my hands shake, but when I look up at the room around me, everybody's nodding their heads, like they all understand, like they've all been there, too.

Will's the first one to break the silence. "So what you're saying is . . . you're still a virgin?"

There's about half a beat, and then I crack up, even though laughing kills my sore ribs, and so does everybody else, even uptight Howard. I punch Will in the thigh, and I'm grateful, so grateful, for him and everybody else—grateful that they listened, grateful that they laughed. Grateful that they see me, the real me, cracks and all.

"Alright, alright," Howard says, shoving the proverbial stick right back in its place. "That's enough."

The laughter settles down, and when it does, all that's left is the stirring in my chest and the burning in the back of my throat. It's dawning on me, all at once, what I did to Savannah, what could've happened, but didn't. Across the room, Red nods at me, and I remember what he said that night in detox. *It's feeling that sucks the hardest.*

Howard thanks me for sharing; he asks the group if anyone would like to respond. But I can't sit here another minute. Every nerve in my body is on fire, and I can't stop jiggling my knees. My chest feels like it's going to explode.

"Can I go?" I blurt, and Howard looks at me, confused.

He glances at the clock. "We've got a few minutes left of group, Eli. Everything ok?"

"Yeah," I tell him, even though it isn't. I need to call Savannah—I need to hear her tell me that she loves me anyway, even after everything. "I was hoping to maybe use the phone."

Howard nods. "Check with your primary counselor after group, okay? In the meantime, I'd like you to hang with us for a few more minutes."

I nod, and I count the seconds to the end of group. When it's over, I don't hang out to chat. I make a beeline to Richard Fisher's office.

Richard Fisher is in session when I barge through his door. The girl in the sagging old couch is wiping tears with a soggy Kleenex, and Richard Fisher glares at me. "Eli, our session doesn't start for another five . . ."

"I need to use the phone," I blurt, because I'm desperate now.

The girl on the couch hiccups into her Kleenex. Richard sighs. "Five minutes," he says. "Please wait in the hall."

"I can't wait," I protest, but Richard Fisher cuts me off with a voice that doesn't take any shit.

"Hall. Now."

I pull the door shut, wondering if prison turned Richard Fisher into an asshole or if he was born that way. I sink down on the floor in the hallway, counting minutes in my head. At three, Libby comes walking down the hall, her purple notebook clutched tight against her chest.

"No way, dude," I say, before she even stops walking. "My session's next, and I don't care if you only need to talk to him for 30 seconds, it's gonna have to wait until I get off the phone."

Libby smirks. "Important conference call with China?"

"I need to call my *girlfriend*," I say, underlining the word for Libby's benefit.

"Girlfriend, huh?" she echoes.

I nod.

Libby shifts her weight to one foot. "Want some company?" She gives me a half-smile. "You know, since I'm going to be waiting awhile for my 30 seconds with Fish."

I peer up at her. "Why does everybody call him Fish?"

Libby shrugs, settling onto the floor beside me, our backs pressed against the pale blue wall. "It's an obvious nickname, right? Why? What do you call him?"

"I tried Dick, but he wasn't exactly a fan."

"I can't imagine why not." Libby giggles, and the sound is so sweet that I hope Hiccups needs a few more minutes with Richard Fisher. And then I remember that Libby's crazy, dangerous even, and that any second, she could flip on a dime and freak out at me. I lean backward, give her a hard look. "You're not going to do that thing again, are you?"

"What thing?" Libby looks genuinely surprised.

"You know, that thing where we're having a nice moment, hanging out or whatever, and then you go all Fatal Attraction on me."

"Fatal *what*?"

I lean away from her. "How have you not seen that movie? It's old, but creepy as shit."

"What does that have to do with me?" Libby asks. "Are you saying I'm attracted to you?"

"No!" It comes out way too loud, and then my neck gets all hot. "I'm not—that's just, it's the name of the movie . . ."

I'm stumbling all over my words until I see the look on Libby's face. Her eyes are shining, and her lips are twitching, and I realize something very important.

"You're fucking with me, aren't you?"

Libby nods. "Yeah. I'm totally fucking with you."

"You knew exactly what I was talking about."

Libby shrugs.

I shake my head, lean back against the wall, and close my eyes. This girl's exhausting.

Her voice, crackling and soft, finds me in the dark. "I'm sorry about the whole weight room thing. I didn't realize—"

I crack one eye open and squint at her. "It's no big deal, really. Only minor permanent damage."

A giggle escapes her lips, and then she tucks her knees against her chest, folding in on herself. "I don't know why I do stuff like that. I'm not trying to be a bitch or anything. I just, I don't know . . ."

She's cute like this, all soft and girly under the dark eyeliner and angry looking hair. She nibbles nervously on a ragged cuticle.

"Apology accepted," I say. And then Richard Fisher opens his door.

He gives the two of us a once-over. "Libby," he says, but it sounds like a question.

"I had a thing I wanted to talk about," she says, looking at me and then back at Richard Fisher. "But it can wait."

Hiccups slips out the office door and scurries down the hall. "Good work today, Myra," Richard calls after her, but she scurries away like a scared little mouse headed for her hole. "See you tomorrow," he calls weakly.

"And I'm still waiting to use the phone," I say. "Like you promised."

Richard sighs. He runs one hand over his head a couple of times. "Tell you what? Go up front and tell whoever's at the desk that I said you could use the phone. I'll call up and let them know."

"Sweet." I jump to my feet.

Richard gestures for Libby to join him in the office.

"One call. Five minutes," Richard Fisher says. "Then come straight back for our session."

I wink at him. "You got it, Fish."

He makes a sound like a cough, but I don't hang out to hear what's next. I jog down the hall, leaving behind Richard Fisher and whatever it was that just happened between me and Libby. I need to call Savannah.

"Five minutes," says the woman at the front desk. She spins the phone around to face me and hands me the receiver. "One call, okay?"

I nod. She gives me a skeptical once-over before turning back to whatever it is front desk people do. My fingers hover

over the buttons, mentally dialing Savannah's cell phone. But something stops me. What if her dad's taken her phone? What if she doesn't want to talk to me? What if she's screening her calls? If I leave a voicemail, does that count as my one call?

My fingers decide for me, dialing Mom's number instead.

"Eli?" Mom's voice is both anxious and hopeful.

"Hi, Mom."

There's silence on the other end, and then I hear sniffles, and I realize that my mom is crying.

"Mom? It's okay, Mom. I'm fine."

"I know," she says after a minute. It sounds like she has cotton balls in the back of her throat. "It's really good to hear your voice."

"It's good to hear yours, too," I tell her, and then my chest gets that shifting, fluttery feeling again.

The front desk lady holds up four fingers. Four more minutes.

"Guess what Fisher made me do?"

"What, honey?" Mom's voice is distant, and I realize she's talking to someone else in the room, probably Benny. "Yes, honey, go get a granola bar. I'll be there in a minute."

"Mom? Mom, I only have four minutes."

"Yes, honey, I'm here. I'm listening. Benny, go watch a show, okay? I'll be there in a minute."

My throat tightens, and my eyes burn. Nothing's changed. I'm here, two hours away, but it's already like I don't exist.

"Eli, I'm listening," Mom says. I hear a door closing, and I know she's shut herself into the office. "Tell me what you had to do."

I swallow the feelings rising in my throat and put on my everything's-fine voice. "I had to read my Step One packet out loud to a whole group of people."

Mom's impressed, even though she probably doesn't know what Step One is. Rehab's got its own lingo. After a week of involuntary immersion, I speak the language, but to Mom, they're just words. I haven't talked to her this much in years, and I only have three minutes, but so much to say. I tell her how Fisher is an ex-con, which doesn't get nearly the reaction I was expecting. I babble about my group, the gym, and the weirdly depressing painting I'm doing in art. I tell her about Will and Red. I leave out Libby, and it feels weird not talking about her, because I have to do it on purpose, because talking about her is right on the tip of my tongue.

Wrap it up, the lady at the front desk mouths, and I resist the urge to flip her off. "Look, I'm going to have to go, Mom." I shoot a scornful look at the Front Desk Fascist. "My time's about up."

"Okay, honey," Mom says. "I can't wait to see you tomorrow."

"Wait, what?" The lady at the front desk is making the "hurry up" motion with her hand, but I hold her off.

"Sunday's Visitation," Mom says. "Didn't Mr. Fisher tell you?"

Relief runs through me, relaxes my shoulders, and loosens the muscles at the back of my neck. I turn my back on the lady at the front desk so she won't see my eyes get all red and watery.

"Do me a favor, Mom?" I ask. "See if Savannah can come?"

There's silence on the other end, and I know Mom's trying to decide if she thinks that's a good idea. Or maybe she already knows something I don't. My stomach gets all tight, and my heart punches me in the chest over and over again. "Mom?"

"I'll have to talk to her father, honey. I'm not sure if . . ."

"Just ask," I say. "Please just ask, okay?"

"Okay."

118

The Front Desk Fascist has decided my phone time's over whether I'm done talking or not. She crosses toward me in two steps, and I know she's going to hang up the phone. I hunch over it, still talking, even as I lower the receiver. "Okay-Mom-I-can't-wait-to-see-you-don't-forgot-to-call-Savannah-I-love . . ."

Click.

"Mr. Fisher said five minutes," the woman says, like that's an apology. I slam the receiver on the phone and shove it back at her.

"You know, I'm paying to be here," I say. "You'd think phone privileges would be part of the deal."

She shrugs, like she couldn't care less. I wait until her back is turned to flip her off.

Day 8

V ISITORS TRICKLE INTO THE REC room, nervously searching the milling crowd of anxious junkies. When families are reunited, it's all hugs and kisses and tears.

It only takes me a few minutes to figure out that waiting for visitors is worse than waiting to see if you got picked for Varsity, or if you were voted Homecoming King, or if your ticket was drawn for the last rocket ship off planet Earth. It's fucking painful. I watch one more family reunite, and then I can't stand it anymore. I grab Red and practically shove him toward the Ping-Pong table. "Play," I tell him, slapping a paddle into his hand.

Ping-Pong passes the time. It gives me something to focus on other than the questions cycling through my brain on auto repeat: Will Savannah show? Will she forgive me? Will her father?

Even with my limited movement, I'm trouncing Red. Then I see her. Savannah and my mom are standing by the door, both of them wearing this what-planet-have-we-landed-on look. I drop my paddle; the ball bounces twice before rolling onto the floor.

"Dude!" Red calls.

I cross the rec room in three long strides, and Savannah's in my arms. She smells like a strawberry Jolly Rancher, and I press my face against her neck. My mom's patting my shoulders and sniffling. There's no Steven, no Benny. Just Savannah, Mom, and me. Hugging, kissing, and crying. Just like everybody else.

"I want to introduce you to someone," I tell them, leading them toward the Ping-Pong table. Red's playing solo, bouncing the ball against the table and tapping it with his paddle. He glances up as we approach, and a wide smile spreads across his face.

"Red's a musician—if he can do with drums what he does with pencils on Styrofoam cups, he's pretty badass."

"Drums, huh?" Savannah (always the social coordinator) tips her heart-shaped chin. "Have I heard you anywhere?"

Red stares at Savannah, taking in her manicured nails and designer jeans. "Doubt it." He sticks out a big bear claw to shake her hand. "You must be Savannah."

It's weird, one part of my life meeting the other. Red's track marks tell his story in scars. He's still jittery, like his nerves are on fire underneath his skin. Chatting with my tucked-in mom and shiny, pink Savannah, Red looks like a junkie. And suddenly I'm embarrassed, and I want to take them somewhere where they don't have to talk to twitching, itching junkies.

Just me.

"I think we're going to go grab some coffee," I say, gripping Savannah's elbow and steering her away from Red.

"It was good to meet you, Red," Mom says. "I hope you . . ." She fumbles over her words, and my brain fills in the blanks. *I hope you feel better? I hope you don't like heroin anymore? I hope you don't die?*

"Mom . . ." I try, before she can say something humiliating.

Red smiles and tips his head at her. "It was nice to meet you, too."

And then I'm the asshole, because I'm about to leave Red to play Ping-Pong by himself, which isn't even a thing, and I have *two* visitors to his none. "You want to join us?" I ask.

Red shakes his head. "Nah, you and I can hang whenever. Go catch up with your family. I've got things to do, places to be." He opens his fist, drops the Ping-Pong ball on the table, and tips it up again with his paddle. "Plus, I'm kinda in the middle of something here."

I shoot him a grateful smile. "You're finally playing against somebody you can beat."

"Get outta here," Red laughs.

"He seems nice," Mom says, as I guide her out of the rec room.

I pretend like she doesn't sound surprised.

Savannah and I sit across from each other in the dining hall. Mom had lasted all of three minutes before she'd run out of things to say and suddenly needed to find the bathroom. Or maybe she wanted to give me and Savannah some space. But now that we're alone, tense silence stretches between us, like when you don't know what to say on the phone, and you just kind of sit there, breathing into the receiver. Too much has happened; there's too much to talk about. Neither one of us knows where to start.

All around us, families sit in tight groups, murmuring to each other over strong coffee and red velvet cake. I concentrate on my coffee; Savannah picks at her cake.

"How are you?" she asks.

"I'm better with you here."

Savannah flushes, so I try again, desperate to steer the conversation away from me and my "problem," and back to common ground.

"How's the team? They miss me yet?"

Savannah stares at her cake, barely touched on its little white paper plate. "Doing okay. Coach has Alex filling in for you . . . you know, until you come back."

"Alex?" I knew Coach Wilson would have to find a temporary replacement, but Alex? The kid's good in the goal, but he can't run for shit. "Well, we can kiss State goodbye."

Savannah won't meet my eyes. "He's okay."

I open my mouth to argue, then shut it just as quick. The silence is heavy, and I know there's something else Savannah wants to say.

I reach across the table and squeeze her hand. "I can't believe your dad let you come."

She stares down at our clasped hands for a minute, her cheeks the color of her sweater. "He doesn't know I'm here." Her eyes dart toward the back of the room, and I follow her gaze.

Mom's shaking hands with Richard Fisher. I wonder if she went looking for him, or if he accosted her on the way out of the bathroom. Either way, their heads lean toward one another in this weirdly secretive way, and I can't help but wonder if they're talking about me.

I try to focus on Savannah. "Does my mom know?"

123

Savannah shakes her head. "Dad's golfing. He'll be gone all day. When your mom called to see if I could come, I just said yes. I didn't even ask because I knew what the answer would be."

I don't know what to say. It's kind of awesome that she snuck out to see me, but I know my mom won't keep Savannah's secret. When Savannah's dad finds out, he'll ground her for life and write me off forever. Unless he already has.

I stroke the back of Savannah's hand with my thumb. "He's going to find out, Savannah. My mom's going to run into him sooner or later, in the grocery store or whatever, and she's going to thank him for letting you come. What's going to happen then?"

"Eli . . ." It's the start of a sentence, but it feels like the whole story. Savannah's eyes are swimming, and she pulls her hand away from mine.

All of a sudden, it's hard to breathe.

"We're done, aren't we?" The words come out cold, icicles with serrated edges, and I see the exact moment they slice into Savannah. Dusky, black tears streak her perfect cheeks.

Around the room, nothing else changes. Mom's still talking with Richard Fisher. Will sits with a weirdly buttoned-up white couple. Red air-drums next to a rosy-faced lumberjack with a severe beer belly. And Mo, who's surrounded by his entire extended family, sits next to a pregnant girl, probably a sister. He puts his hand on her round pumpkin belly, and his face lights up. They both laugh out loud.

Like everything's wonderful.

Like the whole fucking world's not falling apart.

"It's not what I wanted," Savannah whispers. "But then Alex . . ."

One word, and the world stops spinning. The pieces click into place.

I can barely speak. "You and Alex?"

"It wasn't on purpose," Savannah says, her voice taking on a whiny pitch I've never heard before. "I was upset after you left. Really upset. Alex was just trying to be nice."

"Nice?" A kid at the next table shoots me a curious look. I lower my voice to a fierce whisper. "I've been gone a week, Savannah!"

"Eli . . ." Savannah reaches for my arm, but I jerk away from her.

Fucking Alex, swooping in to replace me. Oh sure, he's *real* nice. I've been gone a week, and it's like I was never there at all.

"I'm coming home, you know." My voice catches in my throat, and I hate how weak it sounds. "You said it yourself. Three more weeks, and then I'll be home."

Savannah swipes her hands across her wet cheeks. "It doesn't matter, Eli. My dad's never going to let us be alone together; he's never going to let us go out. He's already screening my calls. Being together . . . it's just not possible anymore." Savannah's words are desperate, pleading with me to understand.

But I can't give her what she wants. I can't be okay with losing her. She says she doesn't want to hurt me, but she's crushing me into a thousand jagged pieces. I want her to hurt as much as I do.

"No, I get it. You and Alex are the King and Queen of LionsHeart now. Happily fucking ever after. At least until the next lacrosse captain comes along."

Savannah's eyes widen like I slapped her; she opens her mouth, then shuts it, because here comes my mom, her eyes red-rimmed, a plastic smile stretched across her face.

The moment's over. There's nothing left to say.

"Do you guys want to go for a walk?" Mom's voice is bright and brittle, ready to break. "Mr. Fisher says the landscape's beautiful. Maybe you could give us a tour, Eli?"

I avoid Mom's eyes—give Savannah a cold, hard stare. "I'm actually pretty tired," I say. "Maybe next week?"

Mom blinks. Her eyes flicker from Savannah to me and back again. "Okay," she says, as if she understands, even though I know she doesn't. "It is a lot, isn't it?"

"Much more than I expected." I point my words at Savannah like poison darts.

Her eyes search my face. I want to hold her; I want to bury my face in her hair and not let go. But she's leaving me. I'm hanging over a cliff, and she's cutting the rope I'm clinging to. She's letting me fall.

Savannah pushes back from the table and stands up. "I'll meet you at the car," she says to my mom, her voice trembling.

Mom stares after Savannah. She knows better than to ask what happened. She picks up her purse, then pauses. "I almost forgot." She reaches into her purse, pulls out a black and white composition book, its corners bent and stained in places. "Benny wanted you to have this. It's the book he made about Disney, remember?"

I stare at the cover. *My Spring Break* is printed in perfect block lettering, clearly his teacher's writing. I'm too pissed and too hurt to give a crap about Benny's artwork right now. "What am I supposed to do with it?"

Mom shrugs. "Maybe he wanted you to have a reminder of him while you're gone. You're important to him, you know. He looks up to you."

Clearly the kid has terrible taste. In the last five minutes, I've lost my team and my girlfriend, probably all of my friends. I'm nothing. A nobody. A complete, fucking loser. I toss the book on the table, and Mom has to catch it before it slides off the other side. "He needs a new role model, Mom. I'm not interested."

Mom closes her eyes for a second, collecting herself. Then she gently slides the book back across the table. "Keep it anyway, okay? Just in case."

She moves to kiss my forehead, but I jerk away. "Savannah's waiting."

Mom sighs. "I love you, Eli," she tells me. "No matter what." Then she slings her purse over her shoulder and heads out of the room.

I glance down at Benny's book, flip unseeing through the crayon-coated pages. I can picture Benny at the kitchen island, feet dangling from the bar stool, his oversized art supply bin on the marble countertop. Mom's cooking dinner, and Steven comes in from work and kisses her on the cheek, then ruffles Benny's hair. The three of them, a perfect family. The loneliness sets in immediately, and it's fucking unbearable, this reminder that life goes on without you, and there's not a fucking thing you can do about it.

I snatch up Benny's book, desperate for something to hold on to, and bolt after Mom and Savannah. Maybe it's not too late. Maybe they're still in the lobby. Maybe I can beg Savannah to change her mind.

But they're not in the lobby. I dart past the front desk, press my face against the glass, and peer down the sidewalk to see if I can catch a glimpse of Mom's car. Nothing.

That's how you do it, isn't it, Eli? You push people so hard they can't get away from you fast enough. You deserve this. You deserve everything you get. The cement of your life is tracked with burned rubber marks and gunning engines.

"Excuse me," the front desk lady says.

I turn to see her leaning over the desk, worry wrinkling her forehead. "Relax," I tell her. "I'm not going anywhere."

That's when I notice Libby, tucked into one of the oversized leather chairs in the lobby.

She's got her purple notebook open on her lap, and her hand's moving fluidly across the page. Her brow's furrowed in concentration, and the tip of her tongue sticks out on one side of her mouth. She doesn't seem to notice me until I'm standing right next to her.

"Hover much?" She doesn't look up.

I sink into the leather chair opposite hers. "Waiting for visitors?"

"The opposite actually." Her wrist moves in tight circles across her paper. Sketching, probably.

"How so?"

Libby sighs and shuts her notebook, like I've killed her train of thought. "I'm keeping watch. This way my mom and her sick fuck boyfriend can't take me by surprise."

I study Libby's face, wondering if this is another dark attempt at humor. "What are you going to do if you see them?"

She opens her notebook again. "Haul ass in the other direction." She studies the page, chewing on the nub of her pencil. "What about you? The whole football team isn't coming for a visit?"

"It's lacrosse."

"What?" Libby glances up at me.

"I don't play football. So even if the whole team was coming to visit me, which they aren't . . ." I get a mental image of Alex on the field, calling the shots, Alex in Savannah's arms, and I have to swallow the bile that rises in my throat. ". . . it would be the lacrosse team. Not the football team."

Libby blinks. "Whatever."

"And for your information, I did have visitors. But they left already."

"So soon?" Libby smirks. "Wow, you really know how to entertain company."

She's fucking with me. I should get up and walk away. But right now, the last place I want to be is alone. Not after what Savannah just did to me. I lean back in the chair and stare at the ceiling. "You don't know the half of it."

"I take it that was your girlfriend who went storming out of here a few minutes ago?"

"How'd you guess?"

"Oh, you know, blonde hair, cheerleader type. Doesn't take a genius."

I close my eyes. "Ex-girlfriend. As of five minutes ago."

Libby's voice softens. "Sorry."

"Yep." I wait for the sting of another jab, but it doesn't come.

Libby's pencil scratches across the paper. "I'm going to be here awhile—at least until visiting hours are over. You can stay, if you want."

I open my eyes and peer down at her. Right now, the dining hall is filled with families happy to see each other, couples working it out, and a thousand other little reminders that I completely suck at life. This chair is where I belong, here in the lobby, where I can watch people walk away from me. "Thanks," I mutter.

Libby nods, without looking up.

So I sit here in the lobby, while Libby sketches in her purple notebook and the front desk lady does whatever it is she does. I sit here, flipping through Benny's book and listening to Libby draw.

Day 9

"SO SHE BROKE UP WITH you." Richard Fisher's feet are propped up on his desk, his hands folded behind his head, like in one of those old timey movies. All he needs is a cigar in his mouth, smoke snaking up to the ceiling. "Did she tell you why?"

"I just told you," I snap. "Because she cheated on me. Because apparently, she'd rather be with my ex-friend, Mr. Fucking Perfect. Alex."

"Ah, the one who throws the parties? With the drunk mom?"

I glance up, surprised Fisher remembers Alex's name. "Yeah, I guess."

"Tell me again: what is it that makes this kid so perfect?"

I hadn't told Fisher everything about that night. I didn't tell him about Alex's mom in the front yard, teetering on one broken stiletto, shrieking at me as I buckled Savannah into the passenger seat of my car. I didn't tell him that the last thing I remember before arriving at Savannah's is seeing Alex through the windshield, half-carrying, half-dragging his mom inside.

The image of Alex's perfect family smears a little, like the lipstick across his mom's cheek. But still. . .

"He's everything Savannah wants, you know? He's good on the team, makes good grades. Popular."

Fisher nods. "So far it sounds like you're describing yourself. At least until you started using dope. Alex isn't in rehab. So I guess he's got that going for him."

His words are pushpins under my fingernails, but I'm not giving in. "Are you actually trying to say this is my fault?"

"No, not your fault," Richard muses. He chews thoughtfully on the earpiece of his glasses. "But an inevitable consequence of your behavior? Maybe."

"Are you freaking kidding me?" I launch off the couch, immediately gripping my ribs where the movement stabs me. "This didn't have anything to do with me. I was gone all of ten seconds before Alex snagged my place on the team and moved in on my girlfriend. That fucker stole my life!"

Fisher slides his glasses back onto his nose. "Drugs stole your life, Eli. Alex moved in on all the pieces you left behind."

"Are you actually defending him?"

"No, I'm not defending him. The kid sounds like an opportunistic son of a bitch. I'm saying that this is a chance for you to accept responsibility for your own part in the events of your life. I mean, c'mon, man—don't tell me this breakup came out of nowhere."

I sink back down onto the beat-up old couch. "We fought," I admit. "We fought a lot, actually. Especially lately."

Richard nods. "What kinds of things did you fight about?"

My mind traces over the last few months like grooves in a well-worn map. Winter Formal was ground zero, the beginning of the end. After that, there were constant fights about me not showing up, not spending enough time with her. "She said I didn't care about her," I say. "That if I did, I wouldn't use."

"Did you care about her?" Richard asks.

"Of course I did. I do. But it started getting hard to be around her, you know? It was like she thought if she nagged me enough, I'd stop."

"And that didn't work." It's a question, disguised as a statement—a trap I fall headfirst into.

"Of course she couldn't make me stop. I couldn't even make myself stop."

"You were powerless," Fisher says.

I've read the literature; I know what he's getting at. *We admitted that we were powerless over drugs, and that our lives had become unmanageable.*

"Yeah," I whisper, digging my nails into the edges of the freshly healed scab on my wrist until blood seeps onto my sleeve. My using was the detonator Savannah and I constantly circled, neither one of us willing to call it by name.

Habit.

Problem.

Addiction.

Fisher tosses me the box of tissues from his desk. I catch it easily and press one against my wrist until the white blooms red. "Do we really have to talk about this?" My voice sounds weak, pleading, and pathetic.

"I'm not trying to hurt you, Eli. I'm trying to hold up a mirror. Since the first day we met, you've been telling me that you want to leave, want to get back to your regular life. But from where I'm sitting, it looks like there's not much of a life to go back to anymore. Your grades have plummeted; your relationship with your family is circling the drain. The only things you had going for you were lacrosse and your girlfriend, and now you've lost those, too. Why do you think that is?"

Fisher's question is a bucket of water on the simmering rage I've felt since Savannah broke up with me. My anger melts into a wave of grief. It's all my fault. Savannah, lacrosse—I let it all slip through my fingers. When I go home in three weeks, I'll be lucky if they let me back into school, let alone onto the team. Spring training 101: No booze. No smoking. I'm pretty sure heroin goes without saying.

I think about Benny's Disney book, the waxy pages I'd flipped through last night, trying to make sense of the pictures. Mom was easy to pick out—the only figure with earrings and long hair. And Benny, the short one. But there were two men in the pictures: Steven and me, I guess.

Except I didn't go to Disney.

The morning of our flight, I was sleeping off a bender. I hadn't even packed. Mom was beyond pissed. She'd shoved dirty clothes into my lax bag and said I could spend the whole week doing laundry in the hotel for all she cared. It was Steven who convinced her that I was too old to enjoy the trip, and I'd be bored watching Benny on all the kiddie rides. I'd told myself that was what Steven wanted anyway, a week alone with his real family. They'd left me behind with a hundred bucks for takeout and strict instructions not to have anybody over while they were gone. While the three of them lived it up in the Magic Kingdom, I'd spent a week on the cracked leather couch in Chase's basement, nodding off into crusty bowls of mac n' cheese, too fucked up to know what I was missing.

Had Benny missed me? Had he drawn what he'd wished for? His big brother beside him on the big kid rides, chowing down on burgers and greasy French fries, fist bumping Mickey. I wasn't there for any of it, but Benny had drawn me anyway.

133

Just because you're hovering at the starting line doesn't mean it's going to turn out any different. You're an addict, Eli.

An addict.

The word is a one-two punch to my gut. I fold over my knees, hands crossed at the base of my neck, and I stare at the floor between my feet.

An addict.

There's nothing left to hide behind. Nothing but this office and Richard Fisher and the truth.

I can't bring myself to look Fisher in the eyes, so I fix my gaze on a worn spot under his desk where his chair has left permanent indentations on the cheap industrial carpet.

"You're right." The words have the bitter tang of humiliation, of despair. I fight rising panic, the urge to run from the room and never look back. But I press on, forcing out the words that claw like a caged monster on the inner walls of my skull. Once I've said it, I can't take it back. Saying it out loud makes it true. I cling to one threadbare strand of hope: if I'm broken, Richard Fisher can fix me.

"I'm an addict," I whisper, the words barely audible. The admission is the rush of crimson from a severed vein—I sink into the couch, drained and bone-tired.

Fisher's eyes are full of knowing. "Acknowledging your addiction is the first step, Eli. Sometimes that step can feel like a thousand miles. But once you've taken it, you can start the real work of recovery. After acknowledgement comes acceptance and then action. My sponsor once told me that recovery is just those three steps, over and over again. The rest is maintenance."

He hands me a white folder from a pile on his desk. *STEP TWO*, the folder reads, and then across the bottom: *We came to believe that a power greater than ourselves could restore us to sanity.*

I'm too exhausted to think past the next thirty seconds, much less a whole new packet. How many freaking steps are there anyway? Fisher must have a whole library of these damn things.

"Remember Step One?" Richard Fisher asks. "Honesty, open-mindedness, and willingness?"

I tip my chin, thumbing through the pages.

"Step Two is about being open to getting help. When we realize that drugs are hurting us, not helping like we thought, we have to figure out a different plan. The Twelve Step program asks us to look outside of ourselves for something positive that can help us choose a different way of life. That's what we call your higher power."

"As in, God?" I ask doubtfully. The only version of God I can muster looks like he walked right out of the Sunday comics— long white beard, hooked staff. A cartoon.

Richard shakes his head. "Not necessarily. Your higher power can be anything that resonates with you, and that usually takes a little while to figure out." He squints at me for a minute, the light crisscrossing his glasses. "The first time I worked this step, I was six months into a three-year prison sentence. My son was dead, and my wife hated me. I was pretty sure that if God did exist, he had to be a raging asshole, and I was better off without him. So I picked the next best thing—the underside of my bunky's bed."

"Seriously?"

"It was bigger than me, and if it could hold my bunky's fat ass up in the air like that, it had to be stronger than me, too. It wasn't much, but it was the best I could do until I started trusting people again."

I toss my bloody tissue toward Richard's trashcan, but it falls to the ground a good foot too short, earning a flicker of a nose wrinkle from Richard Fisher. "Can you hear how lame that sounds," I ask, "or are you immune to cheesiness after thirty years in this place?"

Richard chuckles. "You'd be surprised how cheesy can ring true sometimes. How bad you start craving something simple and real when the rest of your life is a complicated shit show."

I think about my life back home, the arguments it seemed like Mom and I were getting in almost every weekend, the constant effort of resenting Steven, the exhaustion of trying to do everything right, so that I didn't lose Savannah, so that I never had to go back to being a nobody again. The words *simple* and *real* settle in my brain like fallen leaves on campus in October, quiet but just right.

"Sometimes," Richard continues, "people in treatment choose to think of this program, or their small group, as a temporary higher power until they get more clarity. Maybe you could try that."

I think of Prison Tat with his bulging biceps, Will's blue faux hawk, and Mo, who's constantly spouting program-ese. I give Richard Fisher a skeptical scowl. "Seriously?"

"Believe it or not," he says, "the people here have all felt like you at some point, Eli. Lean on them a little. Nobody gets through this stuff alone." Richard glances up at the clock. "We can talk more about this tomorrow. For now, though, I'd like you to get started on the packet. You'll be processing some of the questions in group tomorrow."

"More sharing?" I groan.

"You bet."

I tap the folder against the flat of my palm, and I will myself to look Fisher in the eye. Because I'm empty now, and I need him to tell me that there's something that will fill me back up again.

"If I do this," I begin, and Richard Fisher raises his eyebrows. "If I do these packets, and I share in group, and I come here and talk to you, then I'll get better, right?" The question lodges in my throat, and I blink away tears that burn at the back of my eyes. "I'll get my life back. And maybe—maybe I'll get Savannah back, too?"

Richard Fisher gives me a small, sad smile. "The work of recovery is a long road, Eli, and we can't know how it will turn out. Once we take down all the things we were hiding behind, our lives become more honest, more authentic. We see the world differently, and sometimes we find we don't want the same things we did before. But let's take it one day at a time, okay?" He motions toward the folder in my hand. "That's the place to start."

I promise Fisher I'll start on the packet, but I leave his office in a fog of doubt. I needed him to tell me he could fix me, that A+B=All Better, not give me a bunch of philosophical mumbo jumbo about a "higher power." Because no matter what Fisher says, I know the only person I can depend on is myself.

At first glance, the Step Two questionnaire looks like another dirty laundry list of all the fucked up things I've done. I flip through it, lounging on a picnic table in the visitors' yard after lunch, the afternoon sun so warm at my back I could almost forget where I am, almost forget my admission in Richard Fisher's office.

Almost.

Blacked out? Check.

Driven a car while under the influence? Check.

Lied? Cheated? Run from the cops? Check. Check. Check.

I swear these packets are like flashback tours through the worst kind of haunted house, the kind you can't get out of until you've seen everything there is to see. I've been on an emotional tilt-a-whirl since Savannah left, a constant seesaw between hating her and missing her so bad it hurts. But as I skim through my own answers to these questions, a quiet truth slows my swirling emotions into a dull ache: *No wonder she left you.*

I skip the rest of the questionnaire and flip to the next part. *We came to believe that a Power greater than ourselves could restore us to sanity.* I skim the page.

Sometimes it can be hard to trust anyone other than ourselves, especially if the adults we thought of as our higher powers have let us down.

A memory comes to me like a swift kick in the ribs. I flip open my journal and sketch the night with words.

I was eight years old, and Dad had promised to take me to a baseball game. Steven had just started coming around, and he'd bought me a brand-new Phillies cap special for the game. I'd packed my glove in case a fly ball came my way. Dad told me I might even be able to get it signed. He promised lots of things—pizza, ice cream, the best seats in the stadium. And then he didn't show.

I sat on the front porch steps until it was dark, and Mom came outside.

"He's coming," I told her, as she sat down beside me. A neighbor's TV blared the game through the open window next door. Glowing blue light filtered out into the yard. "He's coming."

It wasn't until later, when a brisk pounding on the living room window woke me from a dead sleep, that I knew Dad had finally shown up. I'd run to my window, pressed my face against the glass. Mom was on the porch. They were arguing, gesturing wildly and yelling so loudly that one of our neighbors shouted at them to keep it down. Mom put her hands on Dad's chest and shoved; I watched him stumble backward.

"No!" I screamed, pounding on the glass so hard it rattled. Dad glanced up. I knew from the look that passed over his face that he had heard me. But instead of coming inside, he turned and headed back to his bike.

"Dad!" I hollered, taking off out of my room and down the stairs so fast I almost tripped on the hem of my pajama pants. "Dad!" I burst through the front door and out onto the porch just as the motorcycle revved to life. "Dad, wait!"

Mom tried to stop me, but I yanked away from her, so that all she held onto was a handful of my pajama sleeve. But it was enough. By the time I jerked free, Dad was already pulling away from the curb. "Dad!" I screamed, running up the sidewalk barefoot, ignoring the stab of chipped concrete in my soles. "Dad! Come back!"

Porchlights flickered on. I darted into the street as the bike's taillights disappeared around the corner. "Dad!"

"Eli," Mom said, panting as she finally caught up with me, "come back inside." She tugged at my hand, her eyes skipping furtively toward the nearest house, where an old lady had lifted the corner of her living room curtain to peer out at us. "People are watching."

When I didn't budge, Mom dropped to her knees in front of me. "Eli, honey," she said, pushing my hair out of my eyes, her fingers gently brushing my scar. "Eli, look at me."

"He left me," I whispered, the truth washing over me like ice water. Dad wasn't coming back. We would never be a family again.

Mom gripped my shoulders, forcing me to meet her gaze. "This didn't have anything to do with you, okay, buddy? This was not your fault."

I stared hard into her hazel eyes, black like holes in the soft glow of light from the street lamps. "I know," I told her, shaking free from her hands. "It's yours."

For a second, Mom looked stunned, as though I'd slapped her. Then her lips pressed into a tight line. She stood up, gripped my hand firmly in hers, and silently led me back to our house.

After that night, Dad didn't come around as much anymore. Birthdays and special events, if I was lucky. At school, I'd stare out my classroom window and imagine his bike pulling into the lot. Then I'd wait for the intercom to buzz on, calling me to the office where my dad would be waiting. We'd eat soft pretzels and cherry water ice, and we'd count the boats, and everything would be the way it was before. And when that didn't happen, I decided maybe Mom was wrong. Maybe it was my fault after all.

"What are you working on?"

I startle, slamming the notebook closed. Libby's standing next to me, dressed in ripped jeans and a t-shirt, her hair pulled up in a high ponytail.

"Geez," I say, quickly ducking my head to swipe at my eyes. "Where'd you come from?"

Libby's eyes narrow. "I've been standing here for like two minutes." Her eyes flicker to my purple notebook, half-hidden under my clasped hands. "Must be some deep dark secrets in there, huh?"

I look past her, thinking of deep dark secrets and the scars on Libby's wrists. "Relatively speaking."

She smirks. "I'm surprised to see you out here. Kinda figured you'd be up in your room, stewing in post-breakup self-pity." She waves her hand, shooing an invisible fly. "The afternoon speaker starts soon. You coming?"

I turn back to my step work, flip to a random page, and pretend to read. "No thanks," I say. "Pretty busy stewing at the moment."

Libby holds up her hands. "Sorry to interrupt."

"No problem."

I peer up from my notebook. Libby's blonde ponytail swings against her back, brushing her shoulders as she walks away. From this angle, I could almost mistake her for Savannah.

Day 10

THE TREADMILL WHINES AS I coax it to 3.0 mph. Red plods along beside me, trying to work up to a jog. I'd give anything to run, but after the push-up incident, the doctor had made me promise not to do anything that might further injure my bruised ribs. Besides, even walking makes me feel like I'm wearing steel ankle weights. At least the pain gives me something to focus on, something other than re-hashing the Step Two share that I'd fumbled through in group earlier this morning.

Afterwards, Howard had opened the floor for guys to share about their higher powers. Mo talked about the AA community; Prison Tat was the only one who talked about Jesus—he kept kissing the heavy gold cross around his neck and holding it to the sky like he was fist bumping the Holy Spirit.

Words like "hero," "trust," and "unconditional love" got tossed around the room like balls of yarn, weaving a web around the circle with me on the outside. Because it's not enough for me. Like I told Richard Fisher this morning in counseling, it's like I've stalled out at Step One. I don't how I'm supposed to pick a higher power when, in my experience, there are no heroes, just regular guys dressed in capes and masks. They're not there when you need them, and they sure as hell don't come when you call.

Red stumbles on the treadmill, struggling to keep his pace. I glance over at the fluorescent numbers on his dash. "You can do better than that," I joke.

Red shakes his head and fumbles for the Pause button. His face is a tomato, and he bends over, clutching his side. "I gotta quit smoking," he wheezes. The treadmill conveyer belt is spattered with sweat. "Whoever said your muscles remember is full of shit."

"How long has it been?"

"Three years, maybe?" Red wipes his face on his shirt sleeve and starts the treadmill again, slower this time. "Nothing since high school."

"I don't think muscles remember *that* well. What sport did you play, anyway?"

Red shoots me a wry smile. "Cross-country."

I laugh. We walk side by side for a minute, like those old ladies at the mall. Except slower. Finally, I work up the nerve to say what's on my mind. "Can I ask you a question?"

"Shoot."

"What's your take on this whole 'higher power' thing? I mean, it's bullshit, right? Some magical being is going to make me better?"

Red gives me a sideways glance. "I guess it depends on who your higher power is."

"Don't tell me you're actually falling for this crap, dude."

Red presses the Pause button again and turns to face me. "You know, after Lisa died, I was really fucked up. I kind of went off the deep end. I think I wanted to follow her, you know? But not the easy way. Not with a handful of pills or a gun to my head. I wanted to do it slowly. One needle at a time."

I wince and glance around the gym to see who else might be listening. Everybody's doing their own thing—a few dudes are lifting weights, and there's a chick on the elliptical. It's just me and Red and the story that unfurls between us.

Red tips up his water bottle, takes a long chug, and wipes his mouth with the back of his hand. "So anyway, there I am, basically homeless, sleeping in flop houses mostly. I didn't have any bags, so I kept everything in my pockets. My stash. My money. I spent a couple of weeks like that. During the day, I'd wander around on the streets and try not to think about Lisa. Then I'd find a place to crash for the night.

"So, this one morning, a couple weeks in, I wake up with a gun to my head. There's this dude in a ski mask, his hand shaking so much that the gun keeps bumping my cheek. 'Give me all your shit,' he says. And so I did. The dude took everything, all the cash I had on me, my stash. Everything. Then he took off. I followed him out into the street, and I remember the sun was so bright, burning, you know? And I didn't know where I was. I didn't know how I'd gotten there. I reached in my pocket for my cigarettes, but they were gone, too. The only thing left was one quarter.

"So I took that quarter to a pay phone, and I stuck it in the slot, and I dialed Lisa's number. Because I knew I was done. I knew it was time to end it. But I was scared, and I wanted to hear Lisa's voice, even just on her voicemail, one more time.

"I'm standing there in the middle of the sidewalk, and I remember there was a used condom on the ground. Nasty, right? But that's what I remember. A used condom on the ground and me at the end of my rope. I dial Lisa's number, and I'm waiting for her voicemail to pick up. But then somebody answers. And it freaks me out, you know, because who could be answering Lisa's phone? And then I realize: it's Lisa's mom.

"I'm so embarrassed that I almost hang up. But get this. She tells me she was praying for me, right before I called. She was praying that I was okay, that I was safe, and that I would get the help I need. So when she asks me how I am, I don't know what comes over me, but I tell her. I tell her that I don't know where I am. I tell her I don't have a dime to my name. I tell her I'm scared, and I'm so sad, and I don't want to do it anymore. I don't want to do any of it. And you know what she does? That woman who had just lost her daughter, she tells me, 'Come home, Ronnie.' And that's when I knew. Lisa didn't want me to die. She didn't want me to join her. She wanted me to get better. She wanted me to have a life.

"So, I let her mom call me a cab. It took me to her house, and then she brought me here."

"Lisa's mom?" I ask.

Red nods. "My pop sure can't afford this place. Lisa's parents are footing the whole bill."

I stare at the dash on my treadmill, watch the seconds tick by. "So, what, you think that was God or something?"

Red shrugs. He presses a button, and the treadmill cranks slowly back to life. "Beats me, dude. Maybe it was God. Maybe it was Lisa. All I'm saying is, maybe it's not all crap."

"Maybe." Maybe Lisa is a ghost or an angel or something; maybe she's looking out for Red. But if that's true, who's looking out for me?

145

Dinner is roast beef and potatoes with carrots, gravy so creamy, you could eat it with a spoon. It tastes like food somebody's grandma would make, not the ex-coke head with five years sober who works the kitchen. But the food sits like stones in my stomach. I pick at a piece of meat, move it around my plate with my fork, and let my thoughts take over.

It's as if my admission in Richard Fisher's office carved something out of me, and while everybody else around here seems to have something or someone to help put them back together, I know I have to do it on my own. It's like on the lax field—I got myself into this mess. Now I have to get myself out.

I hardly notice Red and Will plunk down their trays.

"Ping-Pong later?" Red's fingers drum the table in between bites. "Or are you gonna sit in your room and cry about your breakup again?"

I scowl at him. "I don't cry." In public, anyway, and that is between me and the concrete walls of my shower. "And yeah, I'm down for Ping-Pong."

Across from me, Will groans. "Not me. I've got a week of Self-Reflection during free time."

Red grins. "Apparently, gambling is 'frowned upon' at LakeShore."

Will tosses his fork onto his plate and drops his head in his hands. "I had a whole pool set up and everything."

Red slaps an invisible cymbal with his fork (bum, bum, *CHING!*). Then Libby's voice cuts through our laughter, like the husky bedroom melody of an indie acoustic. "You three losers have plans tonight?"

She's leaning over the end of the table, her palms flat on the laminate. Her two-toned hair hangs in a loose braid over one shoulder, and her wrists are covered in jingling silver bracelets.

Will gives her a half-cocked smile that looks more like a sneer. Libby hasn't exactly been his favorite person since the gym incident. "What, is there a party somewhere we don't know about?"

Libby rolls her eyes. "Howard's taking a van off-campus to an NA meeting in town. He asked me to let people know."

Red clears his throat, casts his eyes my way.

"Yeah," I say. "Maybe."

Libby shrugs. "Consider yourself invited." She flicks her braid off her shoulder and walks away.

Will shoves a piece of gravy-soaked roll in his mouth. "Do I smell a rebound?"

"What? No way, dude." I toss my balled-up napkin at him. It bounces off his shoulder and hits the floor. "She was just doing what Howard told her to. I mean, look, she's probably inviting those people over there, too."

I point across the dining hall, where Libby's chatting with a girl by the coffee bar.

Red grins, punches me lightly on the shoulder. "You could do worse, you know."

"I'd sleep with one eye open, though," Will adds. "That chick's a praying mantis."

"She's not a rebound! I'm not even looking . . ." My words get all tangled up, and I don't even know what I'm trying to say. Savannah and I just broke up, and if I have anything to say about it, we're not going to stay that way. Plus, even if I was looking for a rebound, it wouldn't be Libby. Not because I wouldn't want to, but because she's *Libby*, all sharp edges and jagged angles that bite. Will's right. Libby's not the girl you rebound with. She's the girl that eats you alive.

Will's eyes search my face, an evil grin playing around his mouth. "You're thinking about her right now, aren't you?"

"Shut up," I snap, and Will cracks up.

"Alright, alright . . ." Red makes a big display of zipping his mouth shut. For a second it's quiet at our table. I take a swig of iced tea. Maybe I should go to the meeting. At the very least, it'd take my mind off Savannah. And if Libby's going . . .

I glance around the room casually, my eyes settling on Libby. She's joined Mo at their table, and she must be telling a story or something, because her hands flutter in the air like delicate Chinese fans.

"So . . ." Red's voice cuts through the wandering melody of my thoughts. "Ping-Pong, then?"

I almost choke on my tea. "Um, I was actually thinking . . . you know, a meeting sounds nice . . . or whatever."

Red blinks. Then he and Will crack up.

It's 7:30 and LakeShore's white nine-seater is idling by the front curb. Uptight Howard, dressed in mom jeans and a tucked-in polo, ushers kids into the van like we're already late.

"Evening," I say.

He makes a *hurry up* motion with his hand. "Get in, get in." A thin sheen of sweat shines on his forehead. I climb into the van.

Libby and Mo are already sitting in the back seat. Mo looks like a giant back there, his knees practically in his mouth. "Yo, Roomie!" he calls. "Glad to see you decided to join us."

Libby gives me a half-smile. "No self-pity soup tonight?"

"Not tonight," I tease, sinking into the gray vinyl seat in front of her and propping up my feet. "Turns out you *can* get too much of a good thing."

Mo laughs.

"What about Tweedle Dee and Tweedle Dumber?" Libby asks. "They coming, too?"

I shake my head. "Will's restricted to campus, and Red . . ." I think about the vague explanation Red gave me, the look on his face when he told me he'd have to sit this one out. He'd slipped away right after dinner, and I'd wondered, not for the first time, where he goes to be alone. "He said he doesn't trust himself to leave campus yet." I give Libby and Mo a sideways look. "I mean, what kind of trouble is he going to run into at an NA meeting, right?"

"You'd be surprised, man," Mo says. "I actually got approached in the parking lot one time. Dealers stake out NA meetings. They figure it's a sure thing."

"Like steak in a shark pool," Libby adds.

She and Mo share a dark laugh.

"I'm pretty sure I can handle it," I muse.

Libby raises an eyebrow, and suddenly I feel self-conscious, like I'm bragging about myself or something. "I don't know, I just . . . don't even want it anymore."

A look passes between them, and then Libby gives me this smile that's almost sympathetic.

My stomach curls up like a fist. I know she and Mo are both thinking I've found my "pink cloud," or whatever the shit they call it in group. It's the artificial sense of confidence that comes from being in a place free of temptation. But it doesn't describe me. "I don't!"

Mo chuckles. He reaches over the seat to clap me on the shoulder. "Then consider yourself lucky, bro. You're one step ahead of the rest of us."

A couple more kids get on the bus, and I have to put my feet down so some girl can sit next to me. And then Howard climbs into the driver's seat, all flustered and pink-cheeked.

I lean back in my seat and whisper out one side of my mouth. "Should he be driving? He seems pretty worked up."

Libby giggles. "He's just nervous," she says. "He's speaking tonight."

"What, like at the meeting?"

She nods.

"But what's the point of that?" I ask. "I hear him talk every morning at group. I thought the whole reason we're doing this is for a change of scenery!" Where Libby's voice is the music you peace-out to in the car, Howard's is the radio personality that interrupts the song to sell you self-tanning or laser hair removal. If I'd known I'd be listening to him talk all night, I'd be playing Ping-Pong with Red right about now.

"It'll be good for you to check out a meeting on the outside," Mo tells me. "Trust me, these meetings have saved my ass more than once. They're going to be your lifeline when you go back home."

"More meetings?" Nobody said anything about *more* meetings. Isn't that the point of rehab? It's supposed to fix me, so that when I go home, I can work on getting my life back.

Mo nods. "This is Howard's home group," he continues. "It's where he goes to meetings on his own time. His story's pretty interesting."

"Define interesting."

Libby laughs. "You never know," she says. "He might surprise you."

"Everybody buckled up back there?" Howard asks, and I give him the thumbs-up sign.

"Locked and loaded, capt'n."

Howard glances nervously in the rearview mirror before pulling out of LakeShore's parking lot and onto the empty road.

"The Right Track" Narcotics Anonymous meeting is held at LakeShore United Methodist, a tiny stone chapel topped with an old-fashioned steeple. A small metal side door has a cardboard sign propped outside, welcoming newcomers. "This is us," Howard says, holding the door open.

I follow Libby and Mo inside. The meeting's being held in some lower recess of the church. It smells like coffee and mildew. People sit on metal fold-out chairs that form a semi-circle around an ancient upholstered recliner, apparently the seat of honor. In the far back, one guy's got a black wool beanie pulled down low over his ears; he's hunched over, twitching hands covering his face, like he's coming off a bender. But there are others, too—clean-cut men and women dressed in work clothes. One woman catches my eye; her manicured nails clutch a Starbucks cup, and she douses a teabag repeatedly. She gives me a tentative smile, looking more like someone who should be spending her evening at my mom's book club than at an NA meeting.

Howard helps me and the rest of the LakeShore kids pull out extra chairs, and then he takes his seat up front. I end up sitting between Libby and Mo. Libby takes off her jacket, hangs it over her seat. Her perfume is warm and spicy—like incense or something. Or maybe that's just the way she smells.

Sharp edges, I tell myself. Not a rebound. And as the meeting starts, I do my best to focus on the front of the room instead of Libby's white skin where it sticks out from the unbuttoned cuffs of her denim shirt, or the way her knees bounce in rhythm, like she's singing a song in her head.

Turns out a "real" NA meeting is pretty much the same as our group meetings at LakeShore, except that they start with people who take turns reading a too-long list of rules and regulations—really boring shit, like why members should donate money, and how you're not allowed to interrupt when someone else is talking. We're ten minutes into the meeting before it's time to talk about anything that matters, and considering the speaker's Howard, I'm pretty convinced that the whole thing's going to be a giant snooze fest.

"Good evening," Howard says, in that nasal talk show host voice of his. He thanks the people who read for their service to the group, and then he settles himself back in the upholstered chair and crosses his legs. I can't help but picture a fake fire smoldering on a hearth behind him and a pipe hanging out of the corner of his mouth. "Since this is a Step One meeting," Howard continues, "I've been asked to share about my experience working the step, and the journey that brought me into these rooms in the first place."

Libby gives me a sideways look, and I wonder if she's thinking what I'm thinking, that Howard's own boring personality was probably what drove him to drugs.

"Some of you know this about me," Howard continues. "But I actually played college football. In fact, I was headed straight for the NFL draft when my disease interrupted my life."

Um, what? Howard and the NFL are two things that cannot peacefully coexist in my brain. Mo elbows me in the ribs, a gentle *I told you so*. And he's right, because Howard had me at "draft."

Turns out Howard hasn't always been an uptight group leader with a donut belly and bad taste in jeans. He was, at one point, a football star. Full ride to a state college, town hero, the works. But Howard couldn't manage the pressure.

"It started as Adderall during exams," he tells the group. "Anything to keep me awake so I could cram after double practice days."

Howard's nasty little habit quickly evolved into a taste for coke at parties after they won. But it wasn't until he tore his ACL and had to recover from surgery, that he got hooked on painkillers.

"Suddenly, I wasn't living to play football anymore. I was living for my next score." Howard clears his throat. "I lost my scholarship and my place on the team. My disease took everything—my football career, my education, my friends, and even my family."

Howard tells us about the shitty little apartment he landed after dropping out of college, how he couldn't keep the lights on or food in the fridge. When his mom would give him money, he'd spend it on dope. When he got arrested, she'd bailed him out. And when he'd gotten into a car accident and didn't have insurance, she'd had to foot the whole bill.

"My parents went bankrupt because of me," Howard admits. "My rock bottom was the day they finally wised up and wouldn't let me into their house. In one year, I went from a football hero to a homeless junkie. It took that much for me to see that I was out of control, that my life was unmanageable, and that I was completely powerless over my addiction.

"The best thing my mother ever did for me," Howard continues, "was to lock me out of her house. You know what she said to me?" Howard leans forward in his chair. "I'll never forget it. She lifted a curtain in the kitchen window, where I'd banged so hard I'd cracked a pane. 'You are not your disease,' she said. 'You are a good man and my precious son. But your disease is dark and selfish, and I will not let it step foot into my house again.'"

Howard's laughter shatters the silence in the room like broken glass. "And boy did she mean it. Heck, I've been sober for ten years, and she only let me back in two years ago!" The room rumbles with relieved laughter, relieved that Howard's sober, that his mother let him back in, that for a small second, we can stop thinking about how our own lives have fallen apart.

"I want to emphasize one part of my story for you guys." Howard looks around the circle at me and Libby and Mo and the smattering of other LakeShore kids sitting on the outer rim of the group. "It's those words my mother said to me. You are not your disease."

Libby inhales sharply, and without even thinking about it, I reach for her, drop my hand on her knee—not in a weird creepster way, but in an *I know. I feel it, too,* kind of way. I steal a glance at her out of the corner of my eye. She looks down at my hand for a second, but she doesn't shove it off or tell me to go fuck myself. She looks back at Howard. So I leave my hand where it is. Because I know. Because I feel it, too.

"Ten years," Howard echoes. He shakes his head like he can barely believe it. "The disease of addiction took everything from me. But these rooms gave me back my life. Thanks for letting me share."

The room erupts in a chorus of "thanks for sharing," and then someone opens the floor for individual shares. My hand slips from Libby's knee. She leans into me, whispers, "Good, right?"

I nod. Because like it or not, I felt something while Howard was talking. Like my deepest darkest secrets were written on my skin in permanent marker. Like everyone could see them, but it's okay, because they have secrets, too.

That feeling stays with me until the end of the meeting, when I follow Howard and the other kids out into the parking lot.

I climb into the van ahead of the other kids who linger in the parking lot to chat with people leaving the meeting. I settle onto the cool leather and stare out the window. A few minutes later, Libby joins me. Mo climbs into the front next to Howard, like some kind of NA groupie, no doubt gushing about how this meeting has changed his life. Mo's had so many life-changing experiences, he's practically schizophrenic.

"Ten years," Libby muses, settling back into the seat and wrapping her cargo jacket across her chest. Her eyes are shining, even in the dark van interior. "Hard to believe, right?"

I nod, wondering if we're going to talk about how my hand was on her knee. Or how right it feels for her to be sitting next to me, so close that the right side of my body is warmed by her jacket. So close I'm breathing incense.

"I've almost got thirty days," Libby says.

I turn to look at her. "How long have you been here, anyway?"

"Almost three weeks," she says. "A little over a week left."

I gaze at her for a second, feeling like Benny that time we ran into his teacher at Target, and he finally figured out she didn't live at school. I'd been so focused on getting through my own 28 days, I hadn't even thought about the people who got here before me. Like I'd leave, and they'd all still be here, living their lives at LakeShore. Red, Will, Mo.

Libby.

I open my mouth to say something, but then the girl in the seat in front of us swivels around, hangs her arm over the seat back. "What'd you think about Howard's share?" she asks Libby, and the two are soon lost in conversation.

Howard cranks up the van, and cold air from the overhead vents blasts the top of my head. All around me, kids settle into hushed exchanges as they process the meeting, but I hike up my hoodie and lean against the window. The van is packed, and

Libby's arm is still touching mine. But for some reason I can't put my finger on, I feel completely alone.

Day 11

I 'M SITTING CROSS-LEGGED ON THE floor outside of Richard Fisher's office when he finally shows up for work. He's so engrossed in reading something on his phone that he almost trips over me.

"What the . . . Eli?"

"You shouldn't walk and text at the same time," I tell him. "It's a matter of public safety."

Richard Fisher mumbles something under his breath as he unlocks his office door. I'm pretty sure I catch the words "smart ass." I follow him into his office.

"Come on in," Richard Fisher says, a little unenthusiastically. He drops his helmet on his desk and starts unloading his worn leather brief case.

I drop straight down onto the couch and prop up my feet, eyeing the decals (one peeling) on the shiny side of his black helmet. "Is it true you were in a motorcycle drug ring?"

Richard Fisher rubs his eyes wearily. "Aren't you supposed to be listening to the morning speaker right now?"

"You said you have an open-door policy," I counter. "You said I could come whenever I needed to talk. And I do. Need to talk, I mean."

"I knew I should've stopped for coffee on the way in," Richard Fisher sighs. He drops heavily into his swivel chair. "So talk."

"I went to a meeting last night."

Richard's eyes light up a bit. "Your first NA meeting," he says. "What'd you think?"

"It was fine." I shove a couch pillow under the crook of my neck and lean back against it. "It was good, actually. But now I pretty much feel like crap."

"How so?"

"I don't know," I tell him, because it's hard to explain. Ever since the ride home, I've felt raw, like I'm wearing my skin inside out or something. I snapped at Mo last night when he tried to ask me about the meeting, and I didn't sleep well, so now I'm cranky and achy and tired. And underneath all of that is a steady hunger for something, anything, that will make these feelings go away. I haven't felt like this since Dad died, and the one thing I know for sure will make me feel better, is the last thing I'm going to get my hands on here.

I glare at Richard. "You know, like crap."

He smiles at me. "You're going to have to elaborate."

"I'm pissed, okay?" I can't get comfortable on the couch, and I burrow backward, finally reaching back to yank out the flimsy throw pillow and toss it across the room.

"You're angry," Richard echoes.

"That's what I said," I snap at him, folding my arms across my chest and clenching my fists.

Richard nods. "It's not uncommon for me to hear something in a meeting that reminds me of my own story. Sometimes it can trigger some very difficult emotions."

I sit up on the couch and stare at him. "But you can make it stop, right? I mean, that's your job. That's what shrinks do."

"For the last time, Eli, I'm not a . . ." Richard Fisher rubs his hand down his face, squeezes the bony part at the top of his nose. "They're called feelings, Eli. They're a part of life, and once we stop using drugs to numb them, we have to learn how to deal with them all over again."

"So you're saying I'm going to feel this way forever?"

Richard Fisher shakes his head. "No, not forever. You remember my zit analogy?"

I grimace. "Unfortunately."

"What happens to a zit after you pop it? It scabs over and then what?"

I roll my eyes, thinking Mo's got the story wrong, that Richard Fisher would make a better dermatologist than a shrink. "They heal, I guess."

"They heal," Richard echoes. "Feelings demand to be felt. The important thing is *how* we cope with our feelings while we're having them. As addicts, we have to learn new ways to deal with our feelings—ways that don't involve needles or rolled dollar bills. That's where Step Two comes in: We came to believe that a power *greater than ourselves* could restore us to sanity. Because we *can't* do it ourselves. Think about it: in the past when you've had feelings like this, how have you managed them?"

I don't manage them. I shut them off. I look Richard Fisher straight in the eye. "I get high."

"And how's that worked out for you?"

I think of Savannah, the cloudy February morning when I showed up with flowers. The way she forgave me, the promises I broke. "I'm here, aren't I?"

"Exactly," Richard says. "Shutting down, using drugs, it doesn't work. We have to believe that there's something else out there that can help us choose another way. How are you coming on your step work?"

"See, that's just it," I tell him. "It seems like everybody else around here has something or someone they can depend on to help them out. Red has Lisa, or her mom, or whatever, and Mo has his family and his home group. But when I go home, I'm not going to have anybody. Not Savannah, not my friends."

"What about your family?" Fisher asks.

Anger sears my gut like acid. "What about them?"

"They brought you here. They obviously support your recovery. Can't you depend on them?"

I snort. "Steven only dumped me here so he could avoid the Grandhaven rumor mill. Nobody wants to talk about heroin while they're teeing off. And Mom will do anything he wants, so long as she can keep her sparkly McMansion and the perfect family façade she's got going on."

"It sounds like you're pretty angry at your mom."

"Yes, I'm fucking angry!" I pitch forward on the couch, vomiting the words I've never said out loud. My fury seeps into the carpet, the couch cushions. It drips down the walls. "Dad died, and I was lost. You wouldn't think a ten-year-old could feel so dark inside, but I did. And instead of being there for me, instead of helping me through it, she just picked up and moved on. She married Steven and had Benny. Like Dad never existed. Like our real family was a memory she'd rather forget."

Fisher doesn't seem phased by my outburst. "You feel like she abandoned you," he says.

"It's worse than that," I tell him, my nails sinking into the flesh of my palms. "If it wasn't for her, my dad would still be alive."

He cocks a brow. "How so?"

"My dad died on his way to our house. He was coming to sign divorce papers. He didn't want to. He put it off for as long as he could. If Mom hadn't pushed so hard . . ." My words catch in my throat as I revisit my familiar childhood fantasy, how much better my life would be if Dad was still alive. I swallow hard. "Dad was barely in the ground when Steven proposed."

Fisher leans back in his chair. "Have you ever tried talking to your mom about this?"

I choke out a bitter laugh. "Yeah, right. What am I supposed to say? 'Hey, Mom, thanks for being a selfish bitch.' That'll go over real well."

"Well, I don't know if I'd use those exact words, but the alternative is to not talk about it at all. And then how will it be when you go back home? If you take all this anger with you, how will you keep from falling back into old patterns?"

I consider the possibilities. I might be able to hold out for a little while, but one good fight with mom would have me locked in my room, texting Chase for a hit. But what can I do about it now? How am I supposed to start a conversation eight years in the making?

"I know I should talk to her," I say, hunching my shoulders and hiking my hood up around my ears. "But I don't know how."

"Sometimes it can be helpful to have a family counseling session," Fisher suggests.

"What, like, bring my mom in here?"

Fisher nods.

I sink lower into my hoodie, pulling the cuffs down around my hands. "I don't even know what I would say."

"You'd say all the things you told me. Only you wouldn't have to do it alone. I'd be right here in your corner, backing you up."

I mull it over a minute, my fingers tracing the muted pattern on the sofa cushion. Bringing Mom in to talk sounds terrifying, like heading into surgery knowing full well you're coming out with a vital organ missing. But with Fisher here, she'd actually have to listen for once. There'd be no distractions—no Benny and no Steven. Just Mom and me.

I give a short nod. "No Steven, okay? Just my mom."

Fisher smiles. "Sounds like a plan."

Day 13

THIS MORNING'S SPEAKER IS A 95-pound yogi with more body piercings than orifices. After a brief share on finding her sobriety through yoga and meditation, Ivy has us all put away our chairs and sit cross-legged on the bare floor while she perches on a purple meditation pillow and "oms" like an electric fly zapper.

Red bailed as soon as he heard the word "yoga," sneaking off to wherever it is that he goes. Will sits a few feet away from me. He keeps snickering under his breath, and I'm pretty sure the only thing he's visualizing is the backside of Ivy's yoga pants.

And somehow this is supposed to help me get in touch with my higher power.

Libby sits right next to me. I can't tell if she's into this or if she's fallen asleep, because even though my eyes are supposed to be closed, I keep opening them to make sure that everyone in the room isn't secretly staring at me.

Libby's lashes flutter softly like she's dreaming. Her hands rest palms up on her knees, and the puckered pink skin of fading scars peeks out from under the sleeves of her white t-shirt. I wonder what finds her when she closes her eyes. And then I realize that if she opens them and sees me staring at her, she's going to think I'm a creepy stalker and probably never talk to me again.

I quickly shut my eyes and try not to think about the things that find *me* in the dark: Mom's coming today. And even though Fisher has reassured me a thousand times, I'm still a nervous wreck. What if I chicken out? What if, even with Fisher in my corner, I can't tell her how I've really felt all these years? Deep down, I know that what I want to come from this session is proof—proof that Dad's leaving was Mom's fault so that I can finally let myself off the hook. But what if that proof doesn't come?

"And when you're ready," Ivy finally drones, in this voice that's a weird combo of sexy and nerd, like a guest speaker on NPR or a hot librarian, "open your eyes and come back to the room."

I stretch out my legs, which have fallen so deeply asleep that tiny pins and needles are climbing up my skin like a thousand caterpillars.

"It wasn't that bad, was it?" Libby teases.

"Longest twenty minutes of my entire lifetime." I pound my feet with my knuckles to wake them up. "You?"

"I kinda liked it." She stretches her arms above her head, like she just woke up from a blissful power nap. The smooth white skin of her lower back shows, and I can barely make out the upper edge of lower hip ink. Libby lowers her arms. "I did feel like someone was staring at me, though." She twists around and squints at me, her nose scrunched up like she's sniffing out a lie. "You weren't staring at me, were you?"

For a second I'm not sure if she's talking about when I was watching her meditate or just now, when I was checking out her, um . . . tattoo. Either way, I'm guilty as charged, but I point at my chest like maybe she's talking to someone else and blatantly avoid the question. "Who, me?"

"Yes, you." Libby twists full around on her mat so her knees touch my leg. "Because you know that would be total creepsville, right? To stare at someone while they're meditating?"

I make my face slack-jawed serious. "If you want to get technical about it, staring at someone while they're *sleeping* would be total creepsville. Staring at someone while they're meditating is probably only partially creepsville and, depending on the circumstances, could also be construed as . . . sweet."

Libby blinks.

"Not that I was staring at you or anything."

She shoves my shoulder and laughs, then climbs to her feet, reaching out her hands to help pull me up. "C'mon, perv. Let's get the blood flowing again." I take her hands, pull myself up onto still-wobbly legs, and make some lame joke about how she might have to carry me to group. But as soon as we part ways, the nerves set in again.

I'm a basket case during group, my legs jostling up and down almost as much as Will's, who looks like his very veins are caffeinated. I can't concentrate on anything anybody says. My stomach churns around my breakfast, and my palms are sweating so much they leave wet prints on my jeans. I must look like I'm going to puke or something, because at one point, Howard looks at me all worried and asks if I need to see the nurse. By the time I get to Richard Fisher's office, where my mom and Fish are waiting for me, I can barely see straight. This was a bad idea—a very, very bad idea.

Richard Fisher sits in a chair opposite Mom on the couch, and he's brought in another chair for me. "Come on in and have a seat, Eli. Your mom just got here."

Mom gives me this tiny, tentative smile, and I wonder if she's as nervous as I am. She pats a spot on the couch beside her, but I choose the chair, a safe distance away.

Richard Fisher gives me this expectant look, and I know he's waiting for me to start, but the words that came so freely when it was only me and Fish now seem stuck somewhere between my head and my heart.

"Eli," Fisher begins, laying down a trail of breadcrumbs for me to follow. "Why don't you tell your mother why you've asked her to join us today?"

Mom's face is open and warm, like when she's listening to Benny talk about his favorite kind of dinosaur or the latest episode of *Blue's Clues*. For the first time in a long time, I've got her full attention, and it's absolutely terrifying.

I look at my hands instead of at Mom and force out the words. "I want to talk about Dad."

Mom blinks. "What?" She casts a sideways glance at Richard Fisher. "Why?"

"Because you never talk about him," I push. "Because he's my dad, and you act like he never existed."

Mom's jaw flexes; she picks at an invisible piece of lint on her sweater. I give Richard Fisher a pleading look.

He picks up the trail. "Eli thought that maybe a family session—"

Mom cuts in. "We really should've included Steven."

166

Anger rises in my throat, freeing my tongue. "That's just it!" I say. The words wedge through gritted teeth. "Steven's not my family."

"Honey," Mom tries. She reaches to touch my knee, but I push my chair back out of reach. She sighs. "Steven cares about you a great deal, Eli. And like it or not, he's a part of our family."

Richard Fisher clears his throat. "That may be, but right now it's important that we validate every feeling Eli's having."

"Steven raised him like his own son." Mom talks to Richard Fisher like I'm not even here. "He paid Eli's way into one of the most prestigious college prep schools around. He—"

"He's not my dad!" I explode.

Mom's head swivels to face me, like she'd forgotten I was in the room.

"My dad died, remember? Or did you forget about him when you and Steven were drawing up plans for your new life?"

Mom slides her hands down her face. "That's not fair, Eli. I don't expect you to understand, but I had to do what I knew was best."

"You didn't even ask me! You never once tried to talk to me about my dad. You stuck me in therapy, hoping they could figure out what was wrong with me. Well, guess what, Mom? I could've saved you a boat-load of money—the only thing wrong with me is you!"

Mom turns to Richard Fisher. "I don't think I can do this."

"Now, hang on a second," Fisher tries, his voice coaxing. "Eli, remember how we talked about trying to use I-statements—"

I ignore him.

I want to hurt her. I want her to feel like I've felt all these years. My words freefall like cannonballs. "All I ever wanted was more time with Dad. I wanted to live with him. Did you know that? Did you ever think for a second that maybe I actually needed him around? No, you were too selfish, too self-absorbed . . ."

Mom's face turns to chiseled stone, her voice taut and low. "You have no idea what you're talking about."

"Why can't you just admit it? If you hadn't been so determined to get a divorce, Dad would still be alive."

Mom's shaking her head, deflecting my words. Fury and desperation push me to my feet, and I hover over her, landing a final blow: "It's your fault he's dead!"

Mom's face crumples; she drops her head into her hands. Words, faint and feeble, find their way through her fingers. "It was an overdose, Eli."

An overdose. The word sears my brain, fiery and hot.

"You're lying." My voice cracks, and I hate how pathetic I sound.

Mom peers up at me, her eyes pooling with tears. "I wish I was," she says. "You were so little, and you loved him so much. How could I tell you he was an addict? I had to protect you from the truth."

An addict.

My mind swirls as memories rush in like flood water. "That night," I begin, "the night he left . . ."

The park.

The swings.

Mom's cheeks are glistening, and her eyes are bloodshot. "I went through his dresser," she says. "I'd known for a long time that something wasn't right. We were always short on money, and he was always going out at night, always lying to me. At first, I thought it was an affair. I went through his drawers, looking for receipts, lipstick stains, anything. But I never expected . . ."

Mom dissolves into tears, and Richard Fisher hands her a box of tissues.

I turn my back to them, lean against the wall, and press my forehead against the cool plaster. This new life history sits skin-deep, burning the surface of my knowing, but I will not absorb it. I will not take this in.

Mom's sobbing now, but instead of going to her, instead of comforting her, I reach for the door. "We're done here."

"Eli?" Richard Fisher's voice pulls me up short. A deep crevice furrows his weathered brow. "Can you stay a little longer? I think it's important that we talk about what you're feeling right now."

You know how when you put your hand in scalding water or ice-cold snow, the feeling you get is the opposite? The water feels like ice and the snow burns you? Either way, if you keep your hand there long enough, pretty soon you don't feel anything. You don't notice your hand burning. You don't notice the frostbite.

You don't feel anything at all.

"I'm fine," I say.

"Eli," he presses.

"I said I'm fine!"

Richard Fisher sighs, and I leave without saying goodbye to my mom.

A gnawing hunger grabs me right outside of Richard Fisher's office, tearing at my skin from the inside. I skip the end of group and head to the dining hall, where I scarf down four cream-filled donuts doused in scalding coffee. I leave the cafeteria in a sugar-sick daze. The walk to the art room feels like moving through quicksand, each step heavier than the first. I brush past Libby, almost bumping into her easel, and she grabs my arm.

"Eli? What the hell? What happened?"

Her eyes pass over my face like searchlights, teasing out the story, and for a second I want to tell her everything. But that would make it true.

"I'm fine," I mumble.

I leave Libby at her easel and head for the supply table. I squirt paint on a palette and choose a brush, then fill a can with water from the utility sink at the back of the room. I swipe color after color on my canvas until the paint cakes like mud.

The rest of the class arrives gradually, and the art room settles into quiet, focused activity—a beehive vibrating with the subtle din of brushes against canvases and the soft "oohs and aahs" of the wandering art teacher, with her rustling skirt and wind chime earrings, who stops at each person's easel in turn.

"Tell me about this," she buzzes, hovering near an easel close to mine. Her patchouli smell wafts across the room, stinging my nose.

The girl behind me drones softly about how her self-portrait depicts the pressure of perfectionism.

"I can see the anger here," Queen Bee/Art Teacher hums. "And over here, in these cool tones you've chosen, the loss and isolation."

Her voice is the delicate pitter patter of raindrops in summer—soothing and barely audible. But in the fog of confusion that clouds my brain, they echo like the mega-phoned announcements of a sports commentator. "Anger! Loss! Isolation!"

I stare at my painting, jab more brown here, more yellow and red, until I'm not painting anymore, I'm stabbing the canvas with smudging color. This is supposed to be a self-portrait. This canvas is supposed to tell my story. But my entire life has been a lie.

My dad was an addict.

An *addict*.

Savannah's words sneak in through some back door of my brain. *Your heart stopped, Eli. You were dying.*

Like father, like son.

And suddenly I'm not painting anymore. The paintbrush is gone, and I'm stabbing the canvas with fists that come back streaked with brown. My fragile easel trembles and clatters to the ground. Someone screams. Faces pass in a blur as I run from the room. I don't stop, I don't slow down.

I run until I don't know where I'm going. Until I can't see straight. Until I can't breathe. Down the hall, through the rec room, right out the back doors where visitors stand to smoke. I slump down on the concrete stoop, streaked with ash, and sob into my paint-covered hands. My tears land like clumps of mud.

When the double doors behind me shove open, I'm pretty sure it's an orderly sent by the art teacher to haul me to Richard Fisher's office for more shrinking. Or to the nurse for a sedative. Which actually sounds pretty good right about now.

I wipe my eyes on my t-shirt sleeve. "You don't have to say it," I say, without turning around. "I can take myself back to art."

"Not much point in that," Libby answers, and I twist around real fast, because she's the last person I expected.

She smirks. "Your painting is pretty much a pile of scraps at this point." She sits down on the stoop beside me, her knee bumping mine in greeting. "It sucked anyway."

I choke out a strangled laugh, but the effort pushes out more tears, and I turn my face away from Libby, try to wipe them before she sees.

She doesn't say anything. She doesn't ask what happened. She doesn't even ask if I'm okay. She pulls my head onto her shoulder and pretends she doesn't see me cry.

Paint drips like dried blood from my wrists and hands, mixing with the suds at the bottom of the shower. My thoughts swirl. Mom and Dad on the front porch the night he missed the ball game. Her hands on his chest, pushing him away. The flash of red taillights in the darkness. Mom on her knees in the middle of the street.

She could've told me then. She could've told me a thousand times after. Instead, she married Steven and moved us to Grandhaven, where the ceilings were too high, and everything was closets and corners—a thousand places to hide and nowhere to be myself.

She built our lives on a lie.

I slam the water off, wrap a towel around my waist. Mo sits on his bed; his pen scratches across the pages of a notebook.

My footprints soak the carpet. The picture of me and Mom heckles me from the top of my dresser. Me smiling, totally oblivious, Grandhaven Giants slapped across the front of my jersey like a brand. Like if we moved, we could start over. Like our lives could ever be normal again.

I fling the picture against the wall. The glass cracks but doesn't shatter. The frame lands face down on the floor.

Mo stares at me, his pen suspended above the page.

"Don't ask me if I want to talk about it," I growl. "I'm done talking." I pick up the picture, toss it into the trash. I'm done with all this shit, done with sharing, with memories, with writing in my stupid fucking journal. Done telling the truth.

The truth only brings more pain.

Day 15

I SLEEP THROUGH THE MORNING of my second Visitation. After Mo got up, I turned off my alarm and pulled the curtains closed. I pretend this day is like any other. Savannah won't be here. And I told my mom not to come.

She cried, of course. Over the phone in Richard Fisher's office, she sobbed into the receiver and begged me to reconsider.

"I'll tell you anything you want to know, honey," she'd pleaded. "Anything at all. No more lies. I promise."

I'd handed the phone to Richard Fisher. Thirty seconds of honesty is a drop of water in an ocean of deceit.

"He'll talk when he's ready," Richard assured her. "We can't force him to deal with these feelings if he doesn't want to."

"Thanks, Fish," I'd said on my way out of his office. "I owe you one."

Turns out it's hard to sleep when you're hungry, and the thought of red velvet cake sounds way better than spending the whole day alone in the dark. I fumble under the bed for my sneakers and head downstairs to the dining hall.

It's packed with families, and the red velvet cake is already gone. I grab a plain bagel (the only kind left) and go looking for the only other person I know who won't be spending the day with visitors.

Libby's on the same leather chair in the lobby where I found her last weekend. She's perched with her legs tucked under her like a bird, and even though her notebook is open on her lap, she's not drawing. She's staring through the glass doors into the parking lot.

"Any sign of them?"

Libby startles, nearly jumping out of the chair. I wait for her to laugh or hit me or something, but her face is drawn tight, and she looks back toward the parking lot.

"No," she says. "I don't think she's coming." Her voice is laced with disappointment, and I realize, not for the first time, that I can't figure this girl out.

I drop into the chair opposite her. "I told mine not to come."

This gets Libby's attention. She turns away from the window, her fingers toying absently with the corner of her notebook. "Good for you."

Libby has no idea what happened between me and my mom. But maybe that's the best kind of support there is—the kind that doesn't need to hear both sides. The kind that's on your side no matter what—the kind that backs you up, even if you're wrong.

"So, what's going on?" I ask over a bite of dry bagel. "I thought you didn't want visitors."

"Things change." Libby looks up at the clock above the receptionist's desk. It's already noon—only two hours left of Visitation. Some people are already filtering back out into the parking lot, off to attend soccer games or dance recitals for their non-disappointing children. Libby turns to me suddenly. "Do you want to do something?"

"Like what?"

"I don't know." She closes her notebook, threads her sketching pencil through the wire binding, and stands up. "A walk or something, maybe? I'm tired of waiting around. You snooze, you lose, right?"

"Sure, I guess." I toss the rest of my bagel in the trash by the receptionist's desk. "I hear the landscape here is beautiful," I tease, mimicking my mom's lame attempt at normalizing LakeShore. "Should we take a tour?"

Libby grins and slips her arm in mine. "Lead the way."

Arm in arm, we weave through families and loved ones too focused on one another to care if two scarred junkies decide to go for a stroll. Unnoticed and unclaimed, we slip beneath an EXIT sign and out into the wooded landscape beyond.

We find a path as close to the edge of campus as possible, far enough to feel like we've escaped, but not so far as to actually send the Front Desk Fascist into a conniption. It's a gorgeous spring day, with afternoon sunshine that's melted the morning chill. The trees are so beautiful you can almost forget the security cameras harbored in their branches. The air smells like open woods: damp, earthy, and alive.

"My mom was supposed to come today." Libby clutches her purple notebook to her chest, and for a second she looks like a normal high school girl, walking through a hall of lockers with her books in her arms. Normal, but for the scars.

"I thought you didn't want her here," I say, realizing too late that I've probably crossed a line. Why couldn't I do for Libby what she did for me? No questions, no talking. Just presence.

"She broke up with her boyfriend. Or at least, she said she did. She *said* she kicked him out. It's about time." Libby's lips screw up into a perfect rose petal pout. "Anyway, she was supposed to come today so we could talk about what it's going to be like when I go home next week."

"Next week?" The words push the air from my lungs. I don't know what this is between us, but I know I'm not ready for it to end.

Libby gives me a sideways glance, and I can't tell if she's thinking the same thing as me. "Yep," she says. "Only a few more days." She steps closer to me, on purpose maybe, and her arm gently bumps mine. "What about you?"

"Me?" I run my hand through my hair and let out a deep exhale. "Where do I start?"

Libby smiles. "You don't want to talk about it. I get it. We don't have to talk about it."

"No, it's not that." I don't want to talk about it, but I don't want to *not* talk about it either. "My mom's been the bearer of bad news lately. And I knew if she came, we were going to have to 'talk.'" I bookmark the word in finger quotes, teasing a laugh from Libby. "I just didn't want to, you know? But I also didn't want to bullshit for four hours."

"Totally get it," Libby says. "You can only mention how good the cake is so many times before you start to sound like an idiot."

"Or answer the how-are-you question."

"Oh my god, the how-are-you's!" Libby stops in her tracks and flings out her arms like she's sunning in disgust. "They're the worst!"

177

I pause mid-stride, turn around to face her. "It's like, what do you want me to say? I'm fine, thanks, except for that whole heroin thing."

"Right?"

Libby and I laugh together for a minute, and I can't help but think, screw high school. Screw Mom and Steven, with their trumped-up expectations. *This* is real, this shared laughter and shared pain. Underneath the fake bullshit, where people's secrets hide. That's where Libby belongs.

She touches my arm, and we keep walking. "Heroin, huh?" Libby muses. "I would've guessed pills. Oxy, percs, the good stuff."

"Yeah, well, turns out a taste for H kinda runs in the family." I squint into the distance, remembering the afternoon Mom got the call that Dad had died. The divorce papers were on the table, and Dad was late. Mom had been so pissed; she'd paced the kitchen, mumbling under her breath that it was just like Dad to bail on a promise. I tried to drown out her words with crunchy cheese puffs as I worked on my homework at the kitchen table. When the phone rang, she snatched it off the hook. "Where are you?" she demanded. And then she slid down the wall, crumpling into a heap on the floor, the receiver still clutched in one hand.

Mom didn't cry. Not then, and not later, at the funeral.

I used to hate her for that. I thought she wasn't sad enough about his death, maybe even secretly happy about it. But now I can't help wondering how many sleepless nights she'd spent waiting for that call.

I turn my face away from Libby, blinking away tears. We're halfway around campus, and I can see the rear parking lot up ahead. I'm not ready for this walk to be over; I'm not ready to stop talking. I push my hands deep in my pockets and slow my pace.

"I used to draw on my arms," Libby blurts suddenly.

I peer at her sideways, curious.

"You know, doodles, cool quotes and stuff." She trails her fingers down one creamy arm, her bracelets jingling like delicate wind chimes, sunlight glinting off of silver. "One time I popped too many Xannies before school, three out of Mom's purse while she sweated out her hangover on the Pilates machine in the basement, and two more I'd saved in my locker." She giggles. "I kept nodding off in History, woke up when some asshole pegged me in the head with a balled-up gym sock, my cheek stuck to my hand, drool all over my desk. Everybody laughed, but it wasn't until later, in the bathroom, that I knew why. Everything I'd drawn on my arm was tattooed right across my face. I might as well have written LOSER on my forehead in Sharpie."

She laughs again, a sharp, hiccupy sound, like a bubble of stomach acid, sour and burning. I glance at the notebook she's carrying, thinking of the sketches scrawled there and the scars drawn across her skin.

"Hey, I have an idea," Libby says. "I should draw you."

I give her a doubtful look.

"No, come on, it'll be fun." She's already pulling her pencil out of her notebook. "Here, with the woods behind you." She leads me to a sunny spot between the trees and pushes down on my shoulder. "We both know this is the closest thing to a decent self-portrait you're going to get in this joint."

I hesitate, but Libby's persistent. "No broken limbs or zippers, I promise."

I laugh and sink down into the grass. Libby scoots a few feet away and then sits down facing me, opening her notebook to a fresh page.

I shake my hair down into my eyes, over my scar, and smile like in my driver's license picture.

Libby giggles. "Relax," she says. "This isn't a mug shot."

So I try to cover my awkwardness with humor, go all Blue Steel, and strike a couple poses.

"Be serious, Eli."

And then I don't know what to do, so I lie on my back in the grass and stare up at the bulbous, shifting clouds. It's a sky for daydreaming—the kind of clouds that can be anything, depending on what you're looking for.

Libby drops her notebook, lies on her belly beside me. Propped on her elbows, she plucks the heads of clover, making a little white pile in the grass. "Tell me something else," she says. "Something true."

"What do you want to know?"

My hair has fallen back off my forehead, and Libby's fingers find my scar. She touches it, feather soft. "What happened here?"

"It was a long time ago."

Libby's expectant gaze tugs at the memory of that afternoon. Glistening green grass and the kind of sun that blinds you. Superman ice cream dripping down my arm. Dad's warm hand wrapped around mine.

I swallow. I know I don't have to tell her. But I want to. "It happened in the park, a long time ago. My dad and I were spending the day together, and all I wanted to do was swing. Dad tried to get me to do something else, anything else. The sandbox, the slide. I guess he was tired of pushing me." I laugh. "But I kept going right back to the swings. It was something about that feeling, I guess. Feet in the air, wind in your face. Like flying."

The grass prickles the back of my neck. I shift my hands behind my head. "I kept begging Dad to go higher. He was worried I couldn't hang on, but I begged and begged, and so he made me promise. 'Whatever you do, don't let go.'"

Reliving the scene in the park makes me think of Benny, how he drew me at Disney, even though I wasn't there. He drew me where he wanted me, where I should've been.

"What did I know, anyway? I was just a dumb little kid."

A dumb kid like Benny—too young to understand that my hero was a junkie.

My eyes burn. I swipe at the corners with knuckles that come back wet.

Libby's fingers stroke my brow, my cheek, my jaw. I want to take her hand; I want to press it to my mouth. I want to know what her skin tastes like. "That was the night my dad left us," I whisper. "But the crazy part is, up until the hospital and Mom freaking out afterwards, it's one of my favorite memories."

"The best and the worst," Libby whispers, and I think of Savannah, of her blue dress at Winter Formal, and later, the sour stink of her puke on my suit. The best and the worst all in one.

Libby lowers her elbow, settles down into the crook of my arm, and lays her head gently on my chest. Her hair smells like lavender and sleep, and I close my eyes and breathe her in. It's natural the two of us like this, together on the outskirts, in this quiet place under the trees. I wrap my arm around her, draw her closer, and softly trail my fingers down the length of her forearm, thinking of the things she drew there, of the words I'd write on her skin. "Your turn."

"I don't want to go home."

My chest tightens, and I crane my neck to see her face. "Libby . . ." I begin, but she shakes her head, nuzzling her face into the soft fabric of my shirt. "We all have scars, Eli," she whispers. "They make us who we are."

And I wonder if that's true. If it's our scars that form us, or the other way around—if we choose our own particular brand of pain. If we go looking for it somehow, because it reminds us that we're alive, that we exist, that we're still capable of feeling something. Or if it's because without pain, we forget how good we've got it.

My heart beats in Libby's ear, and I hope she can't tell it's racing. She threads her fingers through mine, and we stay that way until one or both of us falls asleep, and visiting hours are over, and the Front Desk Fascist sends an orderly to wake us.

Day 16

"I HEAR YOU HAD QUITE the weekend." Richard Fisher peers at me over the rim of his reading glasses.

I prop my feet on the scratched surface of the coffee table, its legs wobbly like cardboard, like the kind of furniture we had in our old house, before Steven. "Not you, too."

Ever since Libby and I got hauled back into LakeShore yesterday afternoon, Will and Red haven't been able to shut up about it. Once Visitation ended, nobody knew where we were. It turned into a big to-do, with our names called over the intercom a bunch of times and our rooms checked. By the time some genius thought to check the security cameras, every idiot in LakeShore knew that Libby and I were missing. Together. So when they spotted us sleeping and brought us in bleary eyed with grass on our backs, the rumor mill had already taken on a life of its own.

Richard Fisher takes off his glasses. "You do realize we have a very strict policy about romantic relationships here, right? It

183

should have been reviewed with you and your mom when you first came in."

"Nothing happened," I say, for probably the 800th time in two days. No matter how many times I say it, Will still punches me in the arm and says "Duuude . . ." every time Libby passes.

"I believe you," Fish says, "but I still have to put the two of you on probation. Elizabeth will be leaving soon anyway, but you . . ."

I try to imagine Libby as Elizabeth, with straight black hair, no ink, and no scars. A nameless, faceless girl that I could've passed a million times in the hall at school and never noticed. And then I wonder if Libby's right—if our imperfections shape us, if our scars make us who we are.

"Hello?" Richard Fisher waves an impatient hand in my face. "Are you even listening to me?"

I blink. "Probation, I heard you. Can I go now?"

Richard Fisher gives me a look that's supposed to be stern, I think, but the worry lines around his eyes give him away. "You have two more weeks, Eli. One more mess up, and my hands are tied. You'll have to go home early."

The reality of what he's saying sinks in hard and all at once, like one of those cartoon anvils. If I flunk out of rehab, I'm screwed. At the very least, drug charges mean probation and community service. Forget lacrosse—they'd never let a convict attend LionsHeart. I'd probably never see Savannah again. I let out a heavy exhale like a deflating balloon and slump back onto the couch.

"This is serious stuff, Eli," Richard Fisher says. "Aside from your stay at LakeShore, I'm concerned about what I see happening here."

There's a worn spot on the couch cushion beside me, where the fabric's stretched so thin, I can make out the spongy material underneath. I fiddle with a loose thread at the frayed edge and peer up at Richard Fisher.

"C'mon, man," Richard Fisher leans back in his chair, stretches his arms out wide. "Your girlfriend broke up with you, what, a week ago? And you're already on to the next girl?"

My spine goes stiff. "It's not like that."

"Then tell me what it's like, Eli."

"I don't know. I just . . . when I'm with her, I don't feel so alone."

"Okay," Fish nods. "Tell me what it feels like to be alone."

I pluck at a patch of peeling, dry skin on my knuckle. Ever since Mom left, all I can think about is what she told me about my dad. Because it turns out I was wrong. Dad was an addict—he'd left us long before Mom kicked him out. And what does that say about me?

"Empty," I tell Fish. "Like there's this hole inside me, and all I want to do is fill it up."

"And being with Libby . . . that fills you up?"

I shrug. "Yeah, I guess."

"Can you think of any other time you've gone looking for something to fill yourself up?"

I roll my eyes. I'm not an idiot. I see the connection Fish is trying to make. "This is different," I say. "Libby's different. For as long as I can remember, I've been trying to live up to other people's expectations, you know? Mom and Steven's. Savannah's. It's fucking exhausting. But with Libby, I don't have to prove anything. I can just be myself."

"Ah," Richard Fisher scratches his goatee. "I get it, man, I do. But I want you to consider, even for a second, if it's possible that this is another avoidance behavior. I mean, you've barely said anything about your mom's visit the other day."

I'm shaking my head, but Richard Fisher keeps talking.

"You just found out that your dad was an addict, and that your mom's been lying to you your entire life. And instead of dealing with it, instead of facing it head on, you're hiding out with Libby. As far as I'm concerned, this is the exact same behavior that brought you here in the first place. Just a different drug."

My mouth tastes sour and hot; the hairs prickle on my arms. "You don't know what you're talking about."

"You get caught up with girls, you snort smack, you do it all so you don't have to deal with the one real thing going on. You don't have to deal with your pain."

I'm grinding my teeth so hard my jaw hurts. Who the fuck does this dude think he is? He doesn't know me. He doesn't know Libby. I listen to his bullshit because I have to, because no matter how I feel about Richard Fisher, I'm stuck here. Finishing my time at LakeShore is the only way back to my life.

"You've been given an incredible opportunity here, Eli, and you're wasting it. I mean, what's the plan? Pretend this thing with your mom never happened? That's grade-A thinking right there, man. That way you can skate through the next two weeks without ever learning anything about yourself . . ."

"Fuck you!" I explode, jumping up so fast that the coffee table shakes. "What do you know anyway? You're just some dried up old hack. I'm the one doing all the work here!" I jam my thumb into my sternum. "Me! I've done everything you told me to do—the writing, the fucking sharing! I even let you convince me to bring my mom in, and we both know what a shit show that turned out to be! I've done nothing but hurt since I got here. And now you're trying to tell me it's not good enough? Well, you know what I think? I think you spend all your time trying to fix everybody else so you don't have to think about how much you've fucked up your own life."

Richard Fisher taps his thick index finger on the desk one time, twice. A warning.

I hover over his desk, seething, hot spit collecting in the corners of my mouth. "You spend all your sad sap life muddling in other people's business, but what about yours, huh, Dick?" I snatch up the blue framed picture, the baby in the red bandana, and wave it in Richard Fisher's face like an angry talisman. "When was the last time you spoke to your wife?"

A tight ball forms at the base of Richard Fisher's jaw. He's breathing heavy, fogging up the glasses on the end of his nose. He's about to lose it, and I want him to. I want him to yell; I want him to hit me. Any excuse to let out this fury inside me that threatens to swallow me whole.

I want to peel my skin off. I want to turn myself inside out.

Fish takes off his glasses, wipes them on the hem of his faded green Life is Good t-shirt. "Are you done?" he asks.

Behind me, the dried-up water feature gurgles pathetically like a half-hearted mediator.

Someone else might back down, but not me, not now. I hold Richard Fisher's gaze, the picture of his son still clenched in my fist.

He props his weary elbows on his desk, his shoulders hunched toward his ear lobes. "You're right about one thing, Eli. I've been through hell and back on that side of the desk. But believe it or not, I've learned a few things along the way. The way I see it, you have two choices: You can talk about your dad and about your mom lying to you. We can start addressing some of these feelings you're having, and you can go home armed with strategies for staying clean. You can reclaim your life. Or option two," Richard Fisher holds up two fingers, "you can go home empty-handed, with nothing but a crush on some girl you're never going to see again."

Heat rushes up the back of my neck, flooding my cheeks. I toss the picture frame onto Richard Fisher's desk. The glass rattles in the frame. "Can I go now?"

Richard Fisher gives me a long stare. "Yeah, you can go." And then, to my back on the way out of his office: "But stay away from Libby."

A hard, fast run would wring out my anger like dirty water from a sponge. But I'm still restricted to walking only, and it takes me over an hour on the treadmill to calm down. After the gym, I swing by my room for a quick shower before dinner. Mo's got all his stuff out on his bed, his shirts folded, the surface of his dresser cleared. He's carefully stacking clothes in a half-packed suitcase where his pillows should be. He's giving his final testimony tonight, and even though I've been excited about the idea of having the room to myself, seeing his packed suitcase sucks the wind out of me.

I lean in the doorway, sweaty and out of breath. "You finally figured out I'm a terrible roommate, huh?"

Mo looks over his shoulder, shoots me a wicked grin. "Don't kid yourself, bro. I've known that since day one."

I pull off my soaked t-shirt and toss it into the growing pile of dirty laundry at the bottom of my closet. Mo shoots the pile a wary look. "My point exactly."

I pop my towel at his back playfully. "Hey, I've only missed laundry day once, okay?"

"Tell that to the smell in here."

I duck my head, take a huge whiff of my sweaty pits. "Get a whiff of that LakeShore breeze!"

Mo laughs, and I head into the bathroom. By the time I'm done showering, his suitcase is packed, and he's sitting on the edge of his bed with his eyes closed.

I tread softly across the floor, pull a clean pair of jeans and a t-shirt out of my dresser. I yank on my jeans, and when I turn back around, Mo's opening his eyes.

"Everything, okay?" I ask.

He gives me a shaky smile. "Just nervous, I guess."

"About giving your testimony?" I pull a clean red t-shirt over my head. Part of going home is sharing your testimony with everybody in the building. It's a really big deal, and even though I've only seen a couple of people do it so far, the thought of getting up in front of everybody makes me want to barf.

Mo shakes his head. "Nah, that's the easy part. It's what comes after that's hard."

I hang my towel on the back of my door. "Are you kidding, dude? I'd kill to be in your shoes. You get to go back to your family—you get to see your friends. You get your life back."

"Yep." Mo nods slightly. "And it scares the shit out of me."

I drop down on the end of my bed across from Mo, put my hand on his shoulder. "You can do this, bro. You know this shit inside and out. You're like a walking advertisement for AA."

Mo slips me a sideways grin. "AA doesn't advertise. It's the eleventh tradition."

"See?" I shove his shoulder. "I don't even know what the shit you're talking about." Mo laughs, a big belly laugh that cuts through his nervous tension. "I want to do it right this time, you know? My little sister, she got herself . . ." Mo draws an invisible line out from his own full belly with a caramel-colored hand that shakes a little. "She's gonna need me," he says. "And that *keiki*, I don't want her to come into the world without a man in her life, you know? I want to be there for them both."

I think about Dad, the peel of his tires out of the driveway, the missed birthdays, the baseball game. How he gave up on me. And Mo, who's tried sobriety and failed five times, but still refuses to give up. His niece will be lucky to have him.

"You're the strongest person here," I tell Mo. "If anybody can do this, it's you."

Mo reaches out his hand, his eyes wide and earnest. When I take it, he grasps tightly. "You can do this, too, you know? I believe in you. You just gotta get your head in the game."

I don't know where to look anymore because Mo made it awkward. I try to pull back my hand.

Mo squeezes tighter. "But if you hurt my Libby, I'm going to have to kick your ass."

I give a ha-ha-very-funny kind of laugh, but Mo's crunching my fingers in his palm. "Got it?"

"Geez, I've got it. Promise!"

Mo releases my hand. "Good."

The rec room is packed. I swear Mo's entire family came out to hear his final testimony—the whole two front rows of metal folding chairs are overflowing with highly emotional Hawaiians. His little sister, hoisting her belly in front of her, sits dead center, next to a graying woman who's probably Mo's mom. Mo keeps trying, and they keep coming, everybody hoping that this time will be the last. For Mo's sake, and for his sister's, I hope it will be, too.

I find a seat between Red and Will. Will's leg has been jiggling up and down for the past fifteen minutes, so hard it's creaking his chair and annoying the crap out of me. Red finally digs in his pocket and passes Will a grape Jolly Rancher. Will's leg only stops moving long enough for him to unwrap the candy and pop it in his mouth, and then it's creak-city all over again.

I spot Libby a few rows up from us. Her hair is pulled up, showing the smooth skin at the back of her neck, the baby hairs that hang over the collar of her shirt. I must be staring because Red punches me in the thigh, and I double over, sucking in air that whistles through my clenched teeth.

"Focus," Red hisses, his eyes twinkling.

Mo stands behind the podium, looking out at all the people gathered to hear his testimony. "I sure wasn't expecting this kind of turn out," he jokes. "Is there a party somewhere I should know about?"

Chuckles ripple through the audience.

"Don't worry," Mo says, grinning at Howard, who sits in the front row shaking his head. "I'm just messing around." Mo takes a sip of water from the clear plastic cup on the podium and wipes his mouth with the back of his hand. "In all seriousness, though, this isn't my first trip to the rodeo." He holds up his hand, waggling all five fingers and earning another laugh from the crowd. "You might be wondering what's going to make this time any different." Mo looks right at his sister, then his mom. "Sometimes I wonder that, too." Nobody's laughing anymore. Mo's mom dabs at her eyes with a crumpled Kleenex, lays her head on his sister's shoulder.

"I guess the honest answer is that I don't know," Mo says. "I wish I could see into the future just as much as anybody else, but the fact is, I can't. I have to live life on life's terms. And that means one day, one minute, one fraction of a second at a time. If I've learned anything here at LakeShore, it's that sobriety doesn't come in big sweeping gestures. It doesn't come with promises or negotiations. In fact, those usually come in the pockets of addicts."

He smiles at his own joke, drawing another laugh from the crowd. "What I know for sure is that I want to be there for my family." Mo glances at his sister, whose hands rest on her round belly. "I want to be the man they need me to be. I can't promise that I'll do it perfectly, but I promise that I'll try. Sobriety is a journey, a choice I will make every single day. Today, I'm 28 days sober. And I thank God for that. Thanks for letting me share."

The room fills with applause, and a couple of guys in the second row pump their fists in the air and bark ("Whoop! Whoop!") like Mo just scored a touchdown. Everyone claps as Howard walks across the stage and shakes Mo's hand, cheers when Mo pulls Howard into a bear hug. It's better than graduation, and in that moment of celebration and success, I'm filled with pride and belief. Maybe it doesn't have to be perfect. Maybe not giving up is enough. If that's true, then I know that Mo can do it. And that makes me wonder if I can do it, too.

Mo joins his family in the front row, tucks his heavy arm around his sister, a mother bird pulling her hatchlings close. Howard makes a few closing comments, then leads us all in the Serenity Prayer to close out the meeting. And then the rows of people start to shift, funneling into the center aisle that points toward the refreshment table at the back of the rec room.

Will makes a beeline for the donuts, and Red starts after him. "You want anything?" he calls back to me.

I wave away the offer, spotting Libby in the crowd. "Later."

Red follows Will to the swarming refreshment table. I steal a glance over my shoulder, keeping a sharp eye out for Richard Fisher. But he's in deep conversation with Mo's mom. I weave through the crowd deliberately, moving pieces like Candy Crush, until Libby and I happen to be standing side by side in the haphazard lines that stretch out from the refreshment table like twin rows of marching ants.

I lean in, close enough to whisper, "The wait's a nightmare in this joint. You want to find a better place to eat?"

Her profile stretches into a sly grin, but she doesn't turn around to face me. "I'm not supposed to talk to you."

I look straight ahead into the wavy brown hair of the girl in front of me and talk out of the side of my mouth. "You're not talking to me. You just happen to be standing next to me in line. You happen to be talking, and I happen to be listening."

Libby's fingers find mine. She gives them a quick squeeze, her eyes flitting over my face with a look that sends a rush of nerves through my body. Then she lets go, looks away. And all I am is need.

Libby casts a quick glance in Mo's direction. He's surrounded by hugging, weeping family members, not to mention residents and staff. Libby sniffs. "I hate goodbyes," she mutters, tears thick at the back of her throat.

I steal another furtive glance at Richard Fisher. He's one of many enthusiastic staff members who have gathered around Mo, waiting their turns to say goodbye. "So, let's skip it," I offer.

Libby peers up at me, her eyes questioning.

"Who needs all that mushy goodbye stuff anyway?"

Libby chews on her lower lip, considering. She looks at Mo again. He's hugging another resident, his cheeks streaked with tears. "Okay," she says. "Let's get out of here."

"Really?" I must look surprised because Libby laughs out loud.

"Yeah," she says. "And you better have something good planned, because so far this date's a dud."

A *date*. My brain's fuzzy all of a sudden, and I have to force myself to think straight. It's just like me to come up with some elaborate escape plan and then crash and burn on the execution. I wrack my brain for a place to take Libby. Not outside; the exterior doors get locked automatically after the evening meeting. Nothing like a facility-wide alarm to alert Richard Fisher. And not my room—I don't have to worry about a roommate anymore, but I'm not stupid. A co-ed sleepover would be a guaranteed ticket out of LakeShore. I glance at the refreshment table, still surrounded by residents.

I tip my head toward the kitchen door. "I know a great ice cream place."

"You treating?" Libby teases.

"As long as it's free." I take her hand. "This way."

Libby pulls back, tips her head toward Richard Fisher. "What if someone sees?"

She's right, and as much as I don't want to think about Richard right now, I definitely don't want him barging into the middle of my ice cream date either. Libby and I decide I'll go first, and she'll follow a few minutes later.

I weave through the crowd, keeping my eyes low. Finally, I make it to the door and turn to make sure Libby's following me. At the outer edge of the crowd, she pauses, scanning the room. When she spots Mo, she blows a kiss, quickly, but deliberately, like she's wishing on dandelion seeds. She watches that kiss travel over the expanse of people between her and Mo, and I almost change my mind. She should stay; she should give him a real goodbye.

And that's when I see Red. Head and shoulders above most of the people around him, Red's eyes settle easily on me. His brows raise in a question mark, and then he turns slightly, his searching eyes traveling the invisible thread that connects me to Libby. She turns away from Mo and begins to weave through the crowd, moving in my direction.

Understanding floods Red's face.

Please. I put my finger to my lips, silently begging him not to say anything to anyone.

Red points toward Mo. The look on his face says everything I already know. He's my roommate. He's the first of us leaving. I should stick around; I should tell him goodbye.

I shrug, *I can't help it*, because now Libby's speed-walking toward me, eyes bright with tears or mischief or both, and I don't care if I'm a selfish jerk as long as I'm with her.

Red shakes his head.

"This way." I take Libby's hand and pull her out of the room.

The freezer is full of ice cream, leftover from Sunday Sundaes, LakeShore's catchy weekend dessert. Half-empty cartons offering a variety of flavors line the upper shelf. "Let's see . . ." With my upper body tucked inside the industrial upright freezer, my voice bounces off the walls like I'm exploring a mine shaft or climbing through a heating duct. "We've got mint chocolate chip, cookie dough, peanut butter cup—"

"Any frozen yogurt left?" Libby asks.

"Gross." I rummage through the cardboard cartons until I find some (cherry) and then grab the good stuff (peanut butter cup and mint chocolate chip) for myself. I hip check the freezer door and unload my bounty on the stainless-steel cabinet. "Welcome to Sundae Monday."

Libby casts a nervous glance at the kitchen door.

"Are you going to find us some spoons," I ask, "or do I have to do *everything* myself?"

She flashes me a shaky smile and grabs a couple spoons out of the drying rack. "I have a bad feeling about this," she says, passing one to me. "What if somebody comes in here?"

"Relax." I pop the lid off the yogurt. "All the food's out there, remember? And everybody's going to be way too busy with Mo to come in here for at least another half hour."

She gives me a wary look, forehead puckered, conflicted. I wonder if she's wishing she'd stayed in the rec room. I wonder if she's thinking about Mo. I scoop up a heaping spoonful of cherry fro-yo and offer her the spoon. "Wanna bite of fake ice cream?"

Libby stares at me for a second. Then she hoists herself up onto the counter and takes the spoon, licks it cautiously, like a baby bird. I, on the other hand, spoon a huge chunk of peanut butter cup into my mouth and cringe from the instant brain freeze. Libby laughs.

"It's weird, isn't it," she says, between delicate nibbles from her spoon, "how normal this feels? You and me, I mean."

I nod. If I don't look around me at the industrial range top and doublewide fridge, if I pretend not to notice the Drug Free posters that plaster the white cement block walls, then I could almost imagine that Libby and I are at one of our houses—hanging out in the kitchen after school.

"Especially because you and I would never be friends if we'd met somewhere else."

Libby's words slash at my thoughts. "Of course we would," I say, but she cuts me off with a searing scowl.

"C'mon, Eli. Don't try to tell me that you would even give me the time of day if we went to the same school. I saw your girlfriend. I have guys like you at my school, too, you know." Her eyes flash something dark and painful. "I wouldn't matter to you at all."

I put down my spoon and edge around the counter to face her. I rest my arms on her legs, interlock my fingers behind her hips, and pull her to me until the knobby edges of her knees poke sharp into my chest. "Can I tell you something true?"

Libby nods, small and child-like.

"You are the most interesting person I have ever met," I say.

She blinks, wet lashes smudging black beneath her eyes. I lift a hand to smooth back her hair, softly touch her cheek.

"You scare the shit out of me," I tell her, and she gives a choking laugh.

"When I'm around you, I feel alive, like I'm all the way myself, and I didn't even know until now that I've only been part way myself. But you make me better. You matter to me. I would never let you go unnoticed."

Libby dips her head, wipes her nose on the back of her shirt sleeve. "That was five."

I raise my eyebrows.

"Five true things," she whispers.

"Yeah, well, here's another." I grab her empty spoon and dip it into the cherry fro-yo. I take a big bite and talk out of the side of my mouth. "You have terrible taste in ice cream."

And that's when Libby kisses me.

There's no buildup, no anticipation. No moment of quiet wondering. There is only her mouth on mine and cherry frozen yogurt and a single breathless moment that I never want to end.

And then it does. Libby pulls away, slides down off the counter so that her body presses full against mine, and I can't stand how close she is, I can't stand this wanting. I slip my hand behind her neck, lean down to kiss her again, but she ducks slightly, reaches into her back pocket and pulls out a folded-up piece of paper that she presses against my chest. "I meant to give you this earlier," she says, gently swiping frozen yogurt from the corner of my mouth with one soft finger.

I take the paper and start to unfold it, but she covers my hand with her own. "It's no big deal. Look at it later, okay?"

She watches me slip the folded square into my back pocket, and then she slides out from between me and the counter and heads for the door.

"See you later, Eli," she says.

As soon as the door closes behind her, I take the folded paper out of my pocket. It's a picture of me. Not a disfigured abstract sketch—it's a clear depiction of the day we fell asleep together on the lawn. I'm lying on my side in the grass, tall trees in the background. For a second, I wonder if Libby sketched me while I slept, except that my eyes are open. My hair is swept back enough to reveal my scar. But the eyes are the most prominent. Staring out at me from the page, they are a stranger's eyes, brimming over with feeling. They carry pain and sadness, sure, but it's something else that makes my breath catch and my chest tighten. Another feeling, deeper and powerful enough to penetrate the surface pain. The eyes in the picture are hopeful. They are courageous. They are all the things I want to be but can't.

I trail my finger over the drawing, down to Libby's scrawled message in the bottom corner. *I see you,* and under that a hasty heart above her signature.

I tuck the folded picture back into my pocket and look around the kitchen at the sad remnants of my "date" with Libby: melting ice cream, the lingering whisper of a cherry flavored kiss, and the nagging feeling that Libby just told me goodbye.

Day 17

"WELL, WELL, WELL," WILL SAYS, sliding his breakfast tray down next to mine and slipping into the seat beside me. "Fancy seeing you here."

I shovel another bite of soggy pancake in my mouth and shoot him a sideways look. "Where else would I be?"

Across the table, Red clears his throat and sends Will a warning glare that he promptly ignores. "I don't know," Will says. "Maybe holed up in your room somewhere, jerking off to 'Damaged Girlz R Us?'"

I cast Red a seething glance. "Thanks a lot, dude."

"I didn't tell him anything," Red says. "He saw you leave."

Will smirks. "I had fifteen bucks on you getting kicked out last night. You're lucky I like you. Otherwise you'd owe me big time."

"You have a serious problem, you know that?"

Will chortles into his coffee, and I laugh, too.

Red tosses down his fork. It bounces off his tray, splattering syrup in my direction.

"Dude!" I exclaim. "What's your problem?"

"You're my problem, Eli." Red's face is pink under his freckles, and his hands tremble. "You don't even get it, do you? Will's right! If Mr. Fisher or Howard or any one of the orderlies saw you last night, you'd be gone. And it's like you don't even give a shit."

I peer up at him, surprised at his outburst. "She's leaving soon."

"So what? You're just going to float until she does? Then what? I'm sure there's another crack whore on her way up from detox. Oh, that's right, you got a thing for cutters."

His words sting like tiny shards of glass. "Back off, Red," I say, my voice low, dangerous.

Red snatches up his tray. "You know, being here is a big fucking deal for me. I don't have some polo-playing prick with deep pockets to pay my way." He stares down his freckled nose at me, his pale lids grey and heavy, his voice thick with disappointment. "This place is probably my only chance." His stiff shoulders rise and fall, the helpless gesture of somebody who doesn't know what else to do. "It might be yours, too."

Will and I sit silently for a minute, both of us watching Red lope across the dining hall, dump his tray, and head out through the double doors. Will breaks the silence first. "Damn," he wheezes.

"Yeah." I stare at my tray, my appetite swallowed up by guilt and embarrassment. I stab a piece of pancake and swirl it in aimless circles.

"Well, the good news is, this isn't a long-term problem," Will says.

I peer at him sideways.

"That chick goes home today. She gives her final testimony tonight."

And then I can't breathe. I scan the room for Libby, like it's already too late, like I won't even get to say goodbye. I spot her on the far side of the room, dumping the rest of her breakfast in a trashcan. I pick up my tray and head after her, leaving Will sitting alone.

I catch up with Libby in the hallway outside the dining hall. She's talking to someone, a girl I don't know, with hipster glasses and dreads. I stride right up to them, take Libby's arm rough in mine, and spin her around.

"Hey!" she exclaims.

"Why didn't you tell me?"

The hipster girl gives me a look like she's wondering if she needs to call for help or something, and I realize that I must look deranged, because that's how I feel. Like I'm going out of my mind.

Libby's eyes search my face, and I don't know what she sees there, but her arm relaxes in my grasp. She turns to look at the girl beside her. "It's okay, Celeste. I'll meet up with you in group, okay?"

The girl nods, casts me one more furtive glance before scurrying off down the hall. I drop Libby's arm. I am a madman. I am out of control.

"What the hell, Eli?" Libby demands.

"You're the one that owes the explanation. Why didn't you tell me you were leaving?"

For a second, Libby looks genuinely confused. "You knew I was leaving."

"Not today!" The words explode out of me, and even though I know how ridiculous they sound, there is a tidal pool of emotion rising inside me, and I'm powerless against it.

A small group of kids pass us on their way out of the dining hall. They send suspicious looks our way, and Libby grabs my arm, dragging me farther down the hall, away from the dining hall exit. "Keep your voice down," she hisses.

"I just . . ." I take in her fierce stare, the rigid posture of her back, and all the anger drains out of me. My arms are suddenly dead weights hanging limp from my sides. "I thought we had more time."

Libby laughs. The sound is vicious, and it cuts deep. "More time for what, Eli? More clandestine kitchen visits? More walks in the woods? Or was it more kisses you were after?" Libby's upper lip curls, and her eyes flash dangerously. "Grow up, Eli. This is real life, not summer camp. It's hard and it hurts. I've got enough things on my mind without some rich junkie with a serious case of denial tagging around all the time."

Libby's anger is toxic and sudden, like a plug pulled from a smoke bomb. It seeps out of her pores and annihilates anyone in its path. I thought we were past this, this maniacal need to flatten anyone who gets too close. But maybe I was wrong. Maybe this is who Libby really is.

"Who did this to you?" I whisper, peering down into her face. "Who made you this way?"

Libby winces, and for a second, I can see her, the real her, free of angry, screaming scars. For a second I can see through her pain. Then her expression freezes over, and the look she gives me is one of disgusted pity. "I was always going to leave, Eli. This was always going to end."

She turns and storms up the hallway. I want to swear at her, throw something. I want to beg her to come back. I scream after her, not caring who hears me. "You're crazy, you know that? You're fucked in the head!"

At the end of the hall, Libby shoots me the bird over her shoulder. And something snaps inside me. I aim my words at her heart. "You think I don't see your game? All you want to do is hurt people! But nobody is as damaged as you. You're the one that can't be fixed!"

Libby disappears through the double doors at the end of the hallway without so much as a backward glance. I sag back against the wall, suck in deep, ragged breaths.

"Dude," Will says.

I look up to see him standing in the dining hall door, a steaming cup of coffee in each hand.

"You okay?"

I shake my head.

I'll never be okay again.

At group, I slouch in a chair next to Will, hood up so Howard won't call on me, pass when he does anyway. I skip my session with Richard Fisher and head to the nurse's office where I claim a migraine that earns me a couple ibuprofen and a few precious hours of avoiding Libby.

At lunch, I have to walk right past her, tray in hand. She's sitting with a couple of girls I recognize—the hipster glasses and dreads and a pint-sized goth chick with ear spacers and neon green braces. Libby's hands flutter wildly while she talks, and laughter rises from their table like birdsong.

She's leaving, and I have nobody left.

It's goddamn fucking hilarious.

She glances up at me, her eyes barely registering my presence before she turns back to her friends. My appetite fades like a chalk drawing in the rain. I storm across the dining hall and dump my food, tray and all, into the industrial-sized trashcan.

The rest of the day passes like sludge moving down river. At the gym, I walk on the treadmill at about a 2.0 mph pace while Will and Red sweat it out with Prison Tat. I doze through afternoon group and spend my self-reflection time on the visitors' stoop, surrounded by other people's used up cigarette butts. I skip out on dinner, determined to avoid running into Libby again, and spend the next few hours on my bed, slipping in and out of a restless sleep where my dad rides his motorcycle through dreams painted red, black, and yellow, and Libby's words play on repeat like some kind of fucked-up mantra: *This was always going to end.*

It's dark outside when I wake up; my stomach's complaints are too loud to ignore. Maybe there's still food in the dining hall. At least a bagel or fruit, something to tide me over. I'm lacing up my shoes when there's a quick knock on the door, and Red sticks his freckled face through the narrow opening.

"Hey," he says.

I push up off the bed and head for my closet. "What do you want?"

"Libby's about to give her testimony," he says, stepping fully into the room. "I thought you might want to hear it."

"Pass." I grab my hoodie, stuff my arms into the fleecy sleeves. "I'm going to get some food."

"There are donuts in the rec room."

I stare at Red accusingly. "I'm surprised you give a shit."

"Look, I didn't come here to fight." Red runs his hand through his hair, rippling the orange spikes. "I thought . . ." He stares down at his hands. "Everybody deserves the chance to say goodbye."

I think of Lisa, Red's ex, the goodbye lost to smashed metal and shattered glass. "Thanks," I say weakly.

Red nods. "So I'll see you down there?"

"I don't know," I tell him. "I don't think Libby wants me there."

"She does," Red says. "Even if she doesn't know it."

After Red leaves, I stare at the door for a minute, considering. Libby's picture crinkles in the pocket of my day-old jeans. I pull it out, her words in the hallway seeping from the wrinkled paper like toxic dust.

I crush the picture in my fist and paper ball it to the trashcan. Red doesn't know what he's talking about.

I zip up my hoodie, tug it up high around my ears, and head down the hall. I'm not going for Libby. I'm just going to grab a doughnut, and then I'm out.

Richard Fisher's at the podium when I enter the rec room. He's opening the meeting with a reading from some recovery book, and I pretend to listen as I trail past the refreshment table at the back of the room. I grab a couple of doughnuts and drop into an empty chair in the back row. It creaks loudly, disturbing the kid in front of me. "You know, refreshments are for *after* the ceremony," he whispers.

I lean forward, motioning with the fat jelly doughnut in my fist. "Wanna share?"

His eyes widen as I take a huge bite, squirting red jelly down my chin. Blinking rapidly, he swivels back around. I lean back in my chair, my mouth chalky with powdered sugar. "That's what I thought," I mutter, swiping my knuckle across my sticky chin.

Red and Will are on the opposite side of the room. Even from here, I can see Will's jaws working around a piece of hard candy that's currently saving his life. Red nurses a steaming cup of coffee. I crane my neck for a glimpse of the front row. I spot Libby's rigid shoulders, the shocking contrast of her hair. She's sitting next to a woman who could be her sister, her shoulders slight, her ink black hair bleeding purple at the ends.

After a few minutes, Richard Fisher turns the podium over to Libby. I watch her walk to the makeshift stage. She's wearing grey dress pants, like the kind my mom wears to work, and they look about two sizes too big. Her pale blue shirt is buttoned at the cuffs, and her hair hangs loose around her shoulders. The dark eyeliner's gone, and her pale cheeks are painted with matching pink circles. She's Elizabeth, not Libby. I wonder if that's part of her exit strategy.

She clears her throat, and her shining apple cheeks flush darker. "Twenty-eight days ago, I came here with a list of problems as long as my arm," she begins.

I duck my head to stifle the bitter laugh that rises in my throat, not sure that list has actually gotten any shorter.

"I used to think that having all those problems meant something was wrong with me," Libby continues. "I'd look at the other kids at school, the cheerleaders, the honor roll kids, and I'd think, they have it all figured out. If I could only be like them, everything would be okay. But no matter how hard I tried, I couldn't get it right. I was still me, a tattooed freak with a C average. My problems weren't going anywhere."

I picture Libby walking down the halls of her high school, her hair dyed blonde, her arms hidden behind fat squiggles of permanent marker, black ink smudged on her cheek, and my chest hurts a little.

"When I found Xanax, I found armor. I didn't have to care anymore about what other people thought of me, and I didn't have to think about my problems. I could pretend they didn't exist. It was like a shield I could disappear behind—a cloak of invisibility."

Libby twists her hair up off her neck and holds it there, casting a wry smile around the room. "Being invisible sucks."

Her hair falls soft around her shoulders. She takes a sip of water, swipes the moisture from her upper lip. "I think that's why I started cutting. Because if I could still feel pain, that meant I was still alive. I hadn't all the way disappeared."

An image flashes through my brain, dark and unsettling—Libby drawing a razor across her wrist, blood seeping to the surface like water through sand. Is that what I was to her? A razor blade against her skin? A bleeding reminder that she's still capable of feeling something? Is that what she was to me?

"In recovery, I've learned that problems are a part of life," Libby continues. "In fact, I think the only guaranteed experience in life might be pain. But it's how you handle that pain that matters. You can let it consume you, or you can embrace it and move on.

"For a lot of people here, dealing with their problems means turning them over to a higher power. But I don't buy it."

A few people shift uncomfortably in their seats. Leave it to Libby to give a final testimony that smacks every other testimony full in the face. Maybe I'm imagining it, but I swear her gaze lands on me.

"I don't believe in unconditional love," she says. "I don't believe that it's possible for someone to love you that much, love you in spite of your problems, love you in spite of your pain."

In the front row, the purple-haired woman yawns, makes an obvious show of checking her watch, twisting it on her tan wrist so that it catches the light and sparkles.

Libby's eyes shift away from my face. "I don't know, maybe I'm a pessimist, but in my experience, that kind of love doesn't exist."

Yeah, or maybe that's because you chase it away with a sledgehammer. Right then, I know that I'm not sticking around to tell her goodbye. Will was right. Libby is a praying mantis. She chewed me up and spit me out. But even in my pulverized state, I have too much pride to let her revel in the damage.

I start to stand up, but my chair creaks again, and the guy in front of me gives his neighbor a wide-eyed *Can you believe this guy?* look. I sink back down. I'll sneak out afterwards, when everybody else swarms to congratulate Libby.

"One of the best things that Fish . . ." Libby catches herself, shoots an affectionate glance at Richard Fisher who nods in response. ". . . Mr. Fisher helped me to understand that the second step doesn't have to be about any one kind of God. It's about any source, bigger than myself, that's strong enough to hold the weight of my feelings. For me, that's art."

My mind travels back over the paintings I've seen Libby do in art class—the broken and disfigured self-portrait that first met me in the art room.

"Through art, I can explore any feeling that I have. I can put it all out there—no matter how dark, no matter how disturbing, no matter how painful. My art is big enough to handle it all."

I know I'm not imagining it this time. Libby's gaze settles right on my face, her eyes electric paddles on my heart. And then she looks away, and I can't take this anymore. I stand up, not giving a shit about my squeaky chair, and walk out of the room.

Day 18

THERE'S A NEW PERSON IN Libby's spot in the art room. Instead of Libby's disfigured self-portrait, I'm met with sunshine and flowers.

I stare at the painting, disgust burning at the back of my throat. A girl approaches, a couple of brushes in one hand, a loaded palette in the other. Her thick brown hair, all one perfect color, is tied up with pink ribbon in a cheerleader's ponytail that bobs up and down as she arranges her supplies. "I call it Love," she gushes, even though I didn't ask. "It's my higher power painting. Do you like it?"

"No," I say flatly, then push past her to my own easel where my new canvas has stayed blank for days.

The art teacher greets me with a warm smile. "We missed you yesterday. Are you feeling better?"

"A little."

"I brought something for you." She hands me a thick stack of well-read magazines, several of them with missing covers and most with bent edges.

I rustle through the magazines on the top of the pile. Everything from *Real Simple* to *National Geographic*. "What am I supposed to do with these?"

"I thought you could use them for inspiration." The art teacher casts a meaningful glance toward my blank canvas. "Sometimes it helps to tear out pictures that represent something to you, even if you don't know what that something is. Anything that moves you, that stirs your emotions, tear it out and tape it to your canvas, okay?"

I was kind of planning on spending class staring out the window and feeling sorry for myself. But it's nice she went out of her way to help me, especially since I've pretty much half-assed this class since day one. "If you say so."

She drops a pair of scissors and a roll of tape on the pile in my arms. "It's good to have you back, Eli." She rests a patchouli-scented hand on my shoulder. "Really."

A hard lump rises in my throat. "Thanks," I manage.

I drop the pile of magazines on the floor in front of my easel and settle down cross-legged beside it. Cheerleader Chick shoots me a dirty look from the front of the room, and I'd bet anything that her beaming sunshine has dark, angry edges now, her perfect fucking flowers are wilting, and she's jonesing for her crack pipe or vodka tonic or whatever. What was it Libby said? *This is rehab, not summer camp. Life's hard and it hurts.* Cheerleader Chick might as well get used to it.

I flip lazily through the magazines, wondering what kind of pictures my art teacher expects me to find here. The perfume-scented pages are filled with quick-fixes to life's biggest problems: *Ten secrets to true happiness! Just one pill will make all your pain go away!* There are no pictures of fathers shooting up, no articles about girls slitting their wrists so they can feel the pain.

By the time I get to the last magazine, there's only a few minutes left in art class. It's an issue of *National Geographic*. I thumb hastily through the pages, but one image makes me pause. It's a scenic shot, a breathtaking mountain range that reaches into a watery blue sky. A serene lake stretches out from the closest mountain, its clear depths reflecting the impossible snow-capped heights.

A kayaker, his paddle resting on his lap, floats in front of the mountain. He's tiny in comparison, completely insignificant. His back is to the photographer, but I can imagine the wonder on his face as he peers up at that insurmountable wall of sheer rock.

The art teacher gently taps her delicate gong, marking the end of class. "Time to pack up your materials for the day," she sing-songs.

I start to toss the magazine back into the pile with the others, but something stops me. I tear out that picture of the mountain, the lake and the kayaker, and tape it smack in the middle of my canvas.

At dinner, I push baked ziti around on my plate and pretend like I'm listening to whatever Red and Will are talking about. At one point, I swear I hear her—a raspy laugh lilts across the room, and I whip around, searching for a glimpse of her hair, her face.

Will's voice tugs me back to the table. "I'm sorry, bro—are we boring you?"

I look wide-eyed at Will and Red, like I'm seeing them for the first time. "What?"

"Did you even hear what I said?" Red asks. "I've been talking to you for like five minutes."

I blink. "What? Yeah, sure, I'm listening. I just zoned out for a minute. What were we talking about again?"

Will snorts. "Seriously, dude? Don't rifle through your spank-bank while people are eating. Save it for the shower."

I toss my dinner roll at him. "Shut up."

"I *was* asking if you want to play Ping-Pong after dinner." Irritation saws at the edges of Red's voice. "But you're probably too busy grieving the loss of your two-day relationship, right?"

I stab a forkful of ziti that I have no intention of eating.

"I mean, c'mon, dude! Savannah dumps you, you're wrecked for a couple of days. Until you find Libby. Then it's all sunshine and butterflies until she leaves. And suddenly you're ruined again. How long's it going to last this time? Who's the next chick in line?"

He jerks his head to the table next to us, where Cheerleader Chick nibbles at a plate of plain lettuce, her ponytail bobbing as she chews, an anorexic rabbit on speed. "How 'bout her? Fresh out of detox, ripe for the picking. Just your type."

"I'd hit that," Will says.

My teeth press together, and my fist clenches hard around my fork. "You know, Red, one of these days you're going to have to pick. Friend or shrink? Which one is it? Because I've got enough shrinks in my life right now. And you're starting to sound a hell of a lot like Fish."

Red blinks. I know he's trying to decide whether to let this go, whether he can be my friend when I'm like this, when I'm hurting this way. "Friend," he says softly.

"Good. Because I can take care of myself. And I can definitely kick your ass in Ping-Pong."

Red smirks. "Game on."

The crowded rec room is a new opportunity for distraction, and even as Red and I nudge the Ping-Pong ball back and forth, I scan faces for a glimpse of Libby. I don't know why I'm looking. I know that she's gone. But I'm empty. And I need something, anything, to fill me up again.

Red scores on me for probably the fourth time in a row (I haven't been keeping track). "Dude," he says. "You're not even trying."

"Are we playing or not?" I position my paddle, ready to spike Red's serve.

He lobs it over the net. "You can't do this, you know?"

"What?" I return the ball easily.

"You can't make this about her."

"I thought you were done trying to shrink me."

"I'm not shrinking you. I'm telling you this as your friend."

Back and forth we toss our words; they land lightly at first, and then harder until we're slamming the ball across the net, and I'm not sure if I'm aiming for the point or Red's chest.

"As my friend, I'd wish you'd play the fucking game."

"As your friend, I'm trying to tell you that I've watched you do this since you got here. You made it about Savannah. Now it's about Libby. When's it going to be about you? You leave in what, a little over a week?"

"As my friend, I'd like you to get the fuck out of my business."

"And as your friend, I'd tell you that that's not what friends do."

I spike the ball; it hits the corner of Red's side and spirals up into the air, ricochets off the concrete block wall beside us, and rolls right into a group of kids. One of them is the cheer-leader from art. She picks the ball up, shoots me a withering glare.

I toss down my paddle; it slides across the table, skittering under the net. "I'm not like you, okay? I don't need your help. I'm not some homeless dropout junkie. I have a life."

Red lowers his paddle, stunned. The hurt on his face makes my eyes burn, but my words sense his weakness, move in for the kill.

"I don't need this place, Red. And I sure as hell don't need you." I storm out of the rec room, leaving Red at the table alone.

The darkened lobby is empty, the Front Desk Fascist gone for the day. I take a quick peek down the hall, on the lookout for orderlies. Seeing no one, I lean over the desk, inch the phone closer and pick up the receiver.

When Chase finally answers, I can barely hear his voice, low and sleepy sounding, over the noise in the background: laughter, rumbling voices, and the metallic thunder of animated gunfire.

"Hello?"

"Chase! Dude, I need a favor."

The background noise quiets; I picture Chase pausing the video game, hear him shushing the other people in the room. "Who is this?"

"It's me, Eli!"

"Eli!" Chase laughs, thick and wet, his words slurring. "Where the hell are you?"

I tell him I'm in LakeShore, the rural mountaintop town two hours away from Grandhaven. I tell him I need him to come get me.

Chase is quiet for a second. "Shit, I don't know, bro. Wouldn't that be, like, aiding and abetting a fugitive or something?"

"I'm not in prison!" I hiss, instinctively checking over my shoulder again. Then, lowering my voice, "I can leave whenever I want."

"Yeah, except, that's like a pretty decent drive, and I'm kinda tight on funds right now . . ."

"I'll give you money for gas," I promise hurriedly, my hot breath collecting steam on the receiver. "Whatever you want, just get me out of here."

I tell him to come on Sunday and make a mental note to add him to my list of approved visitors. With the constant coming and going of Visitation Day, no one would even notice I was missing.

There's muffled laughter in the background; I think I hear Alex's voice. I grit my teeth, my fingers tightening around the receiver. Someone un-pauses the game, and Chase breathes heavy into the phone.

"Chase? You still there?"

"Yeah, look, Eli, I'm kinda in the middle of something." His voice is muffled, the phone probably hooked between his cheek and shoulder as his fingers nimbly maneuver the controller. "I'll see what I can do, okay?"

"Sunday," I tell him. "Anytime after ten, but Visitation ends at five. Chase?"

The phone's silent on the other end. Chase has already hung up.

Day 19

WHEN MY ALARM WAKES ME up, I yank the plug out of the wall and toss the clock across the room. I can't go to group. I can't face Richard Fisher. I don't want to talk about how I'm feeling. I don't want to think about it. Right now, I don't even want to exist.

I bury my head under my pillow and beg my brain to shut up. Two hours later, an orderly shakes me awake.

"Get up," he commands.

I crack open one eye and peer up at him. "Dick sent you, didn't he?"

The orderly's mouth twitches. "You're twenty minutes late for your session. Mr. Fisher asked that I come check on you."

"I'm taking a sick day." I cover my head with my pillow, but the orderly picks it up, leaving my whole head exposed.

"This is rehab, not kindergarten, kid," he says. "There's no such thing. Get your ass up."

I don't bother getting dressed. I add a t-shirt and hoodie to the sweats I slept in and follow the thick-necked orderly (who apparently doesn't trust me to get there on my own) to Richard Fisher's office.

Richard Fisher glances up at me over a steaming cup of fresh coffee.

"Morning, sunshine," I mutter, releasing a cloud of stale morning breath.

"Thanks, Nathan," Richard Fisher says to the orderly, who nods and shuts the door behind him.

He picks up his coffee and takes a big swig. The steam fogs his glasses. "Okay, Eli. What's up?"

I sink into my favorite spot on Fisher's crummy old couch. "I want to go home."

Richard Fisher puts down his coffee. "I see."

"I know what you're thinking," I tell him. "I've said this before. And then it was only because I didn't want to share at group or whatever. And you told me that if I left, I'd have to face the judge. So I decided to stay."

Richard Fisher nods, one hand resting on the side of his mug.

"Only this time, I already know all that. And I don't care. I want to go home anyway."

Richard leans back in his chair, propping the mug on his belly. "You've really thought this through." It's a question, disguised as an approving statement, strategically designed to make me ask myself, *wait, have I really thought this through*?

"You're damn right I've thought it through," I tell him. "There's nothing for me here."

"Libby left." Richard Fisher drops those two words in front of me like bait.

I flop backward on the couch and fold my arms across my chest. "So?"

"I know you two were . . . close. You're probably having some challenging emotions about her leaving."

I bark out a bitter laugh. Challenging emotions? All I've felt since the day I got here was confusion and hurt and pain. Libby leaving was the cherry on the crap sundae I've been nursing for the last 18 days. "It's not only that."

"What then?"

"It's not working." The words catch at the back of my throat, and my eyes burn. "I'm not 'better.' Talking about everything makes it all worse."

Richard Fisher gives me a sad smile. "Healing can be a painful process, Eli. Some of us have deeper wounds than others, and it takes a long time for them to heal. I imagine Libby leaving was like a fresh scab getting ripped off. Now you're hurting all over again."

"Everybody leaves," I tell him. "I should be used to it by now."

"You're talking about your father."

"No," I snap, and it comes out louder than I mean for it to. "I mean Savannah and Libby and . . ." I press my knuckles into my eye sockets. "Yeah, I guess I mean him, too."

"Why do they leave, Eli?"

My knuckles are wet, and I hate that I came here, hate that I'm having this conversation. But it's like something's cracked open inside me, and my insides are spilling out, and the only way to stop the flow is to wait until I'm empty again. I pull my hood up and sink inside the fleece cocoon. "Because of me," I whisper.

"Come again?" Richard Fisher presses.

"Because of me!" The words explode with involuntary force, propelling me to my feet. I pace the floor in front of Richard Fisher's desk. "They leave because of me, okay?"

Because I can't make them stay.

Because I'm not good enough for them to stay.

Richard Fisher leans forward on his desk, his elbows pressing into the wood. "Eli, your father leaving didn't have anything to do with you. He loved you, just like I loved my wife. But love doesn't matter to addiction."

"But that's the thing." I spin around to face Richard Fisher. The question inside me claws to the surface, desperate for answers. "If you love someone, really love them, how can you do that? How can you choose drugs over them?"

Richard Fisher peers up into my searching eyes. "Who are we talking about here, Eli? Your father? Or you?"

His question is a fluorescent light bulb in a pitch-black room. I blink, stunned. "I would never do that," I tell him. "I would never pick drugs over my own kid."

"But you chose drugs over lacrosse. Over your family. Over Savannah."

"That's different . . ." I stutter.

"Is it?" Richard Fisher asks. When I don't answer, he continues. "When we let our addiction run the show, who or what we love doesn't matter. Our disease makes our choices for us, choices we can't undo. Some people we don't get back."

I think of Richard Fisher's wife, of the baby in the red bandana. I think of the park, the tang of cherry water ice on my tongue. Starched hospital sheets and Mom's soft fingers on my scar. And Benny, asleep in the car with his head on his chest, his favorite blue crayon still clutched in his hand.

I shake my head furiously, refusing to accept the connection Richard is trying to make. "No. This is different.

219

We're talking about a father here. About a little boy. If he loved me, *really* loved me . . ." I sink back down onto the beat-up couch. Its edges reach up in a broken embrace. "How could he leave me? How could he leave his own son?"

Richard Fisher sighs. He rises from his chair and steps out from behind his desk. The brown clunker groans with his weight as he drops down beside me. For a second I think he's going to hug me. My spine goes rigid, and I pull the drawstrings on my hood even tighter.

"Look at me, Eli."

I shake my head. I can't. Not with my insides on display all over the floor. I don't want to be seen.

Richard Fisher's crotchety voice is a firm hand on my chin, turning me toward him. "Eli. Look at me."

I peer out at him from the circle of protective fleece. My face is wet, and I feel completely ridiculous. But the moment holds me tightly, and I search Richard Fisher's weathered face.

"You are good enough," he says, and the words are like stepping into a hot shower after playing in the snow. They burn at first, and I recoil from the pain.

"You are worthy of love. You are worth sticking around for. The only one who doesn't believe that is you." Richard Fisher places his hand on my shoulder, and the weight of it roots me to the couch, the floor, the moment. It's like I've been hollowed out inside, and I feel everything all at once—the aching grief and fear, the anger, the pain.

"But . . . how?" I ask.

Richard Fisher smiles at me. "One day at a time, Eli. It might sound a little cheesy, but this community, your group, we can be your believing eyes. We can love you until you can love yourself."

I swipe my arm across my face, drying my cheeks with my hoodie sleeve, and give Richard Fisher a sideways glance. "So what now?"

He squeezes my shoulder, then stands up and walks back to his desk. "If it were up to me, I'd tell you to keep doing the hard work you've started. Keep showing up and sharing at group. Keep writing in your journal. I'd tell you that I'd like to get your mom and stepdad in here for another family session and to set up an after-care plan. But it's not up to me. When you came in this morning, you told me you were ready to leave. So you tell me, Eli. What happens next?"

I pull my hands inside the arms of my hoodie and finger the frayed fleece at the cuffs. If I'm ever going to go back home, I'll have to talk to Mom, and it'll be a hell of a lot easier with Richard Fisher in my corner. "I guess . . . I mean, there's only a week left. I might as well stay, right?"

"Might as well."

I plunk my lunch tray beside Red's and sit down next to him. He raises his brow over a mouthful of egg salad sandwich.

I wince at the memory of the scene I made last night, the hurtful things I said. "Look, about last night . . . I was a total asshole."

Will opens his mouth to say something, but Red gives him a swift kick under the table. "Dude!" Will exclaims, dropping his sandwich.

Red flashes a crooked grin over the rim of his glass. "Water under the bridge, bro," he says. "We're just glad to have you back."

"That's all I was going to say," Will complains.

Red tosses his napkin at Will. It bounces off his half-eaten sandwich. "It was!" Will protests, and I crack up.

It's an unfamiliar feeling, showing up like this, with all my cracks and scars exposed. It's uncomfortable, like a new pair of jeans that needs to be worn a few times until they soften, until they sag like second skin. *Thanks*, I want to say, except it'd be awkward. Will's chewing with his mouth open, and Red's talking about something that happened in the morning meeting. And I realize that I don't have to explain anything. Because maybe that's what this whole recovery thing is: breaking down, picking yourself back up. Showing up anyway.

Red takes another bite of his sandwich and talks out of the side of his mouth. "Howard's taking the van to an NA meeting tonight. You in?"

I think about the last NA meeting I went to with Libby. Red didn't go to that one. He said he wasn't ready. Things have changed over the last few weeks, I realize. In big ways and some that seem invisible, everything has changed. Red has changed. I've changed, too.

"Sure," I tell him.

The speaker tonight is a hunkered man who leans heavily on a wooden cane as he walks to his chair at the front of the room. He's been clean for 45 years. As he speaks, shoulders soften; people sit lighter on their chairs. Everybody hears something in his story, some part of their own experience. It's not the specifics of his drug use; it's the common thread of deep suffering that weaves the group together. I wonder if this is what Mo meant when he talked about "turning it over." I wonder if saying it out loud is enough.

The speaker finishes, and the meeting facilitator (a tightly pinched woman with black corkscrew curls) opens the floor for shares. My arm shoots up without asking my brain's permission. Before I can snatch it out of the air, the facilitator's beady eyes land on me. She nods, and suddenly the whole room's looking at me. I open my mouth, hoping that whatever invisible force lifted my arm in the first place can string together a few words for the crowd.

"I, uh, I'm Eli."

"Hi, Eli," the group resonates.

I scan the expectant faces around me. Howard sits a few seats ahead of me. He's twisted around in his chair, and he nods encouragingly. I take a deep breath.

"I, uh, I guess you could say I've been using since I was about fourteen. For fun, at first, and then because I needed it. Because I didn't feel like myself without it. Because I didn't want to *feel* anything at all."

My voice gets stronger as my confidence grows. "Anyway, I overdosed about three weeks ago." The word catches in my throat—it's the first time I've said it out loud. *Overdosed.* I suck in air so hard it hurts and stare out at the sea of faces around me. "I guess I'm pretty lucky to be alive."

I blink back tears that burn behind my eyes and tug at the arms of my sweatshirt, hiding my balled fists inside them. "I lost my girlfriend. And all my friends. And when I go home next week, I don't know what's going to happen. I recently found out that my dad was an addict, too. He died of an overdose. And I guess the only thing I know for sure, is that I don't want to end up like him."

I glance around the room. "Anyway, thanks, or whatever."

"Thanks for sharing," the group answers. It's so weird, the way the group talks as one, and I don't know if I'll ever get used

223

to it. But I feel lighter somehow, like the load I've been carrying around isn't quite as heavy. Like for the space of the next few minutes, this group is helping me carry it.

Somebody else raises a hand, and the group's attention shifts away from me. Beside me, Red quietly offers his fist. I bump it with my own, not bothering to hide the smile that springs to my face.

Afterwards, as NA regulars fold up and put away the chairs, the LakeShore kids head out into the parking lot. There are five of us, not counting Will, who offered to help stack chairs: Me, Red, Cheerleader, and two kids I haven't met—a reed thin chick with charcoal eyeliner and hoop earrings, and a prep-school flunk-out who looks a couple years younger than me. The street lamps illuminate the lot with circles of soft white light that fade into shadow at the edges. We huddle together in the dusky light beside the locked van, waiting for Howard, who stayed behind to chat with a newcomer.

Leave it to Howard to track down the one dude that probably doesn't want anybody to talk to him. His face nearly hidden under a cap and hood, the kid didn't say a word in the meeting, other than raise his hand when the facilitator asked if anybody was new. He was probably hoping to get back to his car without having to say a word to anybody. Not if Howard has anything to do with it. That kid's not going anywhere without an armload of pamphlets.

"What's taking so long?" Cheerleader grumbles. She's got her arms wrapped up inside her sweater like we've been abandoned in the Arctic. It's not even that cold. The chill of early April has nearly passed, and the air carries the warm, wet feel of spring. With a start, I realize that Sunday's Easter. For the first time ever, I won't be spending the holiday with my mom. I haven't even spoken to her since I told her not to come for Visitation. It strikes me that by the time I get home, a whole season will have passed, and I wonder what else will have changed.

"You know Howard." Red's voice interrupts my thoughts. "We're probably taking that poor kid back to LakeShore with us."

I snort. NA regulars are heading out of the meeting in groups of two and three. The parking lot is a chorus of cars unlocking, crisscrossed by blinking headlights. I recognize the new kid as he steps out into the parking lot. But it's not Howard he's talking to. It's Will.

"Over here, dude," I holler, but Will doesn't seem to hear me. He follows the new kid to a jalopy on the shadowed side of the lot. The inside light flickers as the kid unlocks and opens the door.

"What the . . ." Red mutters under his breath. We exchange worried glances.

"Maybe they're just talking," I offer. "Or maybe he's bumming a smoke."

"Yeah," Red licks his dry lips. "Maybe."

Howard's voice carries across the lot. He's heading out of the meeting, deep in conversation with the man who shared his testimony. My stomach clenches. Whatever Will's doing, he'd better hurry up.

"Will," Red whispers in this pathetic hiss that Will can't possibly hear. "Will!" It's louder this time, urgent.

"Shhh!" I elbow him. Howard's midway between the church and the van, helping the old man into a 400-year-old Chrysler.

Like a scene in a movie that you keep rewinding because you're pretty sure you missed something, what happens next is all at once. The Chrysler cranks to life in a cloud of exhaust and flickering headlights. Howard steps away from the car and scans the parking lot. In the dull light cast from the new kid's car, we all see it: the subtle exchange of hands, swift, like a magician's, and Will slips something into his pocket.

Red exhales, and the sound is an audible word: "Fuuuuuuuuuuuuuuuck."

A shadow crosses Howard's face. He flicks up the collar of his jacket, shoves his hands into his pockets, and heads toward the van. "If you're going to LakeShore," he announces, loud enough for everyone in the parking lot to hear, "your ride leaves in thirty seconds." He shoves through our huddled group, unlocks the van, and clambers up into the driver's seat. For a second, his eyes meet mine, and I know he sees the question there. "Get in," he says gruffly.

Cheerleader pushes her way into the van first, followed by the two other kids. Red casts a worried look in Will's direction before climbing into the van. I'm the last one in. Howard cranks the engine, and cold air floods out of the vents onto our already chilled faces. "I'm going to give it a second to warm up," Howard mutters. His eyes meet mine in the rearview mirror. "Shut the door."

I reach across the vinyl seat for the door handle right as Will springs up into the van like a pole-vaulter. "Sorry, sorry," he says to nobody in particular. He drops into the seat beside mine, and I'm seized with hunger. My eyes search his pockets as he buckles his seat belt, looking for any sign of their contents. Mo was right. There are piranhas in the world, and we are the meat they feed on. My brain knows that, but my body doesn't care. I want what Will has.

Will jostles Howard's shoulder, his hand a shadow in the dark interior of the van. "You weren't going to leave without me, were you?"

I glance at the rearview mirror. Howard's face gives away nothing. He stares at an invisible spot on the windshield. "Shut the door, Will," he says.

Will's leg bounces a mile a minute next to mine. Cheerleader snoozes on the prepster's shoulder, and the other girl draws invisible hearts on the rear window with her finger. No one says a word the whole ride back to LakeShore.

When Howard opens the door, we unfold like a clown car. I half-expect Howard to haul Will off, but he just leads our group back through the lobby, signs us in with the Front Desk Fascist, and then checks his watch. "You guys should probably head on to your rooms," he tells us. "Lights out in thirty minutes."

I know what's going to happen when Will goes to his room. And Howard knows it, too. I want him to say something; I want him to search Will's pockets. But he doesn't. He heads off down the hall to his office, and the rest of us find our way to our rooms.

Directing my feet to my own room is a sheer act of mental force. I shut the door behind me, my fingers twitching as I imagine Will emptying his pocket on his bed, unfolding the tiny bag inside. Does he have a lighter? A spoon? A needle? A shameful thought slithers to the surface of my consciousness: Will would share.

The door opens, and I startle a little, skittish. "Lights out," the orderly says. "You're supposed to be in bed."

"Dude, I'm changing," I tell him. He takes a quick peek around the room, his nose quivering like a sniffing drug dog, then shuts the door behind him.

I'm putting on my sweat pants when my door opens again. "Jesus, I'm going to bed, okay?"

But it's not the orderly standing in my doorway; it's Red. His face is ashen and beads of sweat dot his upper lip. He shuts the door, leans against it like he's afraid of what's on the other side. His eyes are closed, and he's panting, his body visibly shaken by the sheer effort of standing in one spot. "Eli," he says, "whatever you do, don't let me leave this room."

And then I know. The hunger that gnaws on me has its claws in Red, too. "Please," he begs, his eyes bloodshot and pierced with pain. And so I promise him. Neither one of us will leave this room. The hunger will subside or consume us, but we'll wait it out together.

Red and I sit side by side on the floor at the foot of my bed. Red rubs his legs up and down. As the evening stretches into night, his body seems to relax, and we pass the hours by swapping stories of our lives before LakeShore.

Red tells me about his days as a street musician, before he landed any real gigs. How he almost beat up a twelve-year-old who tried to bogart his corner with break dancing. How he had to pick a new spot when the kid's older (and much bigger) brother showed up the next day.

He tells me about the gigs, about the parties afterwards, the groupies, the girls. He tells me about Lisa, the girl from back home who meant more than all the rest. The girl who changed everything.

I tell stories, too. I tell him about Savannah and Alex—he listens wide-eyed to the stories about LionsHeart with its stone walls and golden lions guarding the entrance way, a far cry from the mountain sticks he grew up in, the cockroach-infested city slum he found later. I tell him about my dad—lacrosse in the backyard, cherry water ice, and counting the boats. And then I think about how upset Mom was when Dad brought me home that day, how she held me so tightly it hurt, and how some people you don't get back.

We doze on and off until dawn's grey fingers creep across the floor. Red's scrawny elbow pierces my ribcage. "Eli? You awake?"

"I am now." I push myself up off the carpet where I've been sleeping, my elbow as a pillow, drool pooling in the crease at my arm. I wipe the sleep from my eyes, surprised that Red's still here.

Red stands, tugs his jeans where they've ridden up. He's got sleep lines on his face, but he's not as jittery anymore, and his skin has gone back to its normal shade of pale. "I'm going to check on Will. You coming?"

We slink down the hall, carefully avoiding the entrance to the staff lounge where the night orderlies play cards to pass the last few hours of their shift. We pause in front of Will's closed door.

"You sure you want to do this?" I ask Red.

He nods, his eyes glowing in the dim hallway light. "I want to make sure he's okay." He raps on the door lightly, opens it a crack. The room is dark, and both beds are stripped. Will's gone. There's no sign that he was ever there at all.

Day 22

"I HEARD ANOTHER RUMOR TODAY," Red says. He takes a long drag from his cigarette, flicks the dangling nub of ash into the grass. It's Visitation, Easter Sunday, and we lounge on a picnic table outside, waiting for Red's dad to arrive.

I lean backward against the table, my elbows propped on the edge, my face turned up to the morning sun. Over the last two days, as Red and I have tried to piece together what happened to Will, we've heard a handful of possibilities. An orderly searched his room at lights out, found the drugs, and hauled him down to detox. Howard searched the room himself and found Will in the bathroom, semi-conscious. Prison Tat, in the room next door to Will's, swears he heard banging on a door in the middle of the night; Cheerleader Chick thinks Will left on his own, slipped out in the night, his pockets loaded with his stash. Even Howard, plugged with questions, refused to give up the truth.

"This happens sometimes, boys," he told us. "We can only pray that Will finds his way back to recovery."

"What was it this time?" I ask, squinting at Red in the sunlight.

He exhales, two plumes of black smoke puffing from his nose like a dragon. "Stretcher," he says. "The kid at the end of the hall said he got up in the night for some Tylenol. On his way back from the nurses' station, he saw the paramedics pushing a kid through the lobby on a stretcher." He shakes his head, takes another deep draw. "I should've followed him," he says. "If I wasn't so fucking weak . . . maybe I could've helped him, I don't know, convinced him or something."

Red gives me this helpless look, and it's the rawest I've seen him, even in group. His eyes tear, and he drops his head into his palms, pushing his fingers into his forehead. A leaning tower of ash hovers inches from his spiky hair.

Guilt grabs at me with hungry fingers. If Red had said he wanted to go to Will's room, I would've led the way. But not to help him. That's not the way the night would've played out.

My chest aches, and I rummage around for the right words. All I can think about is the last time I was on an airplane, the trip we took to Mexico over spring break sophomore year. The overhead masks and the narrow-waisted flight attendant's morbid instructions to "put on your own mask before you help anyone who needs assistance." I remember looking across the aisle at Benny, his Velcro sandals dangling above the floor, and thinking that's bullshit, I would put his mask on first.

"You did what you had to," I tell him. "It was the best you could've done."

"Maybe."

I stare into the distance; kids gather in small groups with their families, huddled together in the shade beneath the trees. "You think he'll be okay?"

Red shrugs, takes a final drag from the nub in his fingers and flicks it into the grass. "Will any of us?"

Prison Tat hollers from the propped rec room door. "Red, your pop's here."

The table shifts underneath me as Red climbs down. He grounds the smoking stub into the grass with the heel of his boot. "You're a good friend, Eli," he says.

I watch him slip through the door into the rec room. I think about the night we spent in my room, our shoulders pressed together at the foot of my bed, swapping stories that we hoped would save us. And I wonder if I helped Red or if he helped me. I wonder which of us needed the other more.

"No visitors today?" The Front Desk Fascist eyes me skeptically over a thick stack of folders as I stroll through the lobby. I pick a Cadbury egg (crème filled) from the bowl on her desk and plop down in one of the cozy leather chairs.

"Nope." I hook my feet under Libby's empty chair, drag it forward a little, and prop my feet on it.

"Make yourself at home," the Fascist mutters under her breath.

"Thanks." I stretch out, my belly full of the special Easter lunch the cook prepared. Red had offered for me to sit with him and his dad, and I did, until the "how are you's" got too painful, and I had to bail.

I unwrap the candy, thinking about my own family and how they're probably spending the day. Mom still insists on hiding eggs throughout the house, even though Benny has a phobia of mythical holiday characters. It all started after one tragic episode of mall photography involving a particularly creepy bunny costume. That Easter morning, I'd gone into Benny's room to tell him the Easter bunny had brought his basket, and Benny had sat straight up in bed, his face terror-stricken. "Is he still here?"

I'd wanted to tell him the truth right then and there, but Mom had given me a whole spiel about how it would "ruin the magic" or some crap like that. So instead I promised Benny that if I ever caught Triple B ("Big Bad Bunny") hanging around our house, I'd kick him right in his Cadbury eggs.

The memory brings a smile to my face, and I pop the chocolate in my mouth. When I was little, and Dad was still coming around, I'd wake up on Easter to find a green basket filled with dollar store candy and cheap plastic eggs hidden all over the apartment. I remember the jelly beans Dad and I ate afterwards until our teeth felt furry and our bellies sick. Thinking about it now, it was all pretty chintzy, but back then, it felt like magic.

And then I know why Mom didn't let me tell Benny the truth about the Easter Bunny. Because without magic, there's only off-brand crème-filled eggs, plastic green grass, and a bleary-eyed Dad who shows up late and disappears just as quickly.

Because the truth will break your heart.

I crush the foil wrapper into a tight ball between my fingers and roll it until the colors merge, and I can't see the creases anymore. I glance outside. Steven's heading up the sidewalk, dressed in khakis and a blue button down, like he's headed out to lunch at the club. For a split second, I feel like Benny, face to face with "Triple B."

I briefly consider disappearing, faking a migraine and hiding out in my room until visiting hours are over. But I don't. Because it's Easter. Because there's no such thing as magic, and because I don't want to be alone anymore.

Steven steps through the glass, and I stand up. We stand there for a second, neither one of us knowing what to say. "Is Mom . . ." I finally ask, not sure what I want the answer to be.

Steven shakes his head. "You said you didn't want visitors, and she wanted to respect that. But I . . ." His shoulders hunch a little, and he gives me sheepish look. "It's Easter, Eli. I didn't want you to be alone."

I open my mouth to say something, but no words come out. Because all at once I'm realizing what I probably should've known all along: Steven's the kind of guy who shows up.

And so I say the only thing I can think of, offer the only thing that feels right: "Want to get a cup of coffee?"

Steven and I sit across the table from each other in a quiet corner of the dining hall. Most of the visitors have already headed home anyway, back to their real Easter dinners with their non-addicted family members. I ask about Benny's Easter basket; Steven tells me Mom's on a no-high-fructose-corn-syrup kick, so everything in Benny's basket came from Whole Foods. Carob bunnies and muted jelly beans.

"How could you let this happen?" I groan.

"Your mom's a very scary lady when she sets her mind on something," Steven protests. "It was one on one. You weren't there to back me up."

We laugh, but it's awkward, because we don't talk like this, not usually, and because we both know why I wasn't there.

Steven clears his throat. "He misses you, you know? Benny." His gaze shifts to the oily surface of his coffee, thick with cream. "We all do. Especially your mom."

"Is that why you came here?" I demand. "To tell me to forgive her? Because you can forget it." I shove my chair backward, the motion jostling the table and sloshing my coffee. "She lied to me, you know? She lied to me for fourteen years."

I start to stand, but Steven holds up his hand to stop me. "I know," he says. "And you have every right to be furious. But please, hear me out."

The look on his face is so pained, so earnest, that I sink back down into my chair. I fold my arms across my chest and jerk my chin at Steven. "Fine. Talk."

He sighs. His fingers wrap his Styrofoam cup like it's the only thing keeping him afloat. "She wanted to tell you," he says. "We both did. But how do you tell a little boy that his hero is a junkie?"

I think of Benny in the backseat of Steven's car on the way to LakeShore. Benny with his *Blue's Clues* coloring book and his sticky hands checking me for fever. *Eli's not sick like you're thinking of, Benny. He's just not feeling like himself.* I stare down into my empty hands.

"You were too young to understand," Steven continues. "But we waited too long. By the time you were old enough, you'd already pulled so far away. I think your mom was afraid that if she told you the truth, she'd lose you altogether."

I glare at him out from under the fringe of hair that's fallen into my eyes.

"I know that's not an excuse, and it doesn't make it hurt any less. But sometimes, as a parent, there aren't any good choices." Steven runs his hand down his face. His voice is thick, and his eyes are bloodshot at the corners. "I've been thinking about that a lot, you know? Since you left. Every time I look at Benny, I think about you as a little boy, and I get so angry. I can't fathom for a second what kind of cold-hearted person walks away from their son."

My throat clenches, and my own eyes burn. Steven's giving voice to the question I've been carrying around for days.

"I didn't know your dad very well," Steven says. "But I have to believe that something powerful had its claws in him so deep that he didn't have a choice. I have to believe that he didn't want to be the way he was, that he loved you, more than anything in the world, but he was too sick to show it. I can't forgive him, not for what he did to your mom or for what he did to you. But in a way, I guess I owe him my gratitude. Because he gave me you."

I blink, shove the hair out of my eyes, and struggle to meet Steven's gaze.

"Look, Eli, the real reason I came here is because I want to make sure you know that you've never been some add-on, the price I had to pay to marry your mom. You are my family—you, your mom, Benny. We're not a family without you. And what I really want to say . . ." Steven's voice catches in his throat. "I know I'll never be your dad. But I will always be here for you. No matter how hard you push, I will never, ever walk away."

Something breaks inside of me, a fissure splitting apart stone. It hurts, but in a good way. I swipe the tears from my cheeks with the dirty sleeve of my hoodie and let Steven's words settle like salve.

He clears his throat, wipes at the corners of his eyes, and tugs at his collar. "I know I haven't always done a great job, but I want to be better. I want us to be better."

I think of the morning after Winter Formal, my new suit stained with stomach acid, the disappointment sagging heavy under Steven's eyes. I think of his constant presence at lacrosse, all the times he's reached out, and all the times I've pushed him away. Steven's words are a flickering coal under years of dust and ash. I want to lean into their warmth, but the walls I've built are tall and hard to scale. I give Steven a short nod.

"Okay," he says. "That's a start."

Steven stays awhile longer after that. Coffee in hand, we stroll around the outskirts of campus, following the same trail Libby and I blazed only days before. It's awkward at first, but I eventually relax. I tell him about the little things—about the food at LakeShore, and how Richard Fisher's alright once you get to know him. But not the big stuff. I don't tell him about Will disappearing. I don't tell him about Libby.

Visiting hours are almost over by the time I walk Steven back through the lobby. The Front Desk Fascist has already left for the day. One of the counselors slumps lazily in her chair, flipping through the pages of a dog-eared book. She gives Steven a friendly smile as he signs himself out. Then he turns to me.

His arms move awkwardly in his button down, like he's about to try and hug me, but then he sticks out his hand instead.

I take it, ignoring the counselor's curious glance. Steven's hand is warm and sturdy, and when we shake, I feel like we're agreeing to something—a fresh start, a new beginning. "I'm glad you came," I tell him, and then he yanks me closer and clasps me into a clumsy hug.

"Me, too," he says. Steven smells like rehab coffee and spicy aftershave, and I let him hug me, because I'm tired of pulling away.

I watch through the glass as Steven heads back to his car. The Lexus's headlights flicker when he unlocks the car. I wait until I can't see brake lights anymore, until the exhaust fades into the afternoon air. Then I go to the desk, where the Front Desk Fascist's fill-in greets me with a smile.

"Can I help you with something?" she asks.

"I was wondering if I could use the phone? It'll only take a minute."

"Sure." The counselor swivels the phone around and pushes it toward me.

My fingers hover over the buttons, hesitating. What if it's too late? What if things can never be better? What if *I* can never be better?

The glass doors slide open. I glance up as Chase steps into the lobby, a pink button-down rolled to his elbows, his Ray Bans pushed back on his head.

I lower the receiver.

"You said Sunday, right?" he asks, jerking his chin at the counselor behind the desk. "Don't I have to sign in or something?"

I push the phone back around as Chase hurriedly jots his name in the sign-in book.

The counselor considers him over the worn binding of her book. "Visitation ends in fifteen minutes."

"Don't worry, sweetheart," Chase croons. "I'm an in and out kind of guy."

My fingers dig into the shoulder of his pink shirt, pushing him toward the door. "Okay if we go for a smoke?"

She gestures toward the door with the flat of her hand. "Be my guest."

I hurry Chase outside.

"Dude, don't we need to get your shit?"

"Shh!" I send a quick glance through the glass. The girl at the desk flips over her book, her eyes scanning the back cover. "Keep your voice down."

Chase twists toward me. "I thought you said you could leave whenever you want!"

"I can." I sink down onto the curb, thinking of the smooth fabric of Steven's shirt, cool against my cheek when he hugged me. Somebody spit their gum out in the parking lot, and the circle of sticky black tar stares up at me. "I'm not sure if I want to anymore."

"Are you fucking kidding me, dude?" Chase throws up his arms. "You know I left my Mimi's sweet potato soufflé for this shit? And you *said* you'd pay for gas."

"I will," I say, squinting up at him. "As soon as I have cash."

"Motherfucker," Chase mumbles, stepping down off the sidewalk.

"Where are you going?"

"For a smoke," he snaps, shooting me a disgusted look over his shoulder. "I'm guessing you don't have any of those either."

I push up off the curb and follow him to the car. It's his mom's dusty Tahoe, the faded LionsHeart sticker peeling off the bumper. Chase cranks the ignition and lowers the windows. I hover beside the passenger door.

"Don't be an asshole," Chase breathes, blowing smoke out of the side of his mouth. "Get in."

The grey fabric seats are stained. I can't remember the last time I was in this car, probably fifth grade, our last year of Cub Scouts. An open can of red bull sits in one cup holder, a few crumpled tissues in the other. I keep the door propped, one foot safely on the pavement.

Chase offers me his smoke. I take a quick drag and send the wispy exhale toward the sky.

"I brought you something," Chase says. He leans across the seat, flips open the glove compartment, and tosses a small plastic bag onto my lap. Three sandy capsules blink up at me.

"It *was* going to be a welcome home gift," Chase grumbles. "I guess I'll add it to your tab."

I freeze; my spine stiffens, and my fingers twitch. I pick up the baggie, roll around the contents, the shiny capsules taunting me. There's no one here to stop me; it's just me and Chase. I'd do one, not two like before. It wouldn't hurt anybody. Afterwards, I'd go right back inside. Nobody would even know.

I crack open the bag, drop a capsule into my palm. "You know, a kid went home the other day."

Chase sends a perfect smoky donut out the window, then takes a swig of Red Bull.

"He was my friend," I continue. "He scored at a meeting, and then just . . . disappeared."

Chase swipes his hand across his upper lip. "What, like, alien abduction shit?"

I laugh, remembering the telescope Mom and Steven gave me for my eleventh birthday, the hours Chase and I spent at my bedroom window, searching for spaceships, the low flying airplane that sent us screaming downstairs.

"Sort of," I tell him, thinking of Will's stripped white mattress, how it glowed in the dark room, an ominous beacon, like a freshly empty bed in the ICU. "The next morning, he was gone."

"That's fucked up," Chase says. He flicks the cigarette out the window, jerks his chin at the capsule in my hand. "So are we doing this or not? I want to get home before my cousin Artie eats all the damn pie."

I stare down at the creamy capsule, thinking of Will, wondering where he is now. At home, grounded for life, his straight-laced parents watching his every move? Or on the street somewhere, like Red, a park bench, a flop house—face down in a plate full of smack?

And then I think about Benny, and about how some people you don't get back.

I put the capsule back in the bag.

Whatever you do, Red had begged me the night Will left, *don't let me leave this room.*

I have to get out of this car.

A car horn startles me. An ambulance backs up to the curb by the front entrance.

Will, I think as the EMT climbs out of the passenger side, walks around back, and cracks open the door.

The plastic bag falls onto the seat as I lunge out of the car.

"Dude!" Chase hollers. "I'm not waiting around for you! Your ride leaves now."

I ignore him. Because it's not Will the transport nurse is helping up the sidewalk to the lobby.

It's Libby.

The glass doors slide open. The transport nurse grips Libby's elbow with one hand and supports her waist with the other. Her skin is ashen; charcoal circles, deep and dark as war paint, form half-moons underneath her eyes. She's dyed her hair—blue-black like shadows, like secrets. But it's the bandages on her arms that make my throat constrict, my stomach seize. Freshly applied white gauze bandages cover the places where scars once were. My first day in the hospital flashes through my brain like lightening. I remember the doctor tiptoeing around his questions, wanting to know if I did it on purpose.

I turn my back on Chase and the pills in the plastic bag, and I follow Libby inside.

The girl at the desk yells something at me, but I can't even make sense of her words. Libby's the only thing that matters, the only thing that exists.

"What happened?" I am the doctor, hovering close, sizing up my patient, taking in her ravaged arms, her broken body. *Have you ever thought about hurting yourself? Were you trying to take your life?* Libby, what have you done?

I reach out to her, but the heavyweight transport nurse steps full in front of me, blocking Libby with his bulk. "I don't think so, kid."

I dart to one side, but his arm flies out and hits me square in the chest. Pain shoots through me, and I fall back, winded. It's just enough time for the nurse to bustle Libby away from me, through the lobby. I recover and follow them.

"Enough!" The girl at the desk shouts, grabbing the phone. She's probably calling an orderly, but I don't care. I tail the transport nurse to the medical wing.

"Libby!" I shout. "Libby, look at me!"

Libby's hair hangs in greasy ropes down her back. Smudged purple marker peeks out of the white bandages, trailing up her fingers in nonsensical squiggles. She doesn't answer me. She doesn't even turn her head.

At the entrance to the medical wing, the electronic doors swoop open, and two nurses step out. Transport acknowledges me with a jerk of his head. "I have a bit of a situation here."

I rush forward, but the nurses use their bodies to block me, pushing Libby through the doors behind them. They sidle backward one at a time and shut the doors firmly in my face.

I hurl myself against the doors, but they're locked from the inside. Through the narrow glass windows, I watch them lead Libby past the nurses' desk. I bang my hands against the glass, shouting for her. "Libby! Libby!"

Just before she rounds a corner where I won't be able to see her anymore, Libby turns her head ever so slightly. I don't know if she sees me. I don't know if she sees anything. Her eyes are an arctic ocean, frozen solid. Nothing stirs beneath the surface.

I sag back against the wall, my chest heaving as I catch my breath. The swipe pad jabs into my shoulder blade. There's a key pad beneath it, but I don't know the code. I slam my fist into the keypad, over and over again, until the numbers are bruises on my knuckles, and my eyes sting with tears, and an orderly finally catches up to me.

"Do we have a problem here?" The orderly's a young guy, probably new, and barely older than me. His voice is imposing, but his pink cheeks and telltale upper lip sweat give him away. He's nervous.

I eye the swipe card clipped to the chest pocket of his white scrubs. I wonder if I could take him, grab his swipe card, and haul ass through those doors to find Libby. But I'd barely make it past the nurses' desk before someone would call for help. I might not even have time to find her.

I push myself up off the wall, ducking my head to wipe my eyes on my shirt sleeve. "No." I stroll past the orderly as nonchalantly as possible. "No problem at all."

His eyes widen with relief, and his chest deflates a little. "Good," he grumbles. "Move it along then."

"Yes, sir." I give him a sarcastic salute.

He opens his mouth to say something else, but I don't stick around to hear it. I've gotta find a swipe card.

I burst through the door of the gym like someone's chasing me. A couple guys on treadmills look up, surprised. "Is Red here?" I ask.

243

One of them points to the back of the gym, and I spot Red by the bench press, loading up the rack. "Red," I call, breaking into a jog.

One look at my face and Red lowers the weight he's holding. "What's wrong?"

"It's Libby," I tell him, dropping onto the bench. "She's back."

"Shiiiiittt . . ." Red breathes. He heaves the weight back up onto the rack and sits down beside me. "Did you see her?"

I nod. "She looks bad, dude. Really bad. I think . . ." The words catch in my throat. "I think she hurt herself," I whisper.

Red exhales, a heavy wheeze, and lifts the collar of his ripped t-shirt to wipe the sweat from his upper lip. "She told you that?"

I shake my head. "I think they have her drugged or something. She barely even looked at me." The disfigured girl from Libby's painting veers into my memory. *She's broken*, Libby said.

I drop my face into my hands. Crying in counseling is one thing. Crying in the gym is something else entirely. I clench my teeth, willing myself to get it together. But there's a black and gaping hole inside me, and I am dangling from the edge, my grip slipping more each second.

"She's in detox?" Red asks.

I nod into my hands. "I gotta get in there, dude."

A calculating look flickers across Red's face. He stands up, squeezes my shoulder. "Give me a couple hours," he says. "I'll see what I can do."

I sit alone at dinner, swirling my leftover meatloaf with my fork until it looks like gray mush. My body's moved through the motions of the day, but my brain's been with Libby since the second she walked through the door.

Is she sleeping? Is she sick? Is she scared? Is she thinking about me as much as I'm thinking about her?

I barely notice Red drop his tray beside me. He sits down so close to me that his arm jostles mine. "Oh," I say, glancing up at him. "Hey."

Red's cheeks are flushed under his freckles, and his eyes are shining. He casts a furtive glance around the room, then whispers under his breath, "Open your hand."

"What?"

"Just do it," Red hisses.

I drop my fork, slide my hand under the table and rest it on my leg, palm up. Red digs in his pocket, slips something into my hand. Something thin, hard, and plastic.

A swipe card.

"Act normal," he mumbles, shoveling a forkful of meatloaf into his mouth. "Your face is going to give it away."

I copy Red's expression, forcing my face to stay flat and uninterested, but all the while, my eyes are darting around the room, certain that someone knows what I have. My heart is pounding like I just ran a marathon, and it's all I can do not to jump up and run out of the dining hall.

I shove the swipe card in my front jean pocket and pull my shirt low to cover it. "How?" I whisper.

"My counselor never wears hers. Leaves it sitting on her desk in plain view." Red's voice is low, carefully confined to the small space between us. "I may have picked up a skill or two during my weeks on the streets, okay? Not that her office is that hard to get into." He gives me a wry grin, and the pieces suddenly click into place. This is how Red gets around.

I can't hide the grin teasing up the corners of my mouth. "This is awesome."

"Not that awesome," Red says, his eyes darting furtively toward the orderly posted by the dining hall entrance. "She's gone for the day, but she's going to notice it's missing sooner or later. You have one chance, and then you have to get it back to me. Tomorrow morning at the latest, okay?"

My grin dissolves. If I get caught, it won't just be me getting booted from LakeShore. Red will go down for this, too. "We could get kicked out."

Red carves valleys through his meatloaf with his fork. "I know," he says. "But I think it's worth the risk."

My eyes probe Red's poker mask. Red's been anti-me-and-Libby since the beginning. "Why do you want to help me see her now?"

Red lowers his fork, takes a long, slow sip of ice water. "When Lisa died," he begins, "I was lounging on my couch in front of *Jackass* reruns. The accident was less than five miles from my house. And while she died, I ate leftover pizza and laughed at a stupid reality show."

"You couldn't have known it was going to happen," I tell him, because it's what I'd want someone to say to me. "It wasn't your fault." The words are a Scooby-Doo Band-Aid on a fresh gunshot wound.

He shrugs off my reassurance. "I know. I know all that." His fingers toy with the dull tines of his fork, pushing the soft pads of his fingertips against the metal until pinprick indentations mark his flesh. "But even knowing what happened, even knowing the crash would've killed us both, I would've been there if I could."

He looks up at me, his grief palpable. "Not to change it, you know, because I know I couldn't. But to be with her. To hold her hand. To be scared shitless together."

He clears his throat, then takes another swig of water. The emotion dissipates like fog on a bathroom mirror, taking with it secrets scrawled on the glass. "It's worth it," he says.

I nod, and together we start to come up with a plan.

It's after midnight, and the lobby's dark. No one's at the desk. Room checks are over, and the orderlies have ducked into the staff lounge for a game of cards or a quick nap. I've piled all my dirty laundry under my covers, bunched up like a body, and squished my pillow up like a head.

The flickering security lights cast shadows in the corners. I startle at my reflection in the locked sliding glass doors, my hair shaggy around my ears, my face haunted. "Get it together, Eli," I hiss. I stealth-walk down the hall to the medical wing and pause in front of the double doors.

Unlike the rest of LakeShore, the detox unit never sleeps. There are two nurses on duty at all times. The overhead lights are dimmed for the night, but the nurses pop into the rooms every so often to take blood pressure readings, temperature, that kind of thing.

I touch the plastic ridge of the swipe card in my pocket. No way I'm getting into Libby's room and out again without somebody catching me. And I won't have any excuses. I won't have a second chance.

But Libby's alone, probably sick and scared. I think about Red, and though I've never seen Lisa, I imagine them in the car together, hands clutched tightly as the car crashes against a guard rail and careens over the edge.

I take a deep breath and pull the swipe card out of my pocket. With a final peek through the glass to make sure nobody's at the nurses' station, I hold the card up to the flickering red light on the keypad.

It doesn't work.

The light keeps flickering red, and the doors stay shut. Disappointment mingled with a shameful twinge of relief crashes through me.

And then the light's green, and the doors crank open, and they are the loudest freaking doors I've ever heard, announcing to the entire world that I'm breaking into a medical facility.

There's a little alcove for wheelchairs right inside the door. I duck into it, my heart racing.

The medical wing is filled with noise, steady beeps and hums. It reminds me of the morning I woke up in the hospital. I remember how confused and scared I was, my mom's tears, Savannah leaving me, the disappointment and heartbreak etched across her face. It all happened decades ago. Or maybe only moments.

Footsteps come toward me. I press my back against the wall. The footsteps stop, and I peer around the corner. A nurse is at the nurses' station. Her back's to me as she stares into a glowing computer screen, her fingers rapidly skimming the keyboard.

I step out from the alcove. The medical wing's nighttime noises mask my footsteps, and I slip silently past the nurses' station and into the dimly lit hallway beyond it.

The hall is lined with patient doors. It dawns on me that I have no idea which room is Libby's.

Fuck. Fuck. Fuck. Fuck.

What did I think I was going to do? Pop my head into every room and ask for her? I'm such an idiot.

I've almost decided to turn back when I hear her.

"I told you," Libby says, her voice like desert sand. "I can't sleep."

"But it's so late," a nurse says. "You have to try."

I inch forward, past one darkened room, and steal a peek into the next. A dark-haired nurse is standing next to Libby's bed. "You can't get better if you don't sleep, hon."

"I'm keeping watch," Libby tells her, echoing the words she spoke to me in the lobby the first Visitation we spent together. "This way they can't take me by surprise."

"You're perfectly safe here, Libby," the nurse soothes. "Nobody's going to hurt you. Please try and get some sleep."

"I told you I can't!" Libby snarls. "The fucking meds aren't even working."

The nurse sighs, and I wonder if she's thinking that this girl is above her pay grade. That Libby belongs on a psych ward, not in rehab. I wonder if she sees this kind of crazy in detox all the time.

Screams come from the room next door; someone cries out in their sleep. The nurse turns toward the door. "I'll be back soon, okay?"

Quickly, I dart back to the empty room and hide in the doorway. The nurse's sneakers squeak against the tile floor as she heads down the hall to the screamer. "I'm right here, Jerry," I hear her say. She utters soothing words to some poor kid that's thrashing around in the nightmare of withdrawal.

No longer worried about being heard, I step out of the darkness and into Libby's room.

The overhead light is off, and a circle of soft yellow light pools around the lamp on the bedside table. Libby's sitting cross-legged on her bed. She's wearing a hospital gown, knotted loosely at her neck, and her hair spills out of a greasy bun. She's staring at the opposite wall, her glassy eyes fixed on something I can't see. I'm struck by how tiny her feet are, where they stick out from under her gown. The standard issue socks with sticky soles bunch at her toes and ankles.

I ease the door shut behind me, cracked slightly, the way the nurse left it. I'll hear her if she comes back.

I take a hesitant step forward. "Libby?" I whisper.

She flinches but doesn't look at me.

I cross the room and sit down on the edge of the empty bed beside hers. "Libby, it's me." I reach out to touch her, but her whole body shrinks away from me and curls up inside the thin gown that blankets her narrow shoulders. She squeezes her eyes shut.

I lower my hand. "What happened to you?"

Libby shudders. A low moan escapes her lips, and it's the sound of heartbreak, of something once wild, now broken.

Goose bumps careen down my spine. "Libby . . ."

"He came back." The words come out in a hoarse whisper, so soft, I can barely hear.

I lean forward. "Who?"

Eyes still closed, Libby begins to rock gently back and forth. Her arms, stained with faded Sharpie smudges, crisscross her chest, and she clutches her elbows, her nails carving crescent moons into her skin.

"Him."

In a flash, the memory of that first Visitation Day comes barreling back to me. *I'm keeping watch*, Libby had said. *This way my mom and her sick fuck boyfriend can't take me by surprise.*

The boyfriend.

My stomach lurches, and for a minute I think I'm going to be sick. I remember the words I shouted at her the last time we spoke: *What happened to you? Who made you this way?*

The unspoken answer runs like the cold tip of a knife down my spine. "Did he . . ." The words lodge in my throat. "Libby, were you . . ."

"We ate dinner," Libby says. "He brought takeout. Like everything was normal. Like things could ever be normal."

A tear slips out from under Libby's dark fringe of lashes, slicing a shimmering gash down her pale cheek. "But he was looking at me . . ." Her voice catches in her throat, and her words get wider, louder, like her throat can't contain the depth of pain they carry. "...the way he always looks at me."

She's rocking faster now, harder, and it scares me. Her story spills out in a breathless jumble.

"I locked myself in the bathroom. I knew it was never going to be better; he was never going to go away and leave us alone. I found my mom's pills behind the mirror. And then on the bathtub, her razor . . ."

My heart is pounding like it's going to burst out of my chest. I reach out to her because I can't help it; I wrap my arms around her, pull her close. She presses her cold wet face into the side of my neck, grips my back with desperate fingers, and together we careen toward the guardrail, crashing through into the night.

"I didn't mean to," Libby sobs. "I swear I didn't mean to."

"I know you didn't," I tell her, my hands in her hair, on her neck, my mouth against her skin.

I know.

I know.

I know.

We hold each other like this until my t-shirt is soaked through, and Libby's sobs are soft whimpers, and her body goes still in my arms.

And then there are footsteps outside the door. I freeze.

Quick like a darting garden snake, Libby's hand reaches for the lamp. The room plunges into darkness. I slide onto the narrow strip of floor between the two beds. The mattress creaks as Libby lies back against the pillows. The door opens, and a triangle of light reaches across the floor.

I dare only to take soundless sips of air.

White soled sneakers pad toward Libby's bed. Toward me.

"Get out," Libby snaps.

The nurse is nonplussed. "You know I have to check on you, Libby," she clucks.

"I was starting to doze off," Libby whines. "How am I supposed to sleep if you come in the room every five seconds?"

The sneakers pause. "You were sleeping?"

Silence. Maybe Libby nods.

"I'm really not supposed to leave you alone for very long," the nurse frets, rolling up on the toe of one white sneaker. "I could lose my job."

The bed creaks as Libby shifts her weight. "Please," she begs. "I'll be good, I promise. I just need to sleep."

The nurse sighs. "I'll try to give you a few hours. But I'm trusting you, Libby." The sneakers turn, point back toward the door. "Call me if you need anything?"

"Close the door," Libby orders in response.

The sneakers step into the hallway. The door closes, but only halfway. Light floods the room beyond the bed. But it's enough.

I release my breath, take in full gulps of air. Adrenaline pumps through my veins; my arms and legs feel like JELL-O.

Atop the bed, Libby lets out what sounds like a giggle. And I wonder if it's the sound of relief, or if it's like laughing at a funeral. Because you have to do *something*, because you don't have any tears left.

I reach for the mattress above me and haul myself up. "That was close," I whisper, my eyes straining to adjust to the dark.

There's movement, the creaking of the mattress, then the sudden press of Libby's body against my own. Her mouth finds mine in the dark—hungry. Her fingers twist into the hair at the nape of my neck. And I know I am a razor. I know I am a bottle of pills.

But I am hungry, too.

I grip her hospital gown in my fist, reaching for the soft skin beneath. Libby's kisses get harder, desperate. Her dry lips scratch mine; her tongue tastes sour. She cups my face in her hands, and the gauze on her wrists brushes my cheek.

I freeze.

I am a razor. I am a bottle of pills.

She is my addiction.

I let go of Libby's gown. It flutters against her bare legs. Libby pulls back, her eyes searching my face, hurt and confused.

I take her hand in mine and gently begin to unwrap her wrist. Libby's breath quickens, but she doesn't resist. Round and round the gauze goes, until raw skin touches the cool darkness, and Libby's pulse throbs against my thumb. With feather fingers, I trace a puckered trail of stitches along her skin. I kiss her wrist like ointment. Like fresh gauze.

I am salve.

"I didn't mean to," Libby whispers, her voice cracking in the middle.

"I know," I say. I know.

I curl my fingers into Libby's. Her cold hand intertwines with mine, and she tugs me down beside her. I hesitate.

I should go.

I want to stay.

As though she can read my mind, Libby whispers, "Please."

I don't want to be alone either.

I ease myself down onto the bed. Libby scootches over a little, and I tuck my arm underneath her. She lays her head on my chest, ear to heartbeat. I remember the day we napped on the lawn, and I wonder if my heart sounds as different as it feels.

Libby curls up tighter against me, and I stroke her arm, her back, her hair, until I feel her body relax and her breathing slow, and I know that sleep has found her.

I am ointment.

I am fresh gauze.

"Libby?" I whisper.

She makes a murmuring sound but doesn't stir. I slow my breathing until Libby and I are inhaling and exhaling as one, and I marvel at our breath, at our still-beating hearts.

With my free hand, I feel for my scar and run my fingers across the leathery skin. Pain always leaves its mark.

I push Libby's hair back from her forehead, touch my lips to her cool, damp skin. "I see you," I whisper. "I see you."

Libby mutters something in her sleep; she snuggles closer to me, her fingers tightening around mine. My eyelids are heavy, and I let them close for a minute.

Only for a minute.

Day 23

WAKE UP WITH A jolt—panicked and confused.

Grey light streams in through the window. I'm still in Libby's room.

My arm's asleep where Libby's head rests on it, and I crane my neck for a glimpse of the clock on the bedside table.

5:10 AM.

Shit.

Libby's face is nuzzled peacefully against my chest; her breathing is steady and deep. But I am freaking out.

From the hallway comes the sound of the nurse's med cart; she's making her last rounds. I ease my arm out from under Libby, careful not to wake her, and sit up, wracking my brain for a way out of this mess.

I tiptoe to the door and press my ear against it. It doesn't sound like anyone's on the other side. I ease it open and peer out. The nurse's cart is parked outside of the room next door. I can hear her talking to the kid inside. "Good morning, Jerry," she crows. "You're looking better already."

Libby's room is next.

I slip out into the empty hallway. Sleepy chatter trickles down the hall from the nurses' station. The night shift is wrapping up. I know I'm fucked, but desperation makes me brave, and I do the only thing I can.

I walk down the hall and out to the nurses' station like I belong there.

There's an open box of donuts behind the counter, and two nurses hover over it, their backs to me. I'll never make it through the doors without them hearing me. So I make a balls-to-the-wall irrational play and step forward until I'm facing the nurses' station.

"Excuse me," I say.

The nurses startle and turn around quickly. One of them is chewing a bite of donut. She has powdered sugar on her cheek. The other looks at me, confused. "Can I help you?"

"I hope so. You had a patient come in last night? Her name's Libby. I was hoping I could see her."

The donut nurse blinks. "Are you a resident?"

I nod.

"How'd you even get in here?" the other nurse demands. "That door's supposed to stay locked."

I shrug. "It was open, and I just walked through."

Donut Nurse mutters under her breath. "If I've told housekeeping once, I've told them a thousand times. They have to pull that door closed all the way." Her chubby fingers reach for a pen, and she scribbles something on a yellow Post-it pad. I hope I didn't get anybody in trouble.

I clear my throat. "So, about Libby . . ."

Exasperation edges the nurse's voice. "Of course you can't see her," she snaps. "Detox patients are on blackout. No phone calls, no visitors. She'll join the program in a few days. Now get out of here before I call an orderly."

Gladly.

I point toward the double doors I snuck through last night. "Should I let myself out?"

Donut Nurse rolls her eyes. She punches a button behind the nurses' station. The doors crank open like a drawbridge, offering safe passage.

"Thanks," I say, and then I remember that I'm supposed to be disappointed. "I mean, thanks a lot."

The nurses ignore me, already clucking to one another about the irresponsible housekeeping crew. Leaving their grumbling behind me, I haul ass through the empty lobby.

Red's taking forever to answer his door. I knock again, a little louder this time, all the while casting nervous looks over my shoulder for the orderlies I'm sure are about to come barreling around the corner after me. "Red," I whisper. "Red, open the damn door."

Finally, the door cracks open. Red's eyes are squinty with sleep, and he wears a white t-shirt with boxers. "What time is it?" he grumbles.

"Morning," I tell him, and I push the swipe card into his hand.

His fingers close around it, and his eyes widen with recognition, with relief. "You did it."

I nod.

"Did you get caught?"

I throw another furtive glance down the hall. "Not yet."

"Not *yet?*" Red's voice rises. "What do you mean 'not yet'?" Behind him, Red's roommate stirs in his sleep.

"Keep your voice down," I hiss. "I had to improvise to get out, that's all."

"Improvise?" Red's eyes narrow as he takes in my appearance. "Aren't those the same clothes you had on yesterday?"

I glance down at my shirt. "It's probably better if you don't ask questions."

"I'm going back to bed." Red takes a backward step into his room.

"Red?" I say.

"Yeah?"

"If they find out, I swear I won't say it was you. I'll keep your name out of it 100%. Okay?"

Red nods, his mouth curling into a sleepy smile. "Tell me one thing: was it worth it?"

I pause, searching for an answer.

Red means seeing Libby. He means maybe getting caught.

But when I finally answer him, I mean more than that. I mean the last 23 days. I mean cracking open, over and over again.

"Yeah," I tell him. "It was worth it."

"Good." Red retreats into his room and shuts the door behind him.

Back at my room, I'm antsy. There are two hours until breakfast, and I know I can't sleep. I need to do something. I pull on a pair of gym shorts and my sneakers. Screw doc's orders. I need to run.

The lights are off when I get to the gym. I find the switch, and the overhead bulbs flicker on. The room is eerily silent, except for the steady hum of fluorescent lights. I choose a treadmill in the middle of the long line and crank it up to 6.0 mph—a relatively easy jog, but after three weeks of no running, my legs feel cast in iron.

One foot in front of the other. My feet find a steady rhythm. Left foot. Right foot. Inhale. Exhale.

I try to focus on my pace, my breathing, but I can't stop thinking about Libby.

Alone in the bathroom, the pills in her hand, the razor against her wrist.

Didn't she know that there are people who love her? People who would miss her? Didn't that matter to her at all?

My fingers jam the speed button. 7.0 mph.

My breath quickens. My legs burn.

I think about my dad.

How he left me. How he died.

8.5 mph. My lungs ache, and my muscles are screaming.

My feet pound my story into the treadmill. Left foot. Right foot. Inhale. Exhale.

He left me. He left me. He left me.

And then I think about myself, about the people I've hurt, the ones I've left behind.

Savannah's tear-streaked face in the hospital the morning after I overdosed.

Mom's weary head on my chest.

Benny, who still believes in magic and is too young to know the truth.

Benny.

9.0 mph and I can't breathe.

I can't go home. I can't face up to everything I've done and everyone I've hurt. The pain is too much. Red was right. Feeling is the hardest. And I don't know if I want to do it anymore.

And then I think about Chase, the pills I left on the floor of the Tahoe. And I'm wishing I could rewind, scoop them up, and hide them in my pocket. I'd lock myself in the bathroom, and I'd let the whole world fall away. I'd disappear all over again.

And then what? Would I end up like Mo—rehab my second home? Or Red, with a needle in my arm and a gun to my face? Would I end up like Howard, a homeless, panhandling junkie, plunging used needles for a leftover high?

Would I end up like my dad?

I pound out the miles, trying to outrun this gaping hole inside me that nothing, nothing can fill. I grip the dashboard, willing my legs forward until I can't . . .

. . . can't

. . . can't

run anymore.

I jam the emergency stop button, and I lurch forward, barely catching myself before I sink to my knees.

There's not enough air in the world.

I bend over, clutching my sides, heaving in and out until finally, I can breathe again.

Inhale. Exhale.

My breath comes in gasps and wheezes.

And I wonder if Richard Fisher is right—if addiction really is a disease. A disease that doesn't give a shit about love, loyalty, or willpower. No matter how much you love your girlfriend or your family. No matter how much they love you.

Maybe Howard's mom had it right. Addiction is the monster, not the person.

Maybe recovery can be a long and broken road.

Maybe, like Mo said, sobriety is a daily decision.

"Fuck addiction," I mumble out loud.

I pull myself up and ease the speed up to 6.0 mph.

Inhale. Exhale.

One foot in front of the other.

"Fuck addiction," I say again, louder this time. My voice echoes in the empty gym.

"FUCK ADDICTION!" My words graffiti the cement walls.

I'm sitting on the old brown couch in Richard Fisher's office, picking at the worn patch of denim over my knee.

Richard Fisher is reading my purple notebook, the list he'd asked me to write about the challenges waiting for me at home. Every few minutes, he comments on something he's read, but I'm barely listening. All I'm thinking about is Libby, and whether or not I'm going to tell Richard Fisher the truth.

"It seems like going back to school is your biggest concern," Richard Fisher says.

I nod weakly—sure, it's my biggest concern, second to getting kicked out of LakeShore. With only four days left, I finally want to make the most of it. And I'm pretty sure sneaking into detox would be the final nail in my coffin. But I want to know what's going to happen to Libby. I want Richard Fisher to tell me she's going to be okay.

"There are options, you know?" he continues. "You only have a trimester left. We could talk to your mom. There are cyber-schools . . ."

I glance at the clock, the second hand that's maybe frozen because I swear to God it hasn't moved since I got here.

Richard Fisher clears his throat. "Something bothering you, Eli?"

I meet his gaze, and it's so open, so familiar, that I decide to tell him the truth. Sort of.

"Libby's back."

Richard Fisher sinks back in his creaking swivel chair. "You've heard."

I nod.

Richard takes a deep breath. His face gets all serious, like he's about to talk me down from a ledge. And rightfully so. It's a ledge I've been on a few times since I came to LakeShore. Wanting to give up. Wanting to go home. But not this time. This time is different.

"Eli . . ." Richard begins.

"Relax," I tell him. "I just want to know what's going to happen to her."

Richard Fisher taps his pen against my open notebook. "She's going to finish detox, and then she'll rejoin the program."

"And then what?"

Richard raises his eyebrows.

"You know what I mean," I say, fighting the rising urgency in my voice. "How are you going to keep her safe? How are you going to keep her from going back home? Don't you have some sort of long-term program or something? What are you going to do?"

Richard Fisher lets out a heavy exhale. "You know I can't discuss that with you, Eli."

"But I need to know!" I slap the coffee table, and the sound echoes in the tiny office, surprising us both.

I take a deep breath. "I care about her, Richard. I've changed since I got here, you know? I know Libby and I aren't . . . Look, I get it, okay? But I can't handle not knowing what's going to happen to her. I have to know she's going to be okay."

Richard Fisher gives me a small, sad smile. "One of the hardest parts of getting sober, Eli, is finding out that life isn't perfect. There are no guarantees. And for the first time in your life, you're going to have to deal with that kind of uncertainty without using drugs as a crutch."

I sink back into the lumpy cushions, thinking of the pills in Chase's car. The What-If's buzz through my brain like hungry mosquitoes, and I know exactly how Mo felt that night before he left. What if I can't stay clean? What if all the self-control in the world isn't enough? What's going to keep me from coming right back here? Anxiety shoots through me, and my palms grow slick with sweat. "What if I can't?" I ask. "What if I'm not strong enough?"

"None of us are strong enough on our own," Richard Fisher says. "That's what Step Two is all about."

I stare down at my empty hands. "I don't believe in that stuff."

Richard Fisher leans forward, his eyes glinting behind his glasses. "Sometimes you have to fake it until you make it. Act yourself into a new way of thinking. You're not the same kid you were before. You have the tools to stay clean. Whether you use them or not is entirely up to you. But you and I aren't done, you know? We still have to finalize your aftercare program, which is going to involve lots of NA meetings and outpatient counseling. We have a long way to go, kid, but if you're willing to do the work, you'll find that there's another way to live. Eventually, it won't matter how crazy or unfair life is—you can be peaceful inside anyway."

I consider his words. That kind of peace feels a long way off.

"When you say *lots of meetings*, how many are we talking, exactly?"

Richard Fisher rolls his eyes.

"Seriously, give me a ballpark figure."

Richard throws his pen at me. "Get outta town." He points down at my purple notebook. "Are we going to talk about this entry, or not?"

I glance up at the clock again—there's ten minutes left to my session. And I don't want to waste any of them. "Yeah," I say. "Tell me more about cyber-school."

Day 24

RED'S SAVED ME A SEAT at group. He's got a cup of coffee on the floor by his feet, and a couple of cheese Danishes in his hands. "Want one?" he offers.

My stomach growls, even though I just ate breakfast, and I take it gratefully. "Thanks," I say, scattering crumbs.

The other guys settle into their seats, and Howard starts the session.

"Because several of you will be leaving in the next few days," Howard begins, "I thought it would be valuable to spend this session talking about some of the concerns you might have about going home."

Red elbows me in the ribs. "Lucky I'm not one of you," he whispers. "I'm in for another thirty days."

I lick the remnants of cheese filling from my thumb. "The insurance thing got worked out?" Lisa's mom had been working on getting Red an extension for a while, and Red, not at all ready to go back home, had been anxiously waiting for this news.

"Yep. I'm approved for the extended program, and then probably sober living or a half-way house or something."

"Nice."

All around the circle, people offer to share. One by one, fears are named in the safety of this space we've all come to trust.

"Falling back into old habits."

"The stress of going back to school."

"Having to find new friends."

My own fears echo those of the group, and I find myself nodding in agreement, in understanding. When Howard asks the group how they plan on coping with these challenges, I raise my hand.

"Eli," Howard says. "Do you have something you want to share?"

"I, uh, I go home in four days. And I'm not sure I'm ready."

Howard nods encouragingly.

"It's like there's this big hole inside me, and nothing fills it. I know that's why I used, because I was trying to fill that hole. But now that I'm *not* using, the hole feels bigger. It feels *more* empty."

My throat constricts; I force myself to keep talking, even though my words tremble. "You guys all believe in something, but I don't have that. What's going to keep me from falling back in?"

An image of Libby flashes through my mind—alone in her bathroom, a razor pressed against her wrist. Certain there was no other way.

I drop my head into my hands; words pour through my fingers like water. "I want to get better. But I can't do it on my own. I need help, okay? I need help."

Howard's voice tugs me out of hiding. "If there's one thing I've learned over the past ten years, Eli, it's that when you ask for help, it always comes."

I press my palms against my eyes and wipe the telltale wetness onto my jeans. "It just feels so fucking hard."

Howard nods. "I know it does. But you're not alone, Eli. Look around this circle, look at the people in your corner. Individually, we are all vulnerable to the pull of our addictions. But as a group, we are greater. You don't have to do this alone, Eli. The strength and spirit of this group will be with you every step of the way."

I dare to peer around the circle, to meet the gazes of the guys in my group. Some of them haggard, some of them broken. All of them with scars like mine.

A heavy hand drops on my shoulder, and I turn to meet Red's eyes. In them I see the night Will left. Red in my room, both of us weak, both of us hungry for what Will had. But together we were more. Together we made it through.

"Thanks," I whisper.

Red grins at me. "What are friends for?"

I sit cross-legged on the floor in front of my higher power canvas and page lazily through my pile of magazines. The art teacher had them ready for me when I got to class, along with a pair of scissors and a bottle of glue. "Collage is a wonderfully intuitive art form," she'd said, handing over the stack of supplies. "Sometimes you don't even know what you're looking for until you find it."

I sip coffee from my lukewarm cup and eye my canvas skeptically. The picture of the kayaker stares back at me. It's hung there in isolation for the last week. The impossibility of the kayaker's task first drew me to the image—the cliff of sheer rock rising up right in front of him. But it's the water that I notice now, the crystal-clear expanse surrounding the kayaker, holding him up.

I remember something I learned forever ago in Earth Science. Water erodes rock. That mountain face might look impassable, but there are cracks in its seemingly solid surface— narrow spaces where water can get in. Water is powerful. With enough time, water can take down a mountain.

I turn back to the magazine in my lap and examine the pages with sharpened focus. The guys in group talk about their higher powers like they're always available—as handy and accessible as a pack of Kleenex or a tube of ChapStick, right there in your pocket whenever you need them. Not me. I don't believe in some ethereal superpower that can swoop in and rescue me when I'm in trouble. But I believe in my friends. I believe in Red, in the unimaginable courage he has to face down his demons even as he grieves the death of his girlfriend. I believe in Libby, in the quiet strength she finds in her paintings and in her journal, despite her fucked-up family. And I believe in Mo, in falling down and getting back up, over and over again.

I take apart the magazine with frenzied scissors. Within the blaring headlines, I find the words I need. I cut letters from lies, piecing new words together. Page after page, I fill with jagged cracks, until the words spill out like light into darkness, pathways through the mountain.

STRENGTH
COURAGE
HOPE
FORGIVENESS

With dots of glue and fragments of tape, I tell the kayaker the real story. There are cracks in the mountain, I tell him. There are places where you can get through. You may not see them yet. You may not see them for a while.

I fill the sky with words that guide his way like stars.

The lobby's empty after dinner, the Front Desk Fascist gone for the day. I lean over the desk and scoot the phone closer. I lift the receiver, my fingers hovering over the keypad.

You were right.
I need help.
I'm sorry.

Words are insufficient. There's nothing I can say to take back what I've done to my mom, nothing I can say that will change our family's story. The past is already written. My dad died an addict. I'm an addict, too. Nothing I can say will make any of that better.

In the back of my mind, I hear Richard Fisher's voice from so many weeks ago. "That's why we start at the beginning, kid."

And so I do.

I start from where I am.

My fingers crisscross the keypad, dialing the number I know by heart.

"Eli?" she says, before I can say anything at all. "Eli, is that you?"

"Hi, Mom," I say. And then: "Yeah. It's good to hear your voice, too."

269

Day 27

I T'S MY SECOND-TO-LAST morning at LakeShore. Red and I sit in companionable silence over strong coffee and waffles soaked with syrup. We both know I'm leaving tomorrow. We both know Red isn't. What we don't know, what neither of us is saying, is how we'll make it on our own.

Red's the first to break the silence. "It's going to be real boring playing Ping-Pong by myself."

I snort. "At least you'll finally hit a winning streak. Too bad Will's not here to bet on you."

"Yeah." Red gives a small smile. "Too bad."

"He'll be back," I say. "Eventually, he'll find his way."

"I hope so." Red pushes a piece of waffle around his plate, soaking up the syrup. "Have you thought about what you're going to say tomorrow?"

My own bite of waffle is suddenly plaster in my throat. I wash it down with coffee that scalds my esophagus and grimace at Red. "No idea."

Red chuckles. "Winging it, huh? That's brave. If I tried that, I'd just stand there sweating my ass off until somebody put me out of my misery."

"It's not that," I tell him. "I want to plan it ahead of time, but I don't know what to say. I feel like I'm supposed to tell some big story about how I've changed, you know? How I'm better. But what if I'm not?"

Red raises his brow, his loaded fork suspended just short of his mouth. "You don't think you're different?"

The last few days play on random shuffle through my mind, pausing on yesterday. My mom came up—Richard Fisher's idea. It was awkward at first, the space between Mom and I throbbing with the pain of past hurts. But we'd talked, and not just 'good game' or 'please pass the salt,' but *really* talked for probably the first time since before my dad died.

"Things will be different," she'd promised. "You can ask me anything—no secrets, no lies, okay?"

"Different, yes," I say to Red. "But I know I'm not 'cured,' if that's what you mean. I still have a long way to go."

Red smiles; he points his fork at me before popping the bite of waffle into his mouth. "Then maybe you say that."

I nod, considering. Red's voice pulls me from my thoughts. "Is that Libby?"

I swing around, following Red's fixed gaze to the far end of the room. And there she is.

I'm on my feet before Red can say anything else. I weave my way through the dining hall as Libby fills a Styrofoam cup with hot water and selects a piece of fruit from the overflowing bowl. She's turning to leave when I approach.

"Libby?"

271

Her hair's been washed; it hangs soft around her shoulders. Her blue eyes are the placid sea on a clear day. Her lips stretch into a small smile that fills me with relief. "Eli."

I move to hug her, but her hands are full. We share an awkward embrace that jostles Libby's tea. Flustered, I grab a handful of napkins and blot the spill from the floor. When I look back at Libby, her smile is strained.

"I should get going," she says. She nods at the orange in her hand. "I just came for some sustenance. You know ... other than broth."

I force an uncomfortable laugh. "You're feeling better then?" The question is meant to tug at her; I'm not ready for her to leave.

Libby shrugs, pain palpable in her eyes. "Better's a relative word."

"What happens next?"

Libby casts a look around the room, as though searching for an escape. My questions weave a net around her, drawing her in. *Remember that night?* I want to say. *Remember the crash?*

Realization dawns, weighty and sharp. Not everybody gets out. Not Will. Not my dad.

Not everybody's ok.

"They're moving me," Libby says, and even though I'm leaving, too, her words sever me.

"Where?"

"Not sure yet." Libby's lips curl into a sneer. "Turns out LakeShore can't handle my kind of crazy."

Her words are meant to sting, but I reach out to her anyway. Libby, the girl with sharp edges—edges that protect something small and soft and beautiful.

My hand brushes her upper arm, but she shifts her weight, shrugging me off. "What about you?" She rubs her nose with the back of her hand. "You're leaving soon, aren't you?"

"Tomorrow," I tell her, almost guiltily.

"Good for you," Libby says, her voice slightly shrill. "I'm happy for you. I am."

"I'm giving my final testimony tomorrow night. You should come," I offer weakly.

Libby gives me an uncertain smile. "Sure. Maybe." She turns, waves awkwardly with the orange in her hand. "I'll see you around, Eli."

It's like when Mo left. Libby's dandelion seed kiss, her face streaked with tears. *I'll see you around.*

Is this really how it ends? After everything we've been through? After crawling together from the wreckage of our pasts, we're just going to shake hands and walk away?

Everything inside me wants to go after her, wants to keep talking, prolong the inevitable. But while Libby's scars are deep and fresh, mine are finally starting to fade.

I watch her back until she's gone, and then I make my way to the table where Red waits.

Concern flashes across his freckled face. "You okay?"

"Yeah," I tell him, though the words sting, bittersweet. Because all at once, I know they're true.

I'm okay.

I'm going to be okay.

I pick up my tray. "I'll see you later, bro. I'm going to go work on my speech."

Day 28

THE REC ROOM IS FULL tonight. Howard mans the podium, opening group with a few readings and a brief summary of his own story. But tonight, instead of zoning out or counting down the minutes until I can play Ping-Pong, I'm anxious, my stomach in knots. Because tonight I'm the main attraction.

I'm boxed into my front row seat, Richard Fisher and Mom like bookends, Steven next to Mom. I twist around, taking in the crowd. I spot Red a few rows back. He gives me a thumbs-up, mouths *Don't Choke*, and I flip him off as subtly as possible. I scan the room behind him, disappointment like iron weights on my shoulders. Libby's not here.

Richard Fisher nudges me with his elbow, and I turn back around. Howard is ending his share, and it's almost my turn.

My stomach is a cement block, and my mouth is full of dust.

Howard motions for me to join him at the podium, then turns the mic over to me. My legs feel heavy as railway ties as I make my way to the front of the room. I watch Howard walk back to his seat, and then I scan the expectant faces of the crowd. "Uh, I'm Eli," I say into the buzzing mic. My voice sounds foreign as it echoes across the rec room. It cracks a little. "I'm an addict."

"Hi, Eli," the crowd hums in unison, and the steady familiarity of the call and response puts me at ease.

I remember what Richard Fisher and Howard have both said about the spirit of the group. *Let us believe in you until you can believe in yourself.* I picture myself on the lax field, my hands gripping the stick, my muscles tense, ready to play. The bleachers are packed with people that came to support me—Mom, Steven, Richard Fisher, Red. Even Will is out there somewhere, at least in spirit. Libby, too. There are no signs that scream my name, no painted t-shirts. This is a quieter crowd, but constant and faithful.

I stand before a roomful of believing eyes.

I clear my throat and start at the beginning. "I had a pretty awesome life before I came to LakeShore. I was lacrosse captain, I had a gorgeous girlfriend. I was pretty much king of my high school—invincible. I should've felt pretty good about myself, right? And I did, I guess. As long as I was high."

A few heads bob knowingly.

"And I don't just mean high on drugs, even though that was obviously a huge part of it. I also mean being high on winning, high on being popular, high on being wanted. Because when I wasn't, when I was just Eli—not lacrosse captain, not Savannah's boyfriend—but just me, I felt completely empty inside. I felt alone, no matter how many people were by my side. I felt worthless, no matter how many people told me otherwise."

Mom dabs at her eyes with the corner of her Kleenex. Steven shifts in his seat, slings his arm across her shoulder and pulls her into him.

"And so it felt okay, necessary even, to use. Drugs were part of who I was, part of how I got by. I wasn't hurting anyone, at least that's what I thought. And I didn't think I had a problem. I thought I could stop using whenever I wanted. I was wrong. You don't think about these things as they happen. The days, the moments, the final seconds before everything changes. You're invincible. Nothing can touch you. Until it does."

I pause here, knowing that what I'm going to say next will hurt my mom. But it's my truth, and we're not lying anymore. In a voice that trembles with emotion, I tell the group the worst part of my story.

"On the night I overdosed, my girlfriend found me seizing in my locked car. According to her, the paramedics had to break the glass to get me out, had to do CPR. And even then, even when I woke up in the hospital, I didn't think I'd done anything wrong. It was an accident, a temporary setback. All I wanted was for everything to go back to normal. I didn't want to think about what happened or what I'd been doing to myself and the people around me. The people who love me."

Mom squeezes her eyes shut. She lays her head on Steven's shoulder. I hope they hear the apology in my words. I hope they know that I want to be better, that I want us to be better.

A movement at the back of the room catches my eye. Libby leans against the rear wall, listening.

My voice breaks, and I pause for a second, composing myself. "I couldn't see any of that before I came here. But the people here . . ." My eyes land momentarily on Libby, who refuses to meet my gaze. "I've learned that sometimes life has to crack you open before you see the truth of how you've been living. It's painful when you break; the bottom is a very scary place to be. And over the last few weeks, I've cracked open again and again. But I think that's how the light gets in."

I search the crowd for Red's face—he gives me an encouraging nod.

"I can't stand here and promise you that I'm cured," I say. "That's not the way this disease works. But I think if I keep putting one foot in front of the other, life will open up. It will get better. I will get better."

I fix my eyes on Mom and Steven, and I say these last words to them and to myself: "I know I have a lot of work ahead. I know I have a long way to go. But I can only start from where I am."

At the rear of the room, Libby slips out into the hall. I falter momentarily but resist the familiar urge to follow her. I let her go. "Thanks for letting me share."

Richard Fisher is the first to congratulate me. "That was quite the speech," he says, rising from his chair as the people around us head for refreshments. He clasps me on the shoulder. "One might actually get the impression that you learned something here."

I shoot him a sly smile. "Maybe a thing or two. No thanks to you."

Richard Fisher laughs, and I offer my hand. "Thanks, Fish. For everything."

He takes my hand and yanks me into a quick hug. "Don't mention it, kid."

Over his shoulder, Mom and Steven approach cautiously, like they don't want to interrupt our "moment."

"Mom," I say, pulling away from Fish's hug.

Her face brightens; her eyes are shining. I hold out my arms, gather her into a hug, and she half-weeps, half-laughs into my shoulder. "I'm so proud of you, honey," she says. "So very proud."

Steven drops a hand on my shoulder.

"I'm glad you came," I tell him.

He squeezes my arm. "I wouldn't miss it for the world."

As we weave our way through the rows of fold-out chairs toward the refreshment table, the guys from group come up to shake my hand, congratulate me. Red claps me on the back. Prison Tat offers a fist bump, kisses the cross hanging around his neck. And instead of feeling overwhelmed, embarrassed, unworthy, I feel seen—believed in.

Over brownies and coffee, Richard Fisher talks with Steven and Mom at length about discharge procedures and after-care plans. I'll be attending weekly sessions at an outpatient facility closer to home, but Richard is going to check in with me once a week over the phone. "To make sure you're getting all your meetings in," he says. Ninety meetings in ninety days to be exact; my first is tomorrow afternoon, as soon as I'm settled in at home. Turns out this recovery thing is no joke—my twenty-eight days at LakeShore was just the beginning.

Someone touches my arm, and I turn to find Red, his mouth full of chocolate chip cookie and three more in his fist. "That was some speech," he says. "Good thing I've got another thirty days to work on mine."

"Dude, you might wanna stay even longer," I kid him. "Hardest thing I've ever done."

We laugh together for a minute, until the sound fades into the awkward silence of not wanting to say goodbye.

"We'll keep in touch, right?" I finally ask.

Red squeezes my shoulder. "No doubt. We're brothers, aren't we?"

I grin at him and hold out my hand. "No matter what."

Red clasps my hand in his, yanks me toward him, and claps me soundly on the back. "No matter what."

"All packed and ready to go?" My mom's waiting for me in the lobby. It's dark out, and Steven's already gone to get the car.

"Yeah," I tell her, though I linger, my eyes trailing the hallway that leads to the medical wing, hoping to see Libby one last time.

The Lexus sidles up to the curb, and Mom starts through the sliding glass door.

"Just a sec, Mom," I say. "There's one more thing I need to do. I'll be right out."

She nods, takes my duffel from me, and heads out to the car.

The Front Desk Fascist's eyes are skeptical as I approach, but when she speaks, I can hear the smile in her voice. "What is it this time, Eli?"

I flash her a shiny grin. "Could I leave a note with you? There's someone I didn't get to say goodbye to."

She gives a gusty sigh, like scooting the Post-it pad a half inch in my direction is relocating Mt. Everest. She's going to miss me. She just doesn't know it yet.

"Thanks." I reach over the counter for a pen and consider the blank Post-it in front of me. What if this is the last communication I have with Libby? What would I want it to say? Goodbye is tragic—I'll miss you is a waste of words. There is nothing I can write on this two-inch yellow square that will properly sum up everything I feel. My world is ending and be-ginning all at the same time.

I start to scrawl my address on the notepad, then think better of it and push the pad back toward the Fascist. "Never mind."

She gives me a suspicious eyebrow lift. "You sure?"

"Yeah," I tell her. "I'm sure." I turn toward the doors.

"Eli!" I turn around at the sound of Libby's voice. "Eli, wait!" She's hurrying through the lobby, wearing pajama pants and slippers, and all I want to do is wrap her in my arms.

"Looks like you'll get your chance after all," the Fascist says.

"Eli." Libby stops a few feet away from me.

I take a step closer, close enough to touch her, though I don't. Close enough to see the ripples of emotion in her eyes. "I didn't think I'd get to say goodbye."

"I don't do goodbyes, remember?" Libby pushes back the hair from her face with an arm free of bandages. In this light, I can barely make out the scars.

"Right."

Libby smiles, though her eyes glisten. "Look, I just wanted to say . . . don't come back, okay?"

"I won't," I tell her, and then the truth: "I'll try."

Libby swallows hard. Softly, she kisses her fingers, then presses them against my scar. I close my eyes, welcoming the pain. Because I'm alive. Because Libby is alive. Because feeling is the best and the worst all in one.

"See you later?" she whispers.

I nod, even though my eyes burn. "See you later."

With a final wave, I pass through the sliding glass doors and head toward Steven's waiting car.

Mom smiles through the passenger window, and I am flooded with memories of the day they dropped me off. Before I knew about my dad. Before I'd met Red, Will, or Libby. Before my life turned upside down. Less than a month ago, and everything's completely different. *I'm* different. And though it feels like something's ending, I know this is only the start.

I open the back door and slide onto Steven's cushy leather seat that still smells exactly like I remember. Benny's booster seat is empty, but a crayon sticks out from underneath it. Blue, his favorite.

I pull it out and put it in my pocket, so I can give it to him when I get back home.

One foot in front of the other, I tell myself.

This is where I begin.

Author's Note

IF YOU OR SOMEONE YOU love struggles with addiction, you are not alone. Help is available, and recovery IS possible.

For more information or to find a treatment center near you, visit the following online resources:

National Institute on Drug Abuse for Teens
www.teens.drugabuse.gov/have-a-drug-problem-need-help

Substance Abuse and Mental Health Services Administration
www.findtreatment.samhsa.gov

The National Center on Addiction and Substance Abuse
www.centeronaddiction.org/addiction-treatment

Narcotics Anonymous
www.na.org

Support for Family Members and Loved Ones

Al-Anon and Nar-Anon family groups offer support to family members whose loved ones suffer from the disease of addiction. To find a support group near you, visit the following links:

Al-Anon Family Groups
www.al-anon.alateen.org

Nar-Anon Family Groups
www.nar-anon.org

Acknowledgments

WRITING IS TRULY A COLLABORATIVE process. So many hands have touched this book and helped to shape its final form. For that, I am truly grateful. Thank you to Dr. Steven Jaffe from Emory University, who authored *The Adolescent Substance Abuse Intervention Workbook*, which inspired LakeShore's recovery literature and helped to inform Eli's counseling and group sessions. Thank you to Renee Mergen, RN, who helped me understand what happens during an overdose and how it is treated in the hospital. Thank you to the BACS eighth grade girls (2015-16) for their insight on Eli's character arc. Without them, there would be no Steven or Benny. Thank you to the editorial team at Tiny Fox Press, for believing in *Lifeline*, and for helping to shape its final form.

I owe a tremendous debt of gratitude to my own community of believing eyes; you have carried me through when I didn't believe in myself. To Chrissa Pederson, my critique partner extraordinaire, for tirelessly reading (and re-reading) each draft of this novel, for pointing out my writing tics and forcing me to "kill my darlings," for supporting my development as a writer, and for coaching me through each of the many meltdowns I had along the way. To my parents and my brother, who have lived this journey, and who have been tireless examples of courage, strength, and hope. And above all, to Scott and my girls: I am nothing without your faithfulness, love, cheerleading, patience, and constant support. From the bottom of my heart, thank you.

About the Author

B orn to parents with a serious case of "wanderlust," Abbey Lee Nash has lived in some pretty interesting places, including on a Christian farming commune in rural Georgia, above a third-world craft store in Kentucky, and on a Salvation Army retreat center in the Pennsylvania mountains. She currently lives outside of Philadelphia with her husband, two daughters, and one very rambunctious Australian Shepherd. She received her MA in English from Arcadia University in 2011 and currently works at Bryn Athyn College where she teaches writing and literature. She is also an active member of the Society of Children's Book Writers and Illustrators. LIFELINE is her first novel.

www.AbbeyNash.com

About the Publisher

Tiny Fox Press LLC
5020 Kingsley Road
North Port, FL 34287

www.tinyfoxpress.com

CPSIA information can be obtained
at www.ICGtesting.com
Printed in the USA
FSHW021842240219
55915FS